EZEKIAL POOLE: The young Mormon rebelled against his people to rescue the woman he loved—and discovered a new world . . .

REBECCA YORK: She fled an arranged marriage and risked her life to find true love . . .

EARL PEAMONT: An older man, he wanted to make a brand-new life in California—and along the way, he proved he had the courage to do it . . .

JIM STROBRIDGE: The hard-driving construction boss led an army of fearless men to build the Central Pacific. He knew that in the West, it didn't matter where you came from—it only mattered what you could do . . .

The *Rails West!* series from Jove

RAILS WEST!

Sierra Passage

FRANKLIN CARTER

JOVE BOOKS, NEW YORK

SIERRA PASSAGE

A Jove Book / published by arrangement with
the author

PRINTING HISTORY
Jove edition / January 1995

ISBN: 0-515-11527-4

A JOVE BOOK®
Jove Books are published by The Berkley Publishing Group,
200 Madison Avenue, New York, New York 10016.
JOVE and the "J" design are trademarks
belonging to Jove Publications, Inc.

PRINTED IN THE UNITED STATES OF AMERICA

10 9 8 7 6 5 4 3 2 1

CHAPTER 1

Glenn Gilchrist, tall, handsome but a little formal due to his Harvard education and wealthy Eastern background, could hear the Irish rust eaters slamming down rails as the Union Pacific Railroad inched westward. The ringing of steel against steel was a chorus Glenn knew he would dearly miss, but this part of his life was now finished. After working the past few exciting years as Assistant Chief Surveyor for the Union Pacific, beginning with its departure from Omaha, he had been unjustly branded a traitor, a Central Pacific Railroad spy.

It was a cruel and totally unexpected blow for Glenn, who had given every ounce of his energy and talent to helping the Union Pacific win the great railroad race across the West. At twenty-one and fresh out of college, he could have taken the easy road to guaranteed prosperity by going to work in his father's bank, but instead had chosen danger, challenge and excitement. And up until yesterday, he had never regretted that choice.

But Thomas Durant, President of the Union Pacific, had never forgiven Glenn for standing up for the families of the Irish construction workers who had died during the flooding of the Missouri River the very spring the railroad had forged westward from Omaha. Glenn had demanded that some reparations be made for those poor families, and had thus earned Durant's lasting enmity. And now, finally, Durant had concocted this preposterous story of Glenn being a spy for their rivals, the Central Pacific.

"Are you ready?" Joshua Hood, Chief of Scouts, asked, peeking into Glenn's tent. "How much stuff are you planning to take to California?"

Glenn gathered his travel bag, surveying instruments and precious surveyors' maps. "As ready as I'll ever be," he said to the buckskin-clad scout and hunter.

"Best leave those railroad maps, Glenn," Hood said. "You won't be allowed to take them west."

Frustration erupted in sudden anger. "Hell, Joshua, I drew them!"

"Yeah, I expect that you did," Hood said reasonably, "but you did it on Union Pacific time."

Glenn supposed that Hood's point was valid. The maps did belong to Durant's railroad and they were very important to whoever would take his position. The Union Pacific still had a long, long way to go before it finally joined with the Central Pacific, thus uniting the American continent with two thin ribbons of steel.

Glenn laid his maps back onto his surveyor's table. "The surveying instruments and the books I've already boxed and sent to the wagon belong to me," he said, "and I'm not about to leave *them* behind."

"The only thing I wish you were leaving behind is Megan O'Connell," Joshua said, trying to sound as if he were making a joke.

At this remark, Glenn actually smiled. "Joshua," he said, "you lost her and I'm still not sure if I've won her. We both know that she would have married Dr. Thaddeus Wiseman if he hadn't decided to marry her sister Aileen instead."

"I'll never understand why he did that," Joshua confessed with a shake of his head. "Aileen isn't nearly as pretty and she hasn't any of Megan's steel."

Glenn somehow felt compelled to defend Aileen, although he too had difficulty understanding the doctor's choice to wed Megan's sister. "Aileen is . . . is more needing of a gentle husband and there is the matter of her daughter. It's easy to see that little Jenny adores Thaddeus. The three of them are going to make a very happy family. I envy them."

"I don't," Joshua said. "I envy *you* for getting to take Megan all the way to California."

Joshua frowned. He had long, brown hair and dark, piercing eyes. He was a striking-looking man, in a rough, frontier sort of way. "I tell you flat out, Glenn. I'd quit my job as chief scout of this railroad if I thought I had any chance of stealing Megan away from you."

Glenn didn't quite know what to say. They had long been rivals for Megan's affections. Total opposites, they had alternately fought, gotten drunk together and finally and almost reluctantly become trusted friends. Glenn chose to ignore the remark and change the subject.

"Are Thomas Durant and his lackeys waiting outside to make sure that I leave?"

"I'm afraid so," Hood said. "But so are all your friends and their numbers make Durant look foolish. Your friends won't turn their backs on you and Megan."

"Nice to hear that, Joshua."

"Well," the frontiersman said, "no one in their right mind believes any of that bullshit about you being a spy for the Central Pacific."

"Thanks," Glenn said. "And just remember, there is nothing holding you here either."

"This railroad needs me to scout for Indians and hunt for buffalo," Joshua said.

"There are plenty of other men who can shoot all the buffalo that the crews need for meat."

"I expect that's true enough," Joshua admitted, "but there's no one else but me that can palaver with the Cheyenne and the Sioux. I lived with them and maybe that will help me save a few scalps on both sides."

Glenn clapped his friend on the shoulder. "Maybe so, but if you're not damned careful, you're going to 'palaver' yourself into getting scalped. You might speak their language, Joshua, but your eyes are still blue and they'd highly admire your long hair dangling from one of their war lances."

Joshua snorted. "I ride with a lot of fine hunters and we're armed to the teeth. However, you and Megan will pretty much be traveling on your own until you reach Fort Bridger."

"We'll be following the proposed Union Pacific right-of-way."

"Sure, but that won't help you if you get jumped by a war party."

Glenn agreed, and he'd have been lying if he said he wasn't concerned. "Well, there hasn't been any trouble for several weeks. We'll travel at night and lay low during the day. I've ridden out there with you enough to know how to travel in hostile Indian country."

"Yeah," Joshua said, "you have, but it's Megan I'm worried about, not you."

"That's what I figured."

Joshua shifted his feet, then clenched and unclenched his big fists. "All right. After you get beyond the Union Pacific road graders, our forward bridge builders and finally your advance surveyors, you ought to be nearly to Fort Bridger."

"That's right," Glenn said, impatient to leave. "And

then I expect that we can catch an Army escort to accompany us over the Wasatch Mountains into Salt Lake City. From there, we should have pretty smooth sailing all the way across Nevada. The Paiutes aren't too fierce, are they?"

"Don't count on that," Joshua warned. "They almost shut down the Pony Express a few years back. They can get riled as easy as the Blackfeet. Best thing to do is just to steer clear of them whenever possible."

"We'll do that," Glenn vowed.

"Will you telegraph us when you get the chance?"

"Sure," Glenn promised, extending his hand. "And before we go outside and say good-bye to all those people, I'll take this chance to tell you how much I've learned from you, Joshua."

The scout and buffalo hunter actually blushed. After a moment he said, "I thought a college boy like you knew everything already. Didn't figure that you could learn from a grown man that still struggles to read and write."

"What you know can't be taught in a book," Glenn said evenly as they shook hands. "And if the high-and-mighty Thomas Durant ever turns on you the way he did on me, come on to California. We'll find a use for your talents."

"That wouldn't be easy," Joshua said. "There are no buffalo to shoot in those high Sierra Nevada Mountains. There's just pine trees, bears and a hell of a lot of snow in the wintertime. I sure hope you and Megan don't freeze to death like them poor devils that died on Donner Pass about twenty years ago."

"We won't. My plan is to locate this Loudermilk fella that I've been accused of collaborating with as a Central Pacific spy. When I do, I'll wring the truth out of him and clear my name."

"Do that," Joshua said. "But the most important thing

of all is that you take damned good care of Megan."

"I will," Glenn promised.

"You know what I'd do to you if you didn't."

Joshua tried to take the edge off his threat with a smile, but it didn't work because his eyes were deadly serious, and Glenn knew that, friends or not, if he allowed something bad to happen to Megan, this man would go for his throat.

"Yeah," Glenn said, passing by Joshua as he left the tent, "I know."

Outside, a sizable crowd of his friends were gathered. Among them were the Casement brothers, former Union Army General John and his younger brother, Dan. They were both short, dynamic men who had quickly proven their value as leaders and the driving forces behind the actual construction of the Union Pacific Railroad. It had been the Casements who had whipped the often drunken and unruly Irishmen into a well-ordered army of tracklayers and had developed a construction train that moved westward much like a relentless machine on wheels.

Even now, after watching the operation lay rails for hundreds of miles, Glenn still marveled at how the track-laying crews worked. The lead flatcar was laden with rails which were yanked free and slammed down on burnetized rails, then spiked as other flatcars acting as blacksmith, carpentry and repair shops followed. Perhaps most impressive were the immense and specially designed high-sided Union Pacific sleeping cars, each eighty feet long and containing bunks for 144 men. They were followed by enormous dining cars to feed the always hungry railroad laborers. Among the last cars on the long construction train was the famed "Lincoln Car," which had been made specially ordered to protect President Abraham Lincoln. Thomas Durant had paid an enormous amount of money for the plush presidential car, which was ironclad and bulletproof. Glenn was very much aware that a man like Durant who made lasting enemies needed to take every possible precaution against the fate that had befallen Mr. Lincoln.

"Good luck," Dan Casement said, pushing forward to shake Glenn's hand.

"Thanks for being here," Glenn said, aware that even the Casement brothers were not totally immune to Durant's petty vendettas.

"Glenn," General Jack said, in a low voice as he chewed angrily on the stub of a cigar, "you have my letter of recommendation addressed to Charles Crocker. Use the damned thing."

"I will, sir. Thank you!"

"You'll be missed and Durant will no doubt regret the day that he turned you out to work for our competitor."

"I hope so," Glenn said, allowing himself a slight smile. "At least, that's my intention."

Glenn's eyes locked with those of Megan O'Connell. His heart quickened as always, even when seeing her after the briefest of absences. Megan was tall, statuesque and as fresh and lovely as the wildflowers that blanketed these vast prairies every spring. Right now, though, her green eyes were misty and Glenn knew how difficult it was for her to leave her sister as well as her close friends. Friends like Rachel, who had worked in her tent saloon and helped her overcome and eventually bring about the downfall of a particularly vicious competitor, Ike Norman.

"We'd better go," Megan said, hugging Aileen, Rachel and finally Dr. Wiseman. "Let's leave *now*, Glenn."

Glenn agreed wholeheartedly. Megan was on the verge of tears and Glenn could feel a powerful ache in his own throat. They were standing beside a big 4-4-0 locomotive with a sixty-inch driving wheel that had been built by the Taunton Locomotive Works in Massachusetts. The huge engine was huff-huffing impatiently and steam was drifting from its stack. When Glenn glanced up at the engineer, the man removed his cap hat in tribute and waved it with a smile. Glenn couldn't even remember the man's name, although he had seen his face every day for the past couple of years.

"So long," he called to the engineer as he strode toward their light surrey, already packed with trunks containing all their personal belongings.

Huge, gentle but bear-like Dr. Wiseman blocked Glenn's path and the man batted Glenn's hand aside and gave him a crunching hug. "You take good care of my wife's sister," he ordered. "I think you're both out of your minds, but I know it's always been Megan's dream to see California and she couldn't have a finer escort."

"Thanks," Glenn said, finally able to extract himself from the huge man's embrace. "We'll telegraph whenever we can."

"Good," Wiseman said.

Glenn gave Aileen a hug and a quick kiss on the cheek before he helped Megan into the surrey and he followed.

"So long, everyone!" Glenn shouted. "We'll meet again where the rails join!"

The crowd cheered, all except for Durant, whose expression was so sour that he appeared to have bitten into something very distasteful. Glenn, buoyed by this rousing farewell, boldly pointed at the President of the Union Pacific and shouted, "We'll see you in Nevada, Thomas!"

Durant, who had been hanging back from the well-wishers, blanched and hurled his cigar to the ground, then spun on his heels and marched off toward the Lincoln Car.

"Did you have to bait him?" Megan asked with a trace of amusement but also a hint of reproach.

Glenn raised the lines and slowly eased the surrey forward as people parted to let them move on through this latest of the tented hell-on-wheels towns that marked the Union Pacific's steady progress.

"Yes," he finally said as their surrey and its two matched horses moved clear of the crowd, "I did. And I'll tell you something, Megan, that was a damned small satisfaction given what Thomas Durant tried to do to my name and reputation. A reputation I've worked hard to earn since I was hired in Omaha by the Union Pacific."

"Yes," Megan said, "I suppose it was."

She turned and waved back at the receding crowd as gaily as if they were going off to enjoy an afternoon picnic instead of turning their backs on all their family and friends.

"Wave them good-bye again," Megan said, sniffling.

"I already have," Glenn said, guiding their surrey over the tracks and then out into the vast Wyoming prairie where they were engulfed by the enormous expanse of empty land and sky.

Megan finally turned forward and when Glenn looked over at her, he saw that tears were running freely down her cheeks. He reached over and took Megan's hand.

"I can turn this thing around, you know. It's certainly not too late to change your mind about me or California."

"No," she said emphatically as she roughly used the back of her sleeve to dry her tears. "Not unless you want to turn back."

"You know I cannot. There's no turning back for me. But it wasn't your name that was slandered. You have nothing in California to set right."

Megan was silent for so long that Glenn thought she had

not heard him until she finally said, "I have a destiny in California."

"A destiny?"

She dried her tears with a lace handkerchief and raised her chin. Megan's eyes became riveted straight ahead and exuded the fierce kind of Irish determination that Glenn had often witnessed among the tough construction crews. A dogged determination to persevere no matter how difficult the terrain or how terrible the winter weather.

Megan cleared her throat and laid her hand on Glenn's thigh as they bounced along leaving the rail town behind. "Maybe," she said thoughtfully, "destiny isn't the proper word. I don't know for sure except that I've always dreamed of California. I told you that my favorite Uncle Patrick left Boston and sallied off to become a Forty-Niner."

"Yes," Glenn said, "you said that he often wrote you and your family from diggings like Chili Gulch and Fiddletown."

Megan's lips curved to a smile. "That's right. Aileen and I were just sure that everyone in Fiddletown always had a wonderful time dancing and picking up gold nuggets. From Uncle Patrick's letters, we came to believe that California must be a paradise on earth."

"But you know better now," Glenn said. "Right?"

"Of course!" Megan hugged her knees, her expression dreamy. "I know now that Uncle Patrick lied about getting rich and eventually returning home. We learned later that he died a poor, broken man in a town called Columbia. He had a stack of letters that he couldn't even afford to mail. It was a kindness that they were sent to us anyway by one of my uncle's friends."

"So many Forty-Niners went out there, but so few struck it rich," Glenn mused. "I've heard that the only ones who really became wealthy were the merchants."

"Men like Charles Crocker, Mark Hopkins and Collis Huntington."

Glenn smiled. "You know the names of the men behind the Central Pacific, huh?"

"Sure," Megan said. "And everyone I've heard talk about the Central Pacific says that it will never breach the Sierras. They say that the grades are just too steep."

"I've heard differently," Glenn replied. "There was a young surveyor named Theodore Judah who found a route over the Sierras that can be scaled by a railroad."

"I never heard of the man," Megan said. "What happened to him?"

Glenn shook his head sadly. "I don't understand all of the politics and infighting, but I do know that Judah was a visionary and that all he cared about was the realization of a great transcontinental railroad."

"And the others did not?"

"Not entirely," Glenn said. "Huntington, Crocker and the others were only concerned with big profits."

"So what happened?"

Glenn shrugged. "There was a deep rift and Judah sailed out of San Francisco determined to reach New York City and to generate enough financial backing to buy his partners out. But in his haste, he made the fatal decision to cross the Isthmus of Panama instead of going around Cape Horn. He contracted yellow fever and died."

"How terrible!"

"Yes," Glenn said. "I've read some of his engineering reports. He was a brilliant surveyor, Megan. Until he found a route up to Donner Pass, there was never any hope of a railroad crossing the mighty Sierras. Judah, with mathematical formulas backed by his precise calculations and survey reports, proved that the feat could be accomplished, although it will be enormously difficult and extremely expensive."

"I see." Megan thought about that for a moment, then said, "And how is the Central Pacific doing up to this point?"

"Not too well, I'm afraid. To begin with, they've had a lot of trouble getting labor."

"Why?"

"Because," Glenn explained, "the big, hard-rock mines on the Comstock Lode have attracted all the available labor. They're paying unheard-of wages and that means that the only workers that the Central Pacific has been able to hire are misfits, drunkards and troublemakers. Men too unstable or unreliable to work in the deep mines."

"I see. So what is going to happen? Without labor, how can they build?"

"They can't," Glenn said gloomily. "Durant knows this and he'd like nothing better than to see the entire operation fail. He'll drive his rails all the way to Reno, collecting a fortune in land and money every mile of the way. And then . . . well, my guess is he'll just look at the Sierras and declare them impassable."

"You mean he'd quit after coming all the way from Omaha?" Megan's face displayed her amazement.

"Yes," Glenn said, "I believe he would quit. Grenville Dodge and the Casement brothers would be bitterly disappointed, of course, but they'd be helpless. Durant and his partners and major stockholders aren't idealists, Megan. And while they'd like to build a railroad over those Sierras, they're not about to risk their names or fortunes in the grand attempt."

"So it's up to the Central Pacific if we are to have a railroad linking east to west?"

"That's right." Glenn scowled. "And while I admit that

I want to do all that I can to thwart Durant, I'm also committed to Judah's dream of a transcontinental railroad and I'll do everything in my power to see the dream become the reality."

Megan didn't say much for a while as they rode along enjoying the vast silence of the Wyoming plains. So many questions swirled around in her mind about this decision to leave the safety of the Union Pacific and strike out with Glenn for California that she could scarcely believe what she was doing.

Why, at any moment they could chance upon a big war party of Cheyenne and both be tortured and then killed. Like poor Theodore Judah, they both might have their lives abruptly ended, leaving their modest dreams unfulfilled.

But then, Megan told herself, nothing in life was guaranteed. She and Aileen had left the dirty factories of Boston where they'd had no hope of owning their own modest homes or making a decent living. They'd both had husbands then. Boys, more than men, who had thought that life was a game and a gamble. Both of their husbands had drowned in the terrible flood that started when the ice of the great Missouri River had broken and sent a tidal wave down upon them and their riverbank shantytown.

That seemed like a lifetime ago. Now, here she was with Glenn Gilchrist heading off again, older but much wiser. Would he, like her first husband, die suddenly? Would *she* die suddenly or . . . God forbid, suffer a slow terrible death at the hands of Indians?

Despite the warmth of the midday sun, Megan shivered and felt ashamed of herself for her fears. As always, she was charting her own destiny and her destiny was with Glenn now as they made their way to California.

Megan bent her head, made the sign of the cross and

said a silent prayer that they would both reach California safely.

"You want to tell me what you prayed for?"

"No," Megan said quietly, "but it was for both of us."

Glenn chuckled. "Thanks," he said. "I can use all the prayers you want to offer."

"You don't pray?"

"Sometimes," he said, feeling his cheeks warm. "I've always prayed that you'd come to love and marry me."

"I do love you."

"Then marry me," he blurted out.

"No," she said gently. "Not until this is finished."

Glenn felt fit to be tied. "But . . . but why wait!"

Megan's brow furrowed. "I don't know," she confessed. "All I do know for sure is that we have to reach California."

"And then?"

She smiled. "And then we can continue this conversation."

Glenn was filled with exasperation. "You're driving me to distraction, Megan!"

"I'm sorry," she said sweetly, "but *you* need to drive us to California."

He shook his head, took a deep breath of pure Wyoming air and slapped the lines across the rumps of their horses, hurrying them forward in a trot. There would be, Glenn noted, about three more hours until darkness. With any luck at all, they'd not run across a construction crew and he wouldn't have to share Megan's company with anyone else this night. Maybe then, Glenn fervently hoped, they'd talk a little more seriously about love and marriage.

CHAPTER

2

"Look, Glenn!" Megan said, leaning forward. "Isn't that a campfire up ahead?"

Glenn squinted into the sunset, then shook his head. "I don't think so, Megan. I'm pretty sure that it's just the glare from the sun."

"No, it isn't," Megan persisted. "I'm positive that it's a campfire. And I'll bet anything that it's one of our bridge-building crews."

Megan brightened. "Wouldn't that be splendid! They'll have a fire, hot food and offer us plenty of protection on our first night out."

"Yeah," Glenn said, unable to muster any enthusiasm. "And here I was afraid we were actually going to have to spend our first night alone together."

Megan glanced sideways and realized that he actually was disappointed. She laughed. "Why, Glenn, what *did* you have in mind for this evening?"

"Oh, I don't know. Maybe a bottle of wine, a nice dinner and a campfire just for two. Anything except sharing you with thirty or forty lusting bridge builders."

Megan really laughed this time. "I declare that you are a man with ulterior motives. And here I was thinking that you'd be as relieved to find a construction camp as I am."

Glenn realized that he was acting pretty ridiculous. Everyone from Jack Casement on down had urged him to seek protection with the advance Union Pacific construction crews. Nearest to the main construction train were the graders and bridge builders, but farther out were the surveyors, sometimes as many as fifty miles in advance of the construction crews. In all cases, these advance parties were always heavily armed and prepared to fend off sudden Indian attacks. There was safety in numbers and Glenn felt a little ashamed of himself for wanting to risk Megan's safety just so that he could enjoy being alone with her.

"Actually," he hedged, "I am sort of relieved to see a UP construction camp. But I intend to make it clear to them that you are a lady and I won't allow any man to use foul language or—"

"Glenn!" she exclaimed with surprise. "What has gotten into you! I'm a widow, not some starry-eyed virgin. Just like you, I've lived and struggled with these railroad workers all the way from Omaha. Remember? I've heard their stories and there's nothing they could say that would easily offend me."

"But—"

Megan didn't let him finish. "And I'll bet that I know every last one of these men and bought at least half of them a free drink in my tent saloon sometime during the past couple of years."

"Yeah," he said, tight-lipped. "I guess that's probably true. But you're a lone woman out here and it's different."

"Sure it's different," Megan agreed. "There won't be a tent over our heads and liquor won't be served. Poor Henry Harrison won't be around to deal a straight deck and Rachel isn't going to be washing glasses. But other than that, I know and like these construction workers and I certainly will not need protection in their company."

Glenn was stung by her rebuke. What Megan said made sense, but perhaps she didn't know that things really were different out here on the open prairies of Wyoming. Men were rougher in dress and manner, and the unexpected arrival of a beautiful young woman could very well trigger some off-color remark and ungentlemanly behavior.

"Fine, then," Glenn said tightly. "I just thought that you might like to know that I'll be ready if you need me."

Megan's voice softened. "I'm sorry to have lectured you, Glenn. But I've been taking care of myself for quite a long time now and I'm just not ready to have a protector. And frankly, I may never be."

"So what am I supposed to do if someone insults you?"

"Let me handle it."

"And if you can't?"

"Then I'll ask for your help." Megan leaned over and kissed him on the cheek. "Is that agreeable?"

"Sure," Glenn said, only partially mollified.

Megan sighed and was again reminded of how rough men were on the outside and how fragile they could be on the inside, especially concerning matters of the heart. As a tent saloon owner these past years, she had consoled some tough but lonely and despairing young men. They never complained about the brutal, dangerous construction work or the fear of sudden attack by Indians, but let some dance hall or saloon girl break their heart and they could be injured as easily as trusting children. It was even worse if their wives, sisters or mothers died. The death of a childhood friend or sweetheart was enough to send the strongest man into absolute despair.

Glenn was intelligent and even sophisticated, but his feelings were still vulnerable. Megan knew that she had just wounded Glenn and she would have to be more careful. The trouble was, he wanted to protect and care for her, but she gained self-respect by taking care of herself and dealing with life and difficulties on her own terms. It was a great sense of pride to Megan that she had not only survived after her husband's untimely death, but that she had even prospered when she'd hit upon the idea of opening a tent saloon despite nearly everyone's well-intentioned objections. Megan had borrowed and scraped and fought, and eventually she'd established her saloon as one of the most successful businesses on the Union Pacific construction line.

"Let's just be thankful," Megan said as they drew nearer to the construction camp, "that we won't have to worry about Indians tonight."

"Agreed," he said a little stiffly. "And I'll try harder in the future to remember that you are a very self-sufficient woman."

"Thank you," Megan said with a smile as she gave his arm an affectionate squeeze.

As their surrey rolled into the construction camp, the workers stopped their evening chores and came out to greet them. When they realized that Megan was present, their smiles grew even broader.

"Why, if it isn't Miss Megan O'Connell!" the Union Pacific's big Irish construction foreman, Bill Galloway, shouted. "Well, I'll be damned! What are you doing out here alone with a gent like Glenn Gilchrist?"

Glenn reined up and studied the camp. There were about twenty men and they were building a short but heavy trestle across one of the hundreds of unnamed and nondescript ravines that could not be filled in and had to be spanned because they flooded every spring. This particular ravine wasn't even twenty feet across, but it still required an immense amount of timber that had to be freighted all the way from the Laramie Mountains. The local cottonwood that could be harvested along the Platte River and its tributaries could be used for rails in a pinch, but it was too soft and sheared too easily to be used to support the weight of a locomotive and railroad cars. For a proper bridge or trestle, harder woods were required.

"We're on our way to California," Megan called, jumping down to greet by name the men who crowded around her, barraging her with questions.

"How'd you manage this?" a quiet and friendly man named Sinclair Ives asked as he eased over to stand beside Glenn. "Why, any man in this crew would give two years' wages to drive Megan O'Connell all the way California."

"It's a long story," Glenn said. "But the short of it is that Thomas Durant charged me with being a spy for the Central Pacific Railroad and I was fired."

"What!" Ives said, jaw dropping.

"That's right. The charges centered around an Eastern dandy named Peter Arlington."

"I remember him well. Claimed his father owned some big newspaper."

"He's the one," Glenn said. "*The Boston Herald*, circulation fifty thousand. That impressed Durant so much that he made me Arlington's personal escort when the man asked to go hunting for a trophy buffalo. At any rate, it turns out that Arlington *was* a spy for the Central Pacific Railroad."

Ives scowled. "But didn't he get killed by the Indians just a short while ago?"

"That's right and I was with him when it happened. I was lucky to escape alive. I found a sealed letter of

Arlington's that incriminated me as his accomplice. It was addressed to a man named Loudermilk who apparently works for the Central Pacific. The unmailed letter detailed the Union Pacific's progress and strategy. When Durant opened and read it, he saw an excuse to accuse and then fire me."

"That's tough," Ives said as they both watched the rest of the crew escort Megan over to their campfire. The sun was just diving into the western horizon and the land was fired with gold.

"I mean to clear my name," Glenn said with determination.

"You want your job back?"

"No, just my name and reputation."

"Then what'll you do?"

"Try to get work on the Central Pacific Railroad."

Ives blinked. "You'd hire on to compete against us?"

Glenn clapped the man on the back. Ives had been a businessman in New Hampshire before he'd lost his family to typhoid fever and fled west. The man was sensible and well reasoned and had quickly become a quartermaster in charge of construction supplies.

"Well, Sinclair, I don't see it as us against them," Glenn said. "What I see is one part of the country needing to reach the other part of the country. East joining hands with West and both of them the stronger for it. The Civil War pitted North against South but I think that the future is to the west. That's where the open land lies waiting to be ranched and farmed. Where the new and exciting opportunities will be found during the coming century."

"But . . . but we're competitors! Every mile of track that the Central Pacific doesn't lay, *we will*! And we'll be well paid!"

"Not you or me," Glenn corrected. "Durant and all the big Union Pacific stockholders are the only ones that stand to make fortunes."

"But so will Crocker, Huntington and them other fellas out in California."

"That's true, but at least there will be competition if they are successful in beating the Sierras."

It was clear that Ives wasn't in full agreement. "I don't know," he hedged. "I'd like to see us drive all the way across the Utah Territory and then Nevada. Me and all the other men want the railroads to meet at Donner Pass."

Glenn chuckled. "Well," he said, "if I have anything to say about it, we'll meet in the Utah Territory. Maybe even in the Wasatch Mountains. The main thing of it is, we'll make it a good and a fair race."

"You can try, but I'm betting that Crocker's Chinese won't stand up against our Irish."

"I don't know about that," Glenn said. "I've heard rumors that 'Crocker's Pets' are damned hard workers. They never get drunk on payday and about the only thing they do drink is hot tea."

"Humph," Ives snorted. "A little tea-sippin' Celestial pitted against an American who swills whiskey and picks his teeth with a Bowie knife? The Celestials sure don't seem like much of a match to me."

Glenn smiled and clapped Ives on the shoulder. He had to leave and go watch out for Megan, despite her proud talk of being able to completely fend for herself. He found her just as he'd expected, in the middle of a clot of admiring men. Megan was having a good time and, while she wasn't a flirt, Glenn knew that she did enjoy being the center of attention.

"Hi," she called from the middle of the crowd. "Come to protect me?"

Glenn blushed and Megan was sorry for her teasing. But despite Glenn's concerns, she knew that these men would never become crude or offensive. Oh, they were probably quite vulgar when among themselves, but with a lady in their presence, they were perfect gentlemen.

"So why don't you stick around a few days and watch how we build a trestle?" a good-looking young man named Sean McLarity suggested to Megan. "You might even find it interesting."

"I don't think so," Megan said, her eyes reaching to Glenn. "We have to be on our way at first light. We've got a long drive ahead of us. Do you have any idea how far the next surveying team is up the line?"

"Supposed to be working about twenty miles west of us," McLarity said. "Them young college boys passed through here about . . . oh, a week ago?"

"Ten days," another man said. "There were about a dozen of 'em, and the reason I remember it was Sunday was because McCarthy was praying the rosary all day while the rest of us were washin', nappin' and watchin' out for Indians."

"That's right," another man said. "I recollect because a couple of them surveyors wanted to know if they could use our fishing poles and go down by Alder Creek. I helped 'em dig some worms and we musta caught a sackful of brook trout."

"That's right," yet another construction worker said as he sucked wetly on a corncob pipe. "I remember now that we did eat fish that night, along with that damned rotten old buffalo meat that Joshua Hood brought us."

"And I suppose," Megan said, brilliant smile fading, "that's what's for supper?"

"I'm afraid so," McLarity said. "We're expecting Hood and his men any day now to bring us some fresh meat, but so far he's been scarcer in these parts than chicken eggs."

"Well," Megan said, "let's see what we can do to fix up that buffalo meat and make it edible."

The men seemed to think that was a fine idea, and they were grinning when Megan got up and went over to the cook tent and started rummaging around for seasonings.

"She'll make that damned old buffalo meat taste a lot better, I betcha," a man said, looking pleased.

Glenn expected that was the case, and so he wasn't surprised an hour later when Megan and the designated cook for the day produced a dinner that was almost delicious.

"Megan, what did you do to this old buffalo meat?" Glenn asked.

"We found some wild sage and the potatoes and carrots were still pretty fresh."

Everyone ate well and the coffee was good and strong as they gathered under the stars and stared at the campfire. Megan, of course, remained the center of attention, but Ike had told some of the others about the charges that Thomas Durant had made about Glenn and how he'd been dismissed under a cloud of false accusations. Like Ike, the laborers were incensed but also a little troubled that Glenn would go to work for their rival.

"They might not even hire me," Glenn said, thinking it unwise to tell anyone that he had received a letter of recommendation from Jack Casement.

"You wouldn't like working with those damned Chinese anyway," one man said, his voice ringing with conviction. "They're all just runty little fellas and they're real stand-offish. They don't like us anymore than the Indians do."

"That's right," another agreed as he studiously rolled a cigarette with his thick, dirty fingers. "I met a fella that's working for this line back in Omaha at the roundhouse repairing boilers. He was employed by the Central Pacific until Crocker got it into his head to hire them damned Chinamen. He says they're altogether different than us. They stick to themselves and save their money. Never think of gettin' drunk nor nuthin'."

"That's not so terrible," Megan said.

"But," the man quickly added as he jammed the cigarette between his lips, "they have no intention whatsoever of becoming Americans. They all swear they're going back to China just as soon as they can. And I heard that, if one dies in America, he thinks he's going to an everlasting hell if his scrawny little body ain't salted and shipped all the way back to Canton!"

"No!" Megan said, feigning shock.

"It's true," the man vowed, match flaring to cigarette. "I swear it to you, Miss O'Connell."

Glenn had heard the same story but he wasn't convinced that it was entirely true. People had a tendency to exaggerate, especially the Irish. He was considering making this very point when, suddenly, they all heard a shout and the pounding of hooves in the night. In an instant, someone kicked out the campfire and men scrambled for their rifles. Glenn grabbed Megan and pulled her over to their surrey, where he collected their repeating rifles.

"Megan, I trust you know how to use this Winchester if there is Indian trouble on the way."

"You can count on it," Megan said as the racing hoofbeats grew louder and louder.

It was not a bit uncommon for a warrior to take it upon himself to show his bravery by attacking alone. Usually, this was done at first light, but no one was willing to say that either the Sioux or the Cheyenne were predictable.

"Hello the camp!" cried a voice filled with distress. "We've been attacked and overrun!"

Glenn lowered his rifle and a moment later, the silhouette of a horseman emerged from the darkness. The horseman brought his mount to a skidding halt and threw himself off. He staggered over to the smoking remnants of their campfire and almost collapsed.

"Jezus!" he gasped. "I thought they had me! They chased me and some of the others for most of ten miles."

"What happened?" Glenn asked, grabbing the man and helping him back to his feet. "Tell us *exactly* what happened."

"The Indians attacked the surveyors' camp right at sundown. Came racing straight out of the dying sun. They didn't fire a shot or anything until they were almost on us and then they overran the our camp and tried to scatter all our horses. We attempted to make a stand. Tried to keep ahold of our horses and our wits but there were too many of 'em to stand up against. First thing I know, we were being overrun and slaughtered."

The young surveyor's voice cracked and he sobbed brokenly while men worked to rekindle their campfire. When the flames grew higher, it became clear to everyone that the surveyor had been wounded several times.

"Sit down," Megan ordered, pulling the shattered man aside and starting to unbutton his coat, "while I take a good look at your wounds."

But the man rolled his eyes and shook his head. "I can't sit still for that!" he cried. "There may still be a few of my friends alive out there someplace! Maybe a few that got away like me."

"If they did," Glenn said, "I'm sure that they'd come this way."

But the surveyor wagged his head violently back and forth. "No, sir!" he cried. "Not if they were chased in the other direction! I'm telling you, we were overrun and we all scattered like quail, every man runnin' to save his own life."

"Calm down," Glenn said, realizing that the surveyor was on the verge of hysteria.

He turned to the other men. "I know that strong spirits are prohibited out here in the work camps and for good reason. But doesn't someone have a little whiskey that this man can drink to calm his nerves?"

A half dozen of the men all answered at once to the affirmative and before Glenn could turn back around, several bottles were being offered. The young surveyor, whose name was Clyde Evans, grabbed a bottle and upended it, drinking savagely. No one tried to stop him until the bottle was empty and he sat gasping and trembling. His coat was in shreds, his shirt was blood-soaked and even in the firelight, his eyes were glazed with shock.

With Glenn's help, Megan got his bloody coat and shirt off and threw them aside. "I'm going to need more whiskey to clean his wounds. He's been stabbed, shot with an arrow and clubbed. It's a wonder he's still alive, much less conscious."

"We can't just sit here and let them Indians kill off any of his friends that might have got away to make a run for it," a burly Irishman said with excitement as he looked at Glenn. "Mr. Gilchrist, we have to do *something*!"

"We will," Glenn promised.

"We've got to go find that camp and see if we can save any of them boys," another man said eagerly. "We've got some horses. We could all ride out in a wagon, or . . . or even your surrey!"

The men all erupted in a chorus of arguments, some for and some against going, until foreman Bill Galloway's voice drowned out the others.

"All right, men! Listen good! We're *not* going to go gallivantin' around in the night and getting ourselves scalped for no good reason."

This declaration resulted in a cacophony of protests.

"No, sir!" Galloway shouted. "What we're going to do is to wait until dawn and then we'll form a rescue party."

"But they'll probably all be dead by then!"

"Better them college boys than us," Galloway said flatly.

No one argued the point but neither was anyone pleased.

"Galloway is right," Glenn said. "We could be cut down in the dark or attacked at sunrise. We've got to think this out and be prepared. And we need to leave enough men here to protect Megan and our own camp."

Everyone glanced at Megan, who said, "I don't need protection. I want to go with you. There will be other wounded and I'll be needed."

Glenn started to object, but then he caught himself and said, "That might be a good idea."

He could tell that his reply caught her by surprise. Megan stood tall in the firelight and then said, "Thank you, Glenn," a moment before she began to try to save young Clyde Evans's life.

CHAPTER
3

Dawn crept like a thief across the eastern horizon and Glenn watched it struggle to pierce the darkness. It began with a faint, shimmering glow behind the distant mountains, then flowed into a thin crimson line and finally became a fiery orb as the sun shouldered out of the earth.

When he heard Megan stir and then sit erect, Glenn turned his eyes away from the sunrise and said, "You must be very tired, Megan. How is Clyde Evans?"

"He'll be fine," she said with a big yawn. "It's a miracle that he is still alive given his wounds."

Glenn reached out and took Megan's hand. "I doubt if you got more than two hours sleep."

"I can sleep later," she whispered. "That doesn't worry me. But what do you expect will happen when we ride out to find that surveyor camp?"

"I don't know. But I can't see that we have any choice but to forge ahead and try and rescue any other survivors that might have escaped that Cheyenne attack."

"Do you really believe there could be

Glenn released her ha

"But they'd be tracked and slaughtered by the Cheyenne this morning, wouldn't they?"

Glenn had reached the same conclusion. "Probably."

"Then . . ."

"Then we need to find our dead and bury them," Glenn said. "And we need to get moving as soon as possible. Are you sure that you want to come with us, Megan?"

She nodded an emphatic yes. "Besides being needed, I'd feel far safer with you and the rescue party than I would staying here with the rest of the crew."

"All right," he said, noting how other men had begun moving about in preparation to leaving.

"Mr. Gilchrist?"

Glenn turned to see Bill Galloway. "Yes?"

Galloway shifted uneasily. Even in the pale light, the man looked drawn and haggard. Galloway cleared his throat and when he spoke, his voice was low and earnest. "I've been thinking and worrying all night about what we've decided to do this morning. To be honest, I have my doubts."

"What doubts?"

"I just don't see how anyone else could have survived and I'm convinced that, if we go running off looking for bodies, we're just asking to get surrounded out in the open and wiped out."

Glenn took a moment to button up his coat while he considered Galloway's words and waited for the man to elaborate. When it was clear that the foreman wasn't going to add anything more, Glenn said, "So, Bill, what are you trying to say? That we shouldn't do anything? That you want to pretend that our forward survey camp wasn't attacked and keep your crew busy working on this trestle."

"No, dammit!" Galloway exploded. "Of course not! But *I'm* the one that is responsible for this crew—not you. You don't even work for the UP anymore so it's not your ass if things go bad out there with the Indians. It's mine!"

Megan stood up. "Bill, you can't seriously be suggesting that we do nothing."

"No, that's not what I'm suggesting at all!"

Galloway's broad shoulders slumped and he shook his head with despair and confusion. He glanced over at the dark silhouettes of the men who were gathering to leave and hissed, "I just don't know if going out there and exposing ourselves to them murderin' Cheyenne is the right thing to do!"

"We *have* to go find the dead and bury them," Glenn said. "And then Megan and I are moving on."

"Alone! After what just happened?"

Glenn looked at Megan, who nodded her head. He turned back to Galloway and said, "Bill, I've ridden with Joshua Hood and I've fought the Cheyenne. I'm pretty sure the war party that attacked that surveyors' camp will have fled north before the army or the railroad can retaliate. They've learned from hard lessons that their best course is to hit and run."

Galloway nodded but did not look fully convinced. "I'll admit that you know a lot more about the Indians than I do. And I'm not a bit afraid of them, mind you. It's just that . . . well, I might do the wrong thing out of ignorance and I sure don't want to be responsible for gettin' even more men killed. I just don't feel qualified."

"Would you like me to lead our rescue party?"

Galloway's relief was palpable. "You bet I would! I just think that you're the better man for that job. I'll stay here with the rest of the crew and keep working on the trestle. It's damned important that we get 'er finished up this week. That's *my* job, Gilchrist. Like I said, I never hired on to be an Indian fighter."

"Sure," Glenn said, wanting to make it easy on the big Irishman. "Have some of the men also changed their minds about going out to find any survivors?"

"I expect they have," Galloway answered. He looked at Megan. "I sure wish you'd stay here with us. Be a whole lot safer, Miss O'Connell."

"No, thanks," she said, ice in her voice.

"Well," Galloway mumbled awkwardly, "suit yourself. But I expect that some of the men will have changed their minds. None of them hired on to fight Indians either. We can defend ourselves when we're attacked, but to go out there lookin' for . . ."

"I understand," Glenn said. "You don't have to keep explaining."

Galloway looked ashamed of himself but Glenn didn't think any less of the man. The Union Pacific foreman's courage was not in question. Men tough and strong enough to work on the transcontinental railroad were anything but cowards.

While Megan went to check on Evans and make sure that his wounds had not opened again, Glenn hitched up the surrey and mustered the construction workers.

"All right," he said without mincing words, "who still wants to go see if there are any other survivors?"

It was clear that their outrage and passion for revenge had died overnight because only a few men stepped forward. Last night, every man in the camp would have ridden out into the darkness, but in the cold light of dawn, only five UP construction workers, including Ives and McLarity, still had the stomach to venture out among the Cheyenne.

"We'll take our surrey and a wagon and load them with bandages, food, water and extra weapons, just in case we find any more wounded," Glenn said.

"Or in case you get attacked and shot up," a man said in a low but distinct voice.

"That's enough!" Galloway snarled. "I'll hear no more of that talk."

Glenn studied the faces of the five volunteers. They were all young and determined, and he hoped they could use a rifle and stand up under fire if they were attacked. "Men," he said, "we'll leave in a half hour."

While Glenn hitched their horses to the surrey, Megan packed and then spent several precious minutes explaining to Bill Galloway exactly how the badly wounded surveyor should be taken care of and how often his bandages needed to be changed.

"We'll take care of him, don't worry," Galloway promised. "And we'll wait until the day after tomorrow, then take him back to the construction train. Could be that Joshua Hood and his boys will show up in the meantime. Like I explained last night, we're out of fresh buffalo meat and Joshua has got to know we're not fond of maggots."

"If Joshua comes, he'll help," Megan said. "He won't have any trouble finding us."

"I just hope that he finds you alive and with . . ."

Galloway caught himself and clamped his mouth shut, looking ashamed. "Sorry, Miss O'Connell."

"That's all right," she said. "We hope that he finds us back here with many more survivors."

"I should go with you," the Irish foreman stammered, big fists knotting and unknotting at his sides. "I shouldn't let—"

"No," Megan said, cutting him off in mid-sentence. "You're needed here. You can keep the crew working and be ready to fight off any attack."

Galloway nodded, but he looked so remorseful that Megan added, "Bill, if we are attacked out on these plains, we'll need this camp to run to. It's important that we'd have you and your men holding down the fort right here. Otherwise, we'd have little hope of surviving."

"That's the way you see it?"

"That's exactly the way we see it," Megan said with a nod of her head. "I don't think any of us would go out there if we didn't think that we had a place we could run to if the odds proved too great."

Galloway took heart. "Well," he said, squaring himself and standing a little taller, "we'll be here waiting, all right! And if you so much as catch sight of an Indian, you, Glenn and them others come scootin' down the line and don't you even stop to look over your shoulders."

"We'll do that," Megan promised.

A few minutes later, she was back in the surrey with Glenn. The five construction workers had hitched up a buckboard to their fastest camp horses, and everyone had taken the precaution of bridling all of the animals just in case they needed to cut the traces and make a hard run for their lives. Glenn had even seen to it that the fastest animal in camp had been saddled. It was tied behind the surrey and no one had to tell Megan that the sorrel gelding was hers if things really became desperate.

"Let's go!" Glenn ordered with the sun now floating just over the eastern horizon.

Bill Galloway's eyes were bloodshot and worried as he and the others staying in camp wished the rescue party well. Glenn, impatient for them to be on their way, slapped the lines across the horse's rump and the surrey jumped forward.

"Clyde Evans said his survey party was less than fifteen miles away," Glenn explained, "rather than the twenty that McLarity estimated."

"That's better," Megan said, clutching one of the new

Winchester repeating rifles that the forward crews insisted on being armed with against the Indians. "Not so far to run."

"Yeah," Glenn said, tight-lipped. "Only we're not going to wind up running. I'm hoping that the Indians who attacked and almost wiped out that survey party will have made fast tracks. They know that there would be hell to pay if they were caught in that area by the army."

"I hope that you're right about that," Megan said, her green eyes moving constantly back and forth across the sea of empty land and sky.

The hours passed very slowly that morning as they continued along what had once been the Oregon Trail. A blind man could have followed it because of the deep grooves that the wagon trains had cut through the prairie sod on their way west. The land was mostly wild grass but there was plenty of sage broken by occasional pinyon and juniper pines. Far to the north, Glenn could see a huge bluff, maybe two hundred feet high and three miles long. Joshua Hood had once pointed it out to him and called it a "buffalo jump," explaining that, for untold centuries before the arrival of the horse from Spain, the Indians had used the buffalo jump to kill thousands of the great shaggy beasts by driving them off the cliff.

"You can find bones piled fifty feet up from the base of that cliff. Like snowdrifts in the spring where the sun never shines," he'd said. "If you like, we can ride over there and take a look-see."

"Bones hold no fascination for me," Glenn had replied without giving the matter a second thought.

He had also declined the invitation because they'd been hunting not only fresh buffalo meat, but also the vital Wyoming coal deposits that were so necessary to keep the Union Pacific operating. On that expedition, they'd found the precious coal and the buffalo, but also a hunting party of Indians, and the fighting had been desperate.

"What are you thinking?" Megan asked, touching his arm as they rode along in anxious silence.

"I'm thinking about the last time I was out here and we ran into the Cheyenne," Glenn confessed. "And how, instead of five construction workers, we had a bunch of hunters and scouts that knew how to fight and could shoot the eye out of an eagle at five hundred yards."

"Stop worrying so much," Megan urged him. "We're not going to be caught by surprise out here on this flat land and, if we see that big of a war party, we'll just mount our horses and gallop on back to Galloway's construction camp."

"Yeah," Glenn said. "That's exactly what we'll do."

They said little more for the next few hours until, finally, they spotted the buzzards circling a few miles to the west. "I guess we've found the surveyors' camp," Glenn said. "When we get there, I'd like you to wait in the wagon while the rest of us walk up to the camp and . . ."

"I'm not waiting anywhere," Megan said quickly. "So don't say another word."

"Yes, ma'am."

The buzzards were enjoying a late breakfast until Glenn and the driver of the construction wagon put the whip to their teams and drove them off squawking and screeching.

"My God," Megan whispered, hands moving to cover her mouth as she stared at surveyors' corpses scattered around on the field of what had obviously been a terrible battle. "Dear Lord have mercy on them!"

"He'd better," Glenn said pulling the wagon up suddenly, "because the Cheyenne sure didn't."

The camp had been sacked and burned. Where there

had been canvas tents, there were now just burned brown places on the churned-up grass. The dead had been scalped and mutilated. They were lying exactly where they'd fallen, faces bloated and already turning greenish in the warm air. All of the young college-educated surveyors had been stripped of their coats, belts and boots.

Megan bowed her head and tried to stifle a sob. One of Galloway's boys became violently ill and tumbled off the construction wagon, retching.

"Mr. Gilchrist, ain't nobody could have survived," a young man with two Navy Colts tucked into his waistband said in a thin, reedy voice.

"Let's get the shovels and get them buried. Evans said that there were ten men besides himself in this survey party. Let's get a quick count."

The count only took a moment and it came up three surveyors short.

"What do you think?" Ives said, eyes straining outward in all directions for Indians.

"I think we ought to bury these men as fast as we can and then unhitch the horses and ride out looking for tracks."

"Our horses will be shod, theirs won't be," McLarity blurted out, stating the obvious.

"Right," Glenn replied. "Let's get the burying done quick."

They had brought plenty of shovels and even a few picks in case the ground was rocky. Fortunately, the camp was near a small creek and the ground was soft and fertile.

"We'll bury them right here in their camp and rake ashes over their graves," Glenn said to the men. "Maybe that way the animals will leave them alone until Mr. Casement or someone else can either move the bodies or else dig them proper graves."

The men were plenty willing to accept this decision, and they had seven shallow graves dug in less than an hour. During all that time, everyone tried to avoid looking at the poor victims but it wasn't easy. There was something powerful that kept pulling their eyes back to the bodies, and Glenn had never seen faces so morose as he did among the five.

"We can't just dump them into those graves and cover them over without at least saying a few words of prayer," Megan protested.

"I don't have any words to say," Glenn told her. He looked to the others but they all turned away.

"All right then," Megan said, "I'll say a little prayer."

She had been raised a Catholic and had a love for God that had often sustained her during the worst days of the past few years. Megan even had a well-worn Bible given to her by her mother, but it was packed somewhere in her belongings and she knew that these men were extremely anxious to be on their way, so she just bowed her head.

"Lord, these were good men and brave. Receive them to your bosom with love and forgiveness for their sins. Give to them what we all seek, everlasting life with thee in heaven. And protect us now in this time of great trial and danger. Thank you, Heavenly Father, amen."

Neither Glenn nor any of the other men needed to be told to start covering the bodies, and the sad job was accomplished in very short order.

Glenn untied and then mounted the horse they had brought for Megan and said, "I'm going to circle about and see if I can pick up any tracks that might tell us what happened to the three that we figure are still missing."

"Be careful and stay in sight," Megan pleaded. "The

Indians could be hiding in those trees along the stream."

"I doubt it," Glenn said, "but I promise you that I won't be caught napping."

He put the sorrel gelding to a trot and moved away toward the trees, certain that, if there had been any survivors, they'd have headed for the only cover to be found within miles. Glenn had watched Joshua sign read, but he was still mystified by the art of tracking. A good scout or tracker could read the land like a professor would read a book.

As Glenn studied the maze of tracks, the only thing he could be sure of was that there had been a lot of Indian ponies and that only occasionally did he catch a glimpse of a shod hoofprint. It had rained only the day before and the ground was soft, so the hoofprints were clear. The majority of them were also cupped, which meant that the horses had been running.

Glenn came upon a dark patch in the grass and dismounted. His worst suspicions were confirmed when he fingered the stain and realized that it was dried blood. He studied the trees less than a quarter mile away and remounted his horse. Pulling his six-gun, Glenn rode slowly forward, every nerve in his body jangling with alarm.

Glenn was almost to the trees and his heart was hammering the inside of his ribs when he saw a flicker of movement in the shadows. Glenn jerked up so hard on his reins that the sorrel almost squatted on its haunches. Nostrils wide and quivering, the animal snorted and tried to spin away from the trees, but Glenn managed to hold it steady.

Drawing his gun, he yelled, "Hello?"

"Run!" a voice screamed. "For gawdsakes . . . ahhhh . . . run!"

Glenn froze for an instant as rifles spat death toward

him. He spun the sorrel around so violently that it almost
lost its footing and fell before Glenn booted the terrified
beast into a hard gallop.

It was less than a mile back to the others, but when
the sorrel staggered under the impact of two rifle bullets,
Glenn knew that he would never make the distance. The
sorrel was knocked off stride. Then its front legs buckled
and it started to tumble. Glenn kicked free of his stirrups
and everything went blurry as he was hurled into the
air. He struck the ground and felt his left forearm snap.
Somewhere far away he heard screams. It might have been
Indians, it might have been the white man who'd shouted
a warning from the trees, and it might even have been his
mortally wounded horse.

Glenn didn't know. A wave of pain swept over him and
the left side of his body felt numb and unresponsive. He
thought he could hear Megan shouting but could not be
certain. All he knew for sure was that he was a dead man
if he didn't somehow jump to his feet and run.

It seemed to take him forever to get up. Twice, he
lost his balance and fell. When he finally did get to
his feet, he stood swaying and dizzy. He turned to see
a bunch of mounted Cheyenne pouring out of the trees,
feathers streaming, slashes of bright war paint shiny on
their hard faces.

"Glenn!" Megan gasped, grabbing his arm and yanking
him forward even as McLarity grabbed his other arm
while firing at the onrushing Cheyenne. "Run!"

Somehow, he did run. Glenn didn't remember it, but he
must have run because the next thing he knew, he was
being shoved facedown behind their overturned buckboard. Ives had cut the traces on all the horses and ordered
both the surrey and the buckboard to be used as barricades against the Cheyenne bullets. Two of the men were

ordered to hobble the horses and hang onto them at the cost of their lives.

Glenn fumbled for his six-gun, but he was suffering from double vision. He squinted and it was better. Ives, McLarity and the other men opened up with their new Winchester repeating rifles, although a few still had the reliable fifteen-shot Henry repeaters which could fire a steady thirty shots in a minute with a single reloading.

The Cheyenne were also armed with rifles, but they were single-shot weapons and not very accurate. Glenn heard a few heavy slugs slap the bottom of the surrey, but they were of no consequence compared to the Indians' terrible screams of anger as they charged straight into the concentrated fire of the UP riflemen.

Megan was right beside Glenn and was far too busy to be afraid. Her rifle was blazing and she was certain that, if the Indians overran their barricade and got among them, the end was at hand. She kept firing and firing. Then she reloaded and her bullet knocked an Indian pony down. The scene before her was one straight out of Hell as Indians and ponies were crashing to the ground. Again and again, a Cheyenne warrior would rise to his feet after some terrible spill only to stagger forward and be shot down.

Megan fired until her rifle was empty again and the gunsmoke was so thick she could not find a moving target. A lone warrior burst through the smoke, his face contorted with hatred. He was riddled with a volley of bullets and flung backward.

The battle was over before Megan, Glenn, or anyone else even realized it. One moment they were staring into Hell, the next they were blanketed by a great, oppressive silence broken only by the sound of receding hoofbeats.

"By gawd," someone said, "we did it! We beat them bloody bastards!"

Glenn gritted his teeth and had to concentrate in order to release his rifle. He did not feel pain, only a dull throbbing in his forearm and a terrible pounding in his head.

"Reload!" he shouted to the Union Pacific laborers. "Everyone reload!"

Beside him, Megan sobbed and Glenn turned to see her staring at McLarity's bloody face. The man had taken a bullet through the cheekbone which had exited through the back of his skull. He must have died instantly.

"Anyone else hurt!" Glenn shouted. "Anyone else hurt!"

"I've been hit," a man said tightly. "Shoulder wound."

"My ear is missing!" another cried, batting at the side of his head and staring at his bloody palm. "They shot my damn ear off!"

"Shut up!" Ives hissed. "Gawdammit, they may be getting ready to attack again."

Glenn stared through the smoke, which was already beginning to turn thin and wispy. He could see Indians gliding through the smoke like dark shadows, collecting their dead and gathering their scattered horses. A shaken young man beside Glenn cocked back the hammer of his pistol and took aim, but Glenn clamped his hand over the weapon.

"Let's let them go in peace."

"After what they did to McLarity and our surveyors!"

"If we let them go, we can get back to your camp. If we kill a few now, they'll dog us to death. Is that what you want?"

The young man wagged his head back and forth.

"What about the three that are missing?" Ives said.

"I think we'll find them in the trees," Glenn said. "I'll go back and look as soon as this is finished."

The Indians vanished like the gunsmoke leaving a clean

field of battle and very little evidence of death.

Megan helped bandage wounds and steady frayed nerves. "You're so brave," she told one young man who was glassy-eyed with shock. "You fought gallantly."

To another, she said, "We'll have no trouble now. It's finished."

"It was like in the war," the man said. "I was in the War between the States, you know. I was a corporal and I believe that an angel was on my shoulder at Bull Run. It was different than this, bigger and louder and more dead. But . . . but it was the same too."

He looked into her eyes. "Any of that make any sense to you, Miss O'Connell? I thought I'd do better than the others 'cause I been through the killin' . . . but I was wrong."

"Death is death, and it's just as terrible to think you are going to die today as it must have been back then."

"It's worse! I was younger and I didn't think about it so much as now. Look at my hands." He held them up, fingers splayed before her eyes. "See how they're shakin'? Like as if I was a . . . ."

"Shhh. Just be quiet and relax," Megan urged.

She turned to Glenn and said, "Is your forearm broken?"

"I think so."

"I'll splint it. Are you really determined to ride back to the trees?"

"Yeah," he said. "I've got to finish this."

"At least take someone with you. Please?"

"I'll go," Ives volunteered.

Glenn didn't try to stop the man. He was very sure that the Indians were all gone and that he'd find the three dead surveyors in the trees, maybe stripped of their flesh, maybe just dead.

"Let's go," he said, untying the hobbles from the nearest animal.

Now that the fighting was over, Glenn noticed his forearm was throbbing painfully. It was a deep, dull ache that left him slightly nauseous. Ignoring the pain, he managed to get on another horse and then he waited until Ives joined him.

"I hope we're not attacked again," the man said grimly.

"We won't be."

Glenn's words proved to be true this time. They rode into the trees and found the three dead surveyors. All of them had died hard, especially the sandy-haired kid. He'd been tied to a tree and carved up like a holiday turkey.

Slipping off of his horse, Glenn said, "Get some help and then let's bury these poor souls."

Ives climbed back on his horse and galloped away, leaving Glenn with the three dead men, all of whom he knew by name.

One hour later, they were rolling eastward, retracing their path to the construction camp and feeling empty and devastated.

"What are we going to do now?" Megan asked, breaking a long, grim silence.

"I think I should take you back to the train."

"And then go to California alone?"

"I *have* to go," he told her. "You just want to go."

"Make no mistake about this. I'm going to California with or without you, Glenn Gilchrist."

Glenn was silent for a long time and then he said, "All right, we'll rest a day or two and let things blow over and then we'll come back. We'll travel fast and by night and hope that we can sneak through without being caught. But it's a gamble, Megan. That's the only word for it. It's a life-and-death gamble."

"Then let's roll the dice and get on with it," she said quietly.

Glenn took a deep breath and expelled it slowly. He could face his own death, but he couldn't even conceive of Megan being captured by Indians and made to suffer before she was finally killed. And since it did not make any sense to express his deepest fears, he resolved to simply kill her if they were overrun by the Indians.

Anything would be better than what had happened to those they'd found back in the cottonwood trees.

CHAPTER
4

"Indians coming!" one of the laborers cried, pointing east. "Indians!"

Glenn felt his heart stop for a moment but then he relaxed. "They're not Indians," he said. "They're our men."

"It's Joshua," Megan said with relief.

At the sight of the large band of approaching scouts and buffalo hunters, Glenn felt a great weight of responsibility lift from his shoulders. And while it wasn't exactly the United States Cavalry coming to their rescue, the UP scouts and hunters were the next best thing.

When Joshua reined up in front of them and saw that Megan was unhurt, he visibly relaxed although his expression remained set and hard. He stepped down from his horse without a word of greeting, grabbed Glenn by his coat sleeve, then yanked him completely out of the surrey.

Glenn tried to land on his feet but instead fell on his broken arm. A cry of pain escaped his lips and he struggled to throw Joshua off and do battle, but Megan was already jumping into the fray.

"Joshua, are you crazy?" she screamed. "Let go of him or I'll take a whip to you this instant!"

Megan grabbed the buggy whip and reared back with

45

it, ready to strike, and Joshua stepped back, eyes hot and angry.

"I'm going to beat the hell outta Glenn for allowing you to ride out here with Indians on the warpath!"

"If you don't apologize to him this minute, then *I'll* be on the warpath! It was my decision to go to that surveyors' camp despite his objections."

"Don't matter!" Joshua said, taking a step back with his fists knotted in anger.

Glenn pushed to his feet and balled his own fists.

"He's got a broken left arm!" Megan shouted, jumping between the two men. "Joshua, don't you dare fight him!"

"Damn you!" Joshua cussed. "If I had my way, Glenn, you'd have a broken *neck*!"

Joshua's eyes snapped with barely controlled fury, but he backed away and then took a deep breath before letting it out slowly. "All right, Gilchrist. Exactly what happened at the surveyors' camp?"

Glenn, pale and shaking, replied, "Tell him, Megan."

Megan's account was terse and very concise. She ended by saying, "Glenn took all the risk when he rode over to those cottonwood trees. He's lucky to be alive."

"So are the rest of you," Joshua said, looking at Ives and the other men who'd returned in their buckboard. "How many men did you lose?"

"McLarity," Ives said. "We buried him with the surveyors."

Joshua twisted around in his saddle and spoke to a huge buckskin-clad man. "They'll want the bodies buried proper in Cheyenne or maybe even Omaha, same as the last ones. We're going to need shovels and tarps."

"We'll get 'em," the big man said.

Joshua looked back at Glenn, his eyes still hard and

unforgiving. Then, he turned to Megan. "Are you still determined to push on through this Indian country without a proper escort?"

"There's no turning back now," she told him, eyes flashing with defiance.

"Then I'm taking you and Gilchrist on to Fort Bridger," Joshua said after a long pause. "From there, you can connect with the Wells Fargo stage line that will carry you all the way to Sacramento."

"Don't do us any favors," Glenn said angrily. "If Durant discovered you escorted us to Fort Bridger, he'd fire you in an instant."

"To hell with him!" Joshua growled, reining his horse around and riding out. "If he fires me, I'll find a better job."

Megan saw Glenn start to say something and she cut him off quickly. "If he wants to escort us to Fort Bridger, then let's not let pride stand in our way. We need some protection in this country."

"You're right," Glenn said, biting back pain. "Especially now that I've got this damned broken arm."

It took them almost a week to reach Fort Bridger, and they did not see a single Indian, although Joshua said that they were watched from the distant hills by a small hunting party of Cheyenne. On the way to the fort, Joshua told Glenn and Megan something about the colorful history of the fort.

According to Joshua, Fort Bridger had originated as an old trading post founded in 1842 by the famed mountain man and explorer Jim Bridger and his partner, Louis Vasquez. Being well situated near the old Emigrant Trail in the valley of Black's Fork of the Green River, the fort was immediately able to provide for the increasing tide of emigrants bound for both Oregon and California. Fort Bridger prospered almost from the day of its founding. About ten years later, the fort was sold to Brigham Young and the Mormons, who considered it the natural gateway to their community of Deseret. According to Joshua, Bridger and Vasquez had been forced to sell their fort and trading post to the Mormons for the sum of eight thousand dollars. The Mormons had occupied it for another decade, enclosing the fort with a great stone wall some fifteen feet tall. The wall had been constructed to repel Indian attacks, but the fort had always been too well manned to come under serious attack. The present army post had been established in 1858.

"It's a beautiful valley and you'll not find a prettier site for an army post anywhere in the West," Joshua had promised. "Black's Fork, a tributary of the Green River, has five streams that meander through the valley and one of them flows right through the fort itself. The soldiers complain about the winters and the isolation, but for those who love fishing and hunting, it's a paradise. There are deer and antelope, black and grizzly bear, and even beaver are still to be found in the streams."

Joshua had smiled at Megan and said, "At this time of year, the valley will deep in grass and there will still be wildflowers to pick."

"I can hardly wait to see it," Megan had replied. "It seems that all we have had to look at since leaving Laramie is sagebrush."

And now, as they topped a low rise and gazed out on the famous Fort Bridger, Megan could see that the Bridger Basin was every bit as lovely as Joshua had promised.

They rode into the fort and discovered it to be under the charge of Captain Anthony Belton, a middle-aged man well versed in the social graces who insisted that they join the officers for dinner.

"And I have some good news for you," Belton said, "although it is regrettable for us."

"And that is?" Megan asked.

"A Wells Fargo stage is due to arrive tomorrow morning with several Mormon officials I have to confer with. Then we'll all depart in the afternoon for Salt Lake City. I would, of course, prefer that we could enjoy your company for a longer period, but if you are in a hurry to reach California . . ."

"I'm afraid that we are," Megan said, glancing toward Glenn.

"Yes," he said, "we are indeed."

The captain's expression reflected concern as he studied Glenn's arm resting in a sling. "Has a surgeon looked at that?"

"No," Glenn told the man. "But Megan has and that's good enough for me."

"When you reach Salt Lake City, you should have a physician examine it just in case," the captain advised. "Sometimes they can discover that the bones need to be properly reset."

Glenn started to argue but Megan said, "He's right. A doctor should have a look at that arm to make sure that it's going to heal properly."

Glenn nodded agreeably, but he knew that his arm was going to be fine although it did continue to ache and throb. That evening they had a fine dinner with the fort's three officers and talked mostly about the history of Fort Bridger, much of which Glenn and Megan already had learned from Joshua. The conversation was enjoyable, but Glenn's arm was paining him and both he and Megan were very tired, so they were assigned their quarters and went to bed early. Joshua, never one for formality, had declined the supper invitation and had eaten with his scouts and buffalo hunters out in the valley itself where they were camped for the night.

The Wells Fargo stage arrived as promised about midmorning and the three Mormon officials were ushered into the captain's office, where they spent the remainder of the morning. At the noontime meal Glenn and Megan joined them, and they seemed to be in quite good spirits. Glenn sensed at once that the Mormons were pleased with their discussions with the army.

Their leader was a large, officious man named Abner Harrington and he wore muttonchop whiskers and a fancy silk tie. He was in his early sixties and obviously well educated.

"I understand," Harrington said, addressing Glenn, "that you were employed as a Union Pacific Railroad surveyor and engineer. Is that correct?"

"It is."

"And why, may I inquire, are you here so far in advance of your construction crews?"

Glenn's eyes momentarily shifted to Megan. In truth, he did not really care to get into the whole sordid story of Durant's charges of spying. And yet, Glenn realized that this was a question that he could expect time and time again and needed to be prepared to answer.

"Dr. Thomas Durant and I had something of a disagreement," Glenn said, choosing his words carefully. "So rather than work for the Union Pacific, I've decided to go west and to help the Central Pacific, which I understand is having quite a struggle getting tracks down across the Sierras."

"I think," Captain Belton said, "that is quite an understatement."

"Yes," Harrington agreed. "It's my belief that the Central Pacific is hopelessly mired down in the snows around at Donner Pass."

"I disagree," Glenn said. "What I have heard is that the Central Pacific has every intention of tunneling *under* Donner Pass."

"Even so," a Mormon named Everett Smith said, "how do they possibly keep the tracks clear on either side of the tunnel when the snowdrifts get fifteen, even twenty feet deep the way they do on our Wasatch Mountain summits?"

"They will have to design huge snowplows and push them with however many engines it takes to clear the tracks," Glenn said. "If a train with several engines pulling and pushing can drag along fifty heavily loaded railroad cars—as we have often done when hauling construction supplies westward—then it can certainly cut through the very deepest snowdrifts."

"Then how," Harrington asked, eyes narrowing, "would you propose to protect the rolling stock against the threat of avalanches?"

It was a good question and one that Glenn had not considered until this moment. "I don't know," he admitted. "I suspect that the Crocker and his Chinese will have to build huge barricades on the upper slopes strong enough to protect both the tracks and the trains."

"I don't believe," Harrington said, "that man can build anything strong enough to withstand a major avalanche. Have you ever witnessed one, Mr. Gilchrist?"

"I have not."

"So I suspected," Harrington said with a superior smile. "Let me inform you that a major avalanche has the power of a major flood or a even a Midwestern tornado. I have seen them—plenty of them—wipe out roads, cabins, bridges, everything in their path. Could any man-made dam have stopped the Missouri or the Mississippi Rivers from destroying entire riverside towns and communities?"

"No," Glenn conceded. "But a huge river is . . ."

"Is like a huge avalanche, only it's not frozen," the Mormon leader said. "Mark my words, even if the Central Pacific does manage to tunnel under an entire mountain— which I doubt they can do—they still will have to rebuild their line every single spring after the heavy snow and avalanches have wiped it off the face of the mountainsides."

Glenn was an engineer and he had to admit that Harrington's dire prediction was not altogether unreasonable. As an engineer, he had studied mathematics, physics, geology and every science necessary to understand the forces of stress and how to withstand them. But he had never heard of a professor who didn't readily admit that science could never overcome the full force of Nature when she went on the rampage. Acts of God, they were called, and they dwarfed any efforts of man to thwart them.

"I'll admit that the challenge seems insurmountable," he conceded to the officers and their guests, "and no one ever said that the job would be easy. But history has demonstrated that man, when he puts his mind, body, heart and complete energy to a task, can overcome all but the impossible. I think that the Central Pacific *can* beat the Sierra Nevadas and I want to help them do it."

"Here, here," the captain said, raising a water glass in toast. "Well spoken, Mr. Gilchrist!"

"Yes," Harrington said, "but still the naive words of a dreamer."

"A dreamer?" Glenn asked. "There was a time when people believed the world was flat and that ships would fall off its edge if they ventured too far out to sea. There was a time when it seemed as if America would never extend beyond the Appalachian Mountains and yet, here we are on the American frontier enjoying all the comforts of modern civilization."

"Not all," Megan said. "I think that people back East would still find this setting rather primitive."

"Of course," Glenn said, "but we are hardly deprived, and I suspect that our friends from Utah are very comfortably situated in their great Valley of Salt Lake."

"Deseret," the third Mormon, a thin, acerbic-looking man named Hazen declared. "We prefer our community to be known as Deseret."

"Of course," Glenn said. "And I know full well that the Union Pacific is counting on you to help with their construction efforts as they drive into the Utah Territory."

"Our leader, Mr. Brigham Young, was very displeased when he learned that the Central Pacific would *not* be coming through our great city."

"I can only say that the railroad made every effort to do so but the best line, unfortunately, did pass to the north."

"Even so," Harrington interjected, "accommodations should have been made."

"I'm afraid that the line of construction must be approved by the United States Congress," Glenn said, feeling a chill spread across the table. "And as relations between your community and Congress have not always been on the best of terms, you could hardly expect that additional funds would be approved so that the rails would flow through Salt Lake City."

Harrington bristled. "I believe that some recognition of our pioneering efforts should have been made and our communities' needs accounted for by the non-believers."

"I think," Megan said, changing the conversation before

it exploded into argument and smiling at all the men, "that Fort Bridger rests in one of the most beautiful basins I've ever seen. Wouldn't everyone agree?"

Everyone did agree, and the mood at the table thawed until it was time to prepare to leave Fort Bridger.

"Excuse me," Megan said, seeing Joshua outside also preparing to depart with his men. "I want to have a private word with Joshua before he rides away."

Glenn nodded. He knew that Megan thought a great deal of the rough scout and hunter and even found the man attractive. "Sure," he said.

Megan went over to the buckskin-clad scout and slipped her arm though his. "Can we have a moment together?"

"We could have a *lifetime* together if you wanted," he said, taking her aside. "You know that."

"Yes," Megan said, "I do. But I also know that you have too wild a spirit ever to be tamed by a woman or the responsibilities of a family."

"Maybe you do too," he said, dark eyes shifting toward Glenn. "Maybe you're fooling yourself about marrying anyone."

"Maybe," she said as they walked out to the edge of the fort and stood gazing at the distant mountains. "But I want you to know that you will always hold a special place in my heart."

"Fine," he said, trying to control the bitterness he felt. "I'll hang onto that memory and it'll warm me around the campfire."

Megan heard the sarcasm and was hurt. "Joshua," she said, turning to face him, "I'm sorry. I should have been strong enough to hide the attraction I've always felt for you. But I wasn't and it has caused you pain."

"You're attracted to me, but not enough to marry me. Is that the way of it, Megan?"

"Yes," she whispered, wishing she could find the words to make him understand and then forgive her.

He chuckled, but it was not a nice sound. "You know, Megan, I'll bet that I've felt the urge to kidnap you about a hundred times. I've even come to your tent and stood outside ready to do it."

"But you didn't."

"No," he said, sighing deeply. "I kept waiting for you to see that I was the best man for you despite all my rough edges. I thought you'd come around and see that sooner or later. But now . . . now you're leaving and I'll probably never see you again."

"Never is a long, long time," Megan said. "I think we will meet again. I'll be there when the tracks join. Will you?"

He threw back his head and stared up at the blue sky for a moment and, when he dropped his chin, he had that old boyish amusement in his eyes that Megan loved.

"I'll be there, Megan. If I don't get killed, I'll be there. If for no other reason, I'll be there to see you."

"Good," she said, lifting up on her toes and kissing his cheek.

"Now," she said, "if . . ."

Joshua roughly pulled her to his chest and his mouth ravaged her lips. Megan struggled, aware that Glenn and everyone else were staring at this embrace. But she was helpless and, after a moment, his kiss made her forget about everything except the hard heat of his body and the pounding of her heart.

"There," he said, pushing her back to arm's length and grinning to see her breast heaving. "If we never meet again, at least we can say we *really* kissed. You can match that and the way you're feeling right now against any other man and I'll wager you'll remember me."

"I wish that you had not done that," Megan said, feeling angry and a little helpless. "I wish—"

"I wish you'd just shut up and get on that stagecoach before I do more than kiss you, Megan girl," he choked. "I'm just tired to death of talking."

Megan spun around and went back to the others. She knew that her face was crimson and she could not meet anyone's eyes as she gathered her bags and hurried to the waiting stagecoach.

"All aboard!" the driver said, climbing up onto his seat and gathering the lines. "We got a long way to go before sundown!"

Megan sat beside the rotund Abner Harrington while Glenn, Hazen and Smith sat across from her. She knew that Glenn was seething with anger and jealousy but she could not possibly speak to him now. And even if she could, Megan wasn't sure what she could possibly say to make Glenn feel better.

"So long, Megan darling!" Joshua shouted with a wide grin as their stagecoach rolled out of Fort Bridger. "See you where the rails join!"

Megan raised her gloved hand and waved to Joshua and his scouts. And then, she closed her eyes and prayed for a swift and uneventful ride on to Salt Lake City, or Deseret, as these Mormons preferred.

CHAPTER
5

Their stay in Salt Lake City was brief but instructive. After visiting a good surgeon and being assured that his broken arm was properly set and well on the mend, Glenn and Megan were housed in separate hotels. They met and used their one evening to walk about the bustling city and admire the industrious Mormon people who labored hard for a better tomorrow. Brigham Young had led his people out of Illinois, where they had been persecuted, mostly because of their belief in polygamy. He was said to be a dynamic man, pious and completely dedicated to the betterment of the Church of the Latter-Day Saints, which had been founded by Joseph Smith and which had flourished despite great odds.

It was said that, when Brigham Young first saw the Great Salt Lake and its basin, he'd proclaimed, "This is it! This will be the City of Zion!"

"It's hard to believe the enormous work and energy that these people have given to transform this desert into such a beautiful and thriving metropolis," Megan said the next morning as they toured the city while awaiting a stagecoach that would carry them on to Reno, Nevada.

"It is," Glenn agreed. "When those emigrant handcart people finally topped the Wasatch Mountains back in 1847 and gazed down on this valley, it must have looked like a desert wilderness and anything but the promised land. And I understand that they very nearly starved out the first two years because of hard winters and poor crops."

"What happened to change things and allow them to build such a beautiful temple and city?" Megan asked, studying the massive granite buildings that filled Temple Square.

"If my history lessons serve me well, I recall that the Forty-Niner gold rush played a big part in helping the Mormons to survive. An estimated ten to fifteen thousand Forty-Niners passed through Salt Lake City on their way to California. By the time they arrived at this point, their wagons were in desperate need of repairs and their live-stock were all lame or worn out. The Forty-Niners were willing to pay almost anything for supplies so that they could push on across the desert to California."

"All of which I imagine the Mormons were probably only too happy to provide," Megan said as they gazed up at the huge and impressive Mormon Temple adorned with a gold-leaf-covered Angel of Moroni.

"Yes," Glenn said. "And not only did they have this huge and desperate market of California-bound emigrants, but the Mormons were able to buy their repairable goods and footsore animals for giveaway prices. No one has ever accused these people of being either stupid or lazy."

"No," Megan said, watching a tall, well-dressed Mormon in his fifties accompanied by two young wives and a doz-en or more children hurry across Temple Square, "but I have a great deal of difficulty with their practice of polygamy."

"I expect that most women not of their faith do," Glenn said. "And while some men might relish the idea of many wives, others realize that it is a dubious blessing."

Megan frowned at Glenn. "And what is that supposed to mean?"

"Only that the responsibilities must be enormous," Glenn assured her.

"Oh," Megan said, looking bemused.

Glenn took her arm and they headed back to their respective hotels to gather their baggage. They were due to leave at four o'clock and travel all night, circumventing the Great Salt Lake and its vast surrounding flats of salt and alkali.

When they arrived at the stagecoach, however, there was some kind of turmoil which Glenn did not at first understand. Several men were rushing about as if searching for something, looking very upset and angry.

"What's going on?" Glenn asked one of these men.

"None of your concern," the Mormon quickly assured him. "It's just a personal matter."

The answer was not sufficient but Glenn saw no point in making an issue of the disturbance, so he and Megan took a bench at the stage station and waited for the passengers to be called to board. After a few minutes, the half-dozen men gave up their search and left in a huff.

"Say," Glenn called to a rough-looking man who he guessed might be either the stagecoach driver or the shotgun guard. "What were all those gentlemen searching for?"

"A young woman named Miss Rebecca York," the man replied. "She was supposed to marry one of the elders of the Church today but turned up missing."

Megan stepped forward with sudden concern. "Any idea where Miss York might have fled?"

"Nope," the man said without interest as he cradled a double-barreled shotgun. "They thought she was trying to sneak on board this stage but I told 'em they was wrong. They searched the stage and the baggage room, then generally poked their damn noses into every nook and cranny in the office before they were finally satisfied."

"Why would Miss York run?" Megan asked.

"The Mormon she had to marry is old enough to be her father. It was an arranged marriage and Miss York was probably real unhappy. It sometimes happens with young Mormon fillies. Causes quite a ruckus but they eventually are forced into the marriage no matter what their feelings."

"How incredibly cruel!" Megan exclaimed.

"Cruel?" the stage man said with a shrug of his shoulders. "I don't know about that. They marry old men sometimes, but they're always well taken care of and have few wants. It's true that they generally start at the bottom of the household pecking order, but they seem content enough after the children start coming."

Megan's expression told Glenn that she was having a difficult time accepting this before she said, "But what about . . ."

"About what?" the man demanded.

"About love!"

The man actually blushed and then looked embarrassed by the word. "Uh. . . . I dunno about that kind of stuff, miss. Out here, a man and a woman just marry, have kids and hope to live a long time. It's tougher than maybe where you come from."

Megan's green eyes flashed with anger. "Mister, I have been operating a tent saloon on the UP railroad line for over two years and you can't tell me anything about hardship or toughness because I have seen it all. But even so, there is such a thing as love and no woman—or man—should ever even consider marriage without love."

"I wouldn't know about that," the stage man said looking quite annoyed. "I married a widow woman with four little hellions and we've been struggling for the last five years to keep a roof over our heads and the damn wolf from our door. When we talk, it ain't about no love but about how we're going to buy enough grub to last until my next payday."

The stage man turned on his heels and marched away toward the livery leaving Megan before she could form a rejoinder.

"I feel sorry for his wife," Megan said quietly.

"I expect she's too busy with those 'four little hellions' to feel sorry for herself," Glenn said.

"All aboard who's going west!" the ticket man shouted from his office window. "All aboard!"

Glenn and Megan gathered up their handbags. Their larger bags had been put in the stagecoach's rear luggage boot. A pair of huge and obviously heavy trunks were hoisted up onto the roof of the coach, where they were lashed down securely. Glenn soon realized that there would be a total of seven passengers, so they would have a pretty full complement for the long desert journey west.

"Tickets, please," the driver said, flashing a toothless smile. "Give me your tickets."

Glenn and Megan were near the head of the line and able to get good seats together facing forward. One of the other passengers, a sweating, out-of-breath and heavyset cloth salesman from Reno, had the misfortune to be late. This gave him the dreaded middle bench which had no backing to it and thus required its occupant to balance precariously.

"Someone want to trade me their place?" the salesman asked, looking hopefully around the coach. When no one spoke, he said, "I'll pay five dollars for your seat from here to Reno."

There were no takers. "Ten dollars?"

"Make it fifty and you might have something," said a scowling passenger who had introduced himself as Joe Fisher.

"Fifty dollars!" the salesman wheezed. "Why, that's almost as much as the fare!"

"Fifty is what it would cost to take my seat." Fisher looked around. "Anybody else willing to sit perched like a damn bird for the next five hundred miles?"

When no one answered, the man cackled like a crow. Glenn took an instant dislike to Fisher, but he was not about to trade his place for fifty dollars either.

"Maybe someone is getting off sooner," the cloth salesman said, still hopeful. "Perhaps at Elko?"

When everyone just looked at him, the salesman's eyebrows raised and his voice took on a note of pleading. "Listen," he appealed, "there are five of us gentlemen and just two ladies. And while I'd never expect a lady to take her turn here on this middle bench, I do believe it only fair that we all trade places and share in the discomfort on an equal basis."

"I'll trade with you once in a while," Glenn offered. "But not fifty-fifty."

"Why thank you, sir!" the salesman cried. "Now who else will display a sense of fairness?"

"No one else is such a fool," the hawk-faced man said, shooting Glenn a tough glance.

Glenn bristled. "Are you calling me a fool?"

Joe Fisher leaned forward, right hand slipping across his waistband toward the handle of his gun. "Only a fool or a weakling would give up his seat because of this man's whining."

Glenn didn't reach for his gun as Fisher expected. Instead, he drove a straight right hand into the man's Adam's apple with such force that it caused Fisher to slam back in his seat, choking and trying to breathe. Glenn quickly disarmed the man.

"Are you going to do something to help him?" the salesman cried. "He may die!"

"No," Glenn said, "he won't. But I guarantee that he's not going to be very pleasant company during the next twenty-four hours."

"That was uncalled for," a middle-aged man said angrily as he tried to calm his small and frightened-looking wife. "Totally uncalled for!"

Glenn looked at Megan, who squeezed his good arm and said, "Mr. Fisher insulted you and got what he had coming."

Glenn felt better after that. The hawk-faced man finally managed to get his breath but when he recovered, he was livid with anger.

"Give me back my gun!"

"Not until I'm ready."

"I'm going to speak to the driver about you at our next stop!" Fisher raged.

"I'm also going to speak to him," Glenn warned. "And I'm going to suggest that you be removed from the inside of this coach and made to ride up on top."

"No!" The salesman lowered his voice. "I just don't think that will be necessary. I'm sure that we can all become good friends."

"To hell with that!" Fisher wheezed, his eyes watery but filled with pure hatred as he studied Glenn. "You're going to pay for this, mister."

"Is that right," Glenn said, "well, in that case . . ."

"Stop it! Can't you see that all this is upsetting my

wife!" the middle-aged man complained with obvious exasperation. "We don't want any trouble in here! We just want to travel in peace and as much comfort as we can. We all need to get along and try to make this trip endurable."

"He's right," another passenger argued. "We've got to go too far to be feuding and fighting."

"Of course he's right," Megan said, "let's be friends."

"I'm willing," Glenn said, studying Fisher.

"I'm not!"

"Suit yourself," Glenn told the man. "But I'm going to insist to the driver that you be removed from this coach at the first stage stop."

"You sonofabitch," Fisher breathed. "I'll get even."

"Oh, stop this at once!" the woman cried, wringing her hands in her lap. "You men are *upsetting* me!"

The anguish of her words caused Glenn to sit back and relax, while Fisher kept swallowing and trying to clear his injured throat.

"What is your name?" Megan asked the woman.

"Mildred," she replied. "And my husband is Noel."

Megan was trying to lighten the mood. "And how far are you traveling?"

"We're going all the way to California to visit our son. He lives in San Francisco and is a very successful banker."

"How nice," Megan said, encouraging the woman to elaborate on her son and thus calm her fears as the miles rolled past.

When Glenn became convinced that he was not about to be attacked by Fisher, he turned his attention to the Great Salt Lake. It was an immense body of water surrounded by huge tracts of glistening white salt and alkali deposits dotted with patches of crusted and stunted sagebrush. Its colors seemed to change as the sun began to sink toward the western horizon. In some places, the water looked milky, but in others, it took on alternating shades of the purest greens and blues. Glenn thought the lake had a striking and deathless quality about it that he had never seen before in any body of water. And its size, as he well remembered from seeing it from atop a Wasatch Mountain summit, was truly gargantuan.

"Did you know that you cannot drown in that lake? That it is so salty that it suspends you on the surface?" said a young man in a brown suit who had been reading the Book of Mormon and silently praying.

"Is that a fact?" Noel asked with surprise.

"It is," the ascetic-looking Mormon answered. "The water, unfortunately, is much too salty to be of any agricultural use but it has a remarkable buoyancy. We do glean the salt, of course, and sell it at a nice profit."

"Does it ever flood?" Glenn asked.

"Yes," the man said, removing his cheap bowler hat and nervously curling its brim. "When the snows are especially deep in the surrounding mountains, the lake rises. When that happens, we do lose farmland, which is very difficult to reclaim and requires several years of leaching the salts out of the soil before it can become productive. As you might suspect, our farms in the general proximity of that lake are nearly worthless and are used primarily for grazing sheep, horses and cattle."

"Very logical," Glenn said, thinking how well-spoken this quiet and yet informative young man was. The man introduced himself as Ezekial Poole. "And how far westward are you traveling, Mr. Poole?" Glenn asked.

"Please call me Zeke," the young man said, offering his hand. He had a strong grip and his palms were heavily calloused. It reminded Glenn that all Mormons, no matter how educated, were expected to work hard in the fields to ensure the harvests. "And I am going as far as this line takes me."

Zeke turned his eyes to the cloth salesman. "That would be . . ."

"Sacramento," the man said. "And as long as we are introducing ourselves, my name is Earl Peamont. And please," the cloth salesman said, "my back is killing me from trying to sit here. Do you think we could trade places, just for a while?"

"Sure," Glenn said.

"I'll take a turn too," Zeke said. "That way, it will make things easier all the way around."

"Thank you!" Peamont said, flashing the Mormon a quick, grateful smile.

They traded places and watched the sunset turn the surface of the huge salt lake into a pot of liquid gold. The sky burned with a fire and everyone except the hawk-faced man craned their necks to enjoy the spectacular show. When the sun finally died, their Concord stagecoach sailed on through the dusty moonlight. The passengers talked little, lost in their own private reflections. Glenn was relieved when Joe Fisher slumped against the side wall and began to snore.

It must have been nearly midnight, and Poole had taken his turn on the center bench, when the stage finally rolled into its first stop. Half of the passengers were sleeping and there was confusion as they awakened and were told that the stop would be brief.

"Just some beans and bread and a few minutes for every-one to stretch their legs and make a nature call, if they need to," the driver said.

The stage station was humble and, while the horses were replaced, the passengers filed slowly into a rock shanty and were told to take their places at a long, rough-hewn table and benches. Without greeting or ceremony, an Indian woman entered the room and began to ladle out big spoonfuls of beans on a tin plate. They looked like they were weeks old and were even crusty, but no one complained. When the woman disappeared back into her kitchen she left the pot of beans, and it was no time at all until the pot was scraped clean.

"I'm still hungry!" a passenger complained, but then smiled as the woman brought in two big pans of cornbread.

The bread was excellent and the coffee strong, with a hint of licorice. It wasn't until Glenn was nearly through with his meal that Megan tugged on his sleeve and whispered, "Where is Zeke?"

Glenn had been so famished that he hadn't even noticed that the young Mormon was missing. "Didn't he come in here and fill a plate?"

"Yes, he did," Megan said. "But then he left quickly."

"Maybe he prefers to eat alone," Glenn said, emptying his coffee cup and then helping Megan to her feet.

They were the first ones outside, and it felt good to stretch their legs and gaze up at the stars. Glenn was about to say something when he caught a movement against the sky over the stagecoach.

"What the . . ." Glenn blinked. "Megan, someone is up on top of the stage."

"Why in heaven's name would they be up there at this hour?"

Glenn's first thought was that one of the stage line employees might be up there rummaging through the passengers' big trunks. But then, he recognized the bowler and Zeke's slender form. "It's that young Mormon, Zeke!"

Glenn hurried over to the wagon, and when he stepped up onto the coach and grabbed the top railing that held the trunks in place, Zeke's face appeared silhouetted against the moon and starlight.

"What are you doing up there?"

"I . . . I was just trying to get into my trunk," Zeke said. "Wanted to get a clean shirt."

"Oh," Glenn said. "Well, do you need some help?"

"No, no!"

"Is something the matter, Zeke?"

The Mormon shook his head. "Nope. I got what I needed. All the food gone?"

"Might be some cornbread left. It was the best part of the meal."

Zeke hopped down from the coach, straightened his coat and tie, then hurried on into the rock shanty.

"He's a strange one," Glenn said. "One minute he's as cool and collected as could be, the next he acts as jittery as a June bug in a hot skillet. What do you make of him, Megan?"

"I don't know," she confessed. "He's really the first Mormon that I've ever been around. But I will have to admit that he acts a little queer."

Glenn climbed down from the coach and waited beside Megan until the other passengers were ushered outside. In a few minutes, everyone piled into the Concord and they were rolling west again. Megan laid her head on Glenn's shoulder and slept, though fitfully. Glenn tried to sleep, but Joe Fisher had not gone up on the top and Glenn had forgotten to talk to the driver about him. The man's hatred was palpable and Glenn did not trust himself to close his eyes for fear he'd get a knife plunged into his throat.

It was a long night and when dawn finally came, they were still laboring across the vast and inhospitable Salt

Lake Desert somewhere west of the huge lake. At nine o'clock, they made a halt in the desert as a Wells Fargo employee appeared driving a buckboard to bring five barrels of water for their stagecoach horses. The poor beasts were coated with alkali dust and extremely thirsty. The dust and their sweat had formed a gray coat that blanketed their bodies, making Glenn wonder how the animals would ever be clean again.

"We'll be here just a half hour and then push on," the driver announced. "Everyone better do their business because we ain't stopping till noon."

"What about breakfast?" Earl Peamont cried. "My God, you mean to say that we'll have no breakfast?"

"You had an early one last night at the rock station," the driver said, drawing a piece of jerky from his coat pocket and biting off a big hunk. "Too bad."

The shotgun guard chuckled and then bit off a big hunk of his own jerky and chewed it with a superior grin. Glenn wasn't all that hungry, but Peamont was famished.

"How about sharing some of that jerky?" the cloth salesman said with a big smile.

"Nope," each of the Wells Fargo employees replied.

"Then how about I *buy* some from you?"

"Cost you five dollars for this bitty piece and it'll probably make you sick," the shotgun guard said, holding up what little was left of his jerky.

Peamont swallowed and licked his porcine lips. "I sure am hungry," he whined. "I sure would like some of that."

"Five dollars," the guard repeated, not grinning any longer.

"I'll take it," Peamont said, jumping forward with a bill suddenly materializing in his chubby hand. "But by gawd, this isn't right! They promised we'd be properly fed!"

The pair chuckled and the guard looked very pleased

about the money, stuffing it into his dirty vest.

Glenn was red-eyed from lack of sleep. He pulled the driver aside and told him about Joe Fisher's threat of retaliation.

"I can't make him ride up on top," the driver said. "He paid for a ticket same as you did."

Glenn could see the man's point, but he wasn't ready to give in and have to be on guard for another day and night, always wondering if Fisher was going to attack him the minute he dozed. Turning on his heels, he marched over to his adversary and said, "Fisher, I'm giving your gun back to you unloaded."

"I got extra bullets. It ain't going to change anything."

"Fine," Glenn said. "Why don't we just settle this right here and now, and that way no one will get hit with any stray bullets. Just because my left arm is in a sling, it doesn't mean that my right arm and hand can't do what is necessary."

Glenn took a step back and pushed his coat aside to reveal the gun that he wore on his hip. Joshua Hood and he had spent a lot of time practicing and Glenn felt confident that he was a better-than-average shot, although he was a long way from being a gunfighter.

"Well?" he asked.

The hatchet-faced man was not of a mind to settle the issue this way. With a snort of derision, Fisher turned his back on Glenn hissing, "I'm tired of the smell of all you people anyway!"

Then, Fisher climbed up top of the coach and wedged himself in between the two trunks.

"Hey," Peamont cried in protest. "Be careful with my trunks."

Glenn looked at Megan and saw that she had the same thought and that was that Zeke had told them he owned one of the trunks. Had the refined and well-educated Mormon been trying to steal something from it? If so, it would certainly explain his excitable and erratic behavior. Glenn turned to look at Zeke, but the fellow was jumping into the stagecoach.

"Now no one will have to sit on the middle bench," Zeke said, trying to force a cheerful smile.

"What's wrong?" Glenn blurted out. "You look pale."

"I'm fine," Zeke snapped. "Just . . . just a little tired, I think."

"I see," Megan said, looking sympathetic. She smiled at Zeke and then at Mrs. Appleton. "Well, at least things will be a little less cramped now that—"

"Hey!" Joe Fisher shouted from up above. "There's someone *inside this trunk*!"

Zeke threw open the stagecoach door, and Glenn only saw the flash of the gun in his hand as he jumped to the ground and cried, "Fisher, leave her alone!"

Glenn started to move, but Megan grabbed his arm and held him for a moment. "What do you want to bet we've found that young Mormon bride-to-be stowed away in a trunk?"

"Yep. I'm sure that's what all this has to be about," Glenn said, not doubting it for an instant as he eased out of the coach while the other passengers talked excitedly among themselves.

"Move back from that trunk, Mr. Fisher!" the Mormon shouted. "Just put your hands in the air and scoot back as far as you can."

Fisher obeyed but when the shotgun guard reached for his weapon, Zeke thumbed back the hammer of his six-gun and coolly shot the man's hat right off his head. The team of horses bolted forward spilling Fisher off the roof. The man landed on the back of his neck and his cry of surprise and alarm was abruptly cut short.

Megan rushed over to him and bent low. When she raised and looked at Glenn, she whispered, "He landed on his neck and it must have broken. He's dead!"

Zeke's jaw dropped and he stared. "I . . . I didn't kill him," he finally stammered. "It wasn't my fault that Mr. Fisher fell off the roof and was unlucky enough to have broken his neck."

"No," Glenn said, "it wasn't your fault, but a judge might think you had something to do with it."

Zeke raised his gun and waved it back and forth. "I'm not going back and neither is Becky!"

"Easy," the driver said. "Ain't no one going to say you killed that man. Now just put the gun down and help your girlfriend outa that trunk and everything will be fine."

Zeke nodded and climbed up onto the boot, then jumped onto the roof of the coach as the other passengers disembarked. A moment later, a very pretty but frightened-looking young lady was emerging from Peamont's big trunk.

"He . . . he said I'd come to harm if I didn't play their game!" Peamont explained in a rush. "Young Mr. Poole said he'd kill me if I didn't let him put the girl in that trunk so she could be snuck out of Salt Lake City."

"That's a lie," Zeke flatly stated. "I paid you twenty dollars."

"Did not!"

"Did too," Zeke said, taking the girl's hand and drawing her close. "And since I figured you might lie to everyone just like you are right now, I even marked the bills I paid you to hide Becky in your trunk."

Peamont gulped. "You're crazy!"

"What's the mark?" Megan asked.

"A heart with an arrow through it and our initials, E. P.

and R. Y. You'll find them on money he's carrying in his pocket."

"Why," the guard said reaching for his vest pocket, "that five-dollar bill that he gave me for the jerky has that damned heart and initials!"

To prove his words, he waved the bill in front of the passengers.

Glenn shook his head. "It really doesn't matter anymore," he said.

"Does to me!" Peamont cried. "If them Mormons back in Salt Lake City ever find out I was helpin' young Poole, I'll never be allowed to sell cloth there again!"

"And I damn sure *will* tell them," the driver said. "Unless I'm well paid to keep my mouth shut."

"And so will I," the shotgun guard said, folding his arms across his chest and looking like the cat that swallowed the canary.

Glenn, Megan and everyone else seemed to reach the same conclusion and that was to allow the young couple to travel on at least to the next stage station. Clearly, the pair were in love and very frightened. And while the accident had been partially Zeke's fault, it could also be argued that the driver had been negligent because he had not properly set his brake. Had he done so, the wagon would not have jumped forward and the accident would not have happened.

So they left the watering stop with Fisher's body lashed down on the roof between the two big trunks. Zeke and Rebecca squeezed into the coach and, since they were both slim, they didn't take much more room than a single man with the considerable girth of Earl Peamont.

Nobody said much of anything as the stagecoach rolled all morning across the desert heading toward Nevada. Glenn knew that the young couple did not want to openly discuss their plans for the future. Quite clearly, that future did not and could not take place in the Utah Territory.

No matter, Glenn thought. The pair were young, bright and very much in love. They would probably be married at the first opportunity and find a way to make a good life for themselves. You could see the confidence and joy in their eyes. They looked very happy.

Glenn shot a sideways glance at Megan and their eyes met. He wondered if she was also noting how happy and how much in love these Mormon kids were and if she also felt envious.

Glenn sincerely hoped so.

CHAPTER
6

By the time their stagecoach had rolled into Elko, Nevada, the young Mormon couple had so charmed the passengers that a collection was taken up and enough money donated to take the couple on to Reno or even Sacramento. A few days later, on a windy afternoon during a wheel-repair delay at a tiny stage stop in Central Nevada, Glenn and Megan found themselves alone with the young Utah couple as they watched tumbleweeds race and bound across the desert.

"Zeke, I've been very curious," Glenn said. "What would you have done if your people had discovered Becky in that big trunk and tried to force her to marry against her will?"

Zeke held Becky's hand and his answer was slow and thoughtful. "I had armed myself and I was prepared to fight to the death for her."

"You would have shot one of them?" Becky asked, blue eyes widening.

"I . . . I don't know," Zeke confided. "I'd not have let them take you away to marry Mr. Parks, I know that much."

Glenn nodded with understanding. "Sometimes we just don't know what we will do when we're pushed to the wall. But I suspect, Zeke, that you'd have pulled the trigger."

"Probably," Zeke agreed. "But that's all behind us now. Becky and I may go back to our people someday and settle around Salt Lake City. It's hard to leave family and friends. To be honest, we've never lived among ... among other kinds. We're both a little worried."

"There will be some adjustments," Glenn said, not wanting to alarm the young couple but also wanting to warn them that they were about to enter a much less orderly and much less law-abiding society. "You'll have to be wary of strangers."

"I know," Zeke said. "We have always enjoyed the protection of Brigham Young and our Church, but I have dealt with many emigrants and I understand that some are bad."

"Some are," Megan agreed, "but others are completely honest and God-fearing people who would never harm or cheat their fellowman. There are all different kinds and you'll soon learn how to read which ones bear watching and which ones you must never turn your back on."

"You sound," Becky said, "like you've known some very bad men."

"I have," Megan confessed. "Less than a month ago, back in Wyoming, a man and a woman who owned a competing tent saloon actually tried to murder me."

"They did?" Becky paled.

"Yes, and if it had not been for a dear friend and employee, they would have succeeded."

Megan forced a smile. "But remember that most of the people you meet will be kind and honest. Things were much safer in Salt Lake but you'll find that the opportunities might be much greater out west in a less orderly society. Since there are fewer rules, each individual has much greater freedom to make whatever they can of themselves."

Becky hugged her young man proudly. "Zeke and I have talked a lot about that and I know that he is going to excel at anything he undertakes. And I want to help him."

"You'll both do very well," Glenn said. "But if the adjustment is too difficult, I'm sure that you would be welcomed back to Salt Lake City after it's clear that you were meant for each other and when you perhaps even have a family."

But Becky shook her head. "I don't want to ever go back. Sure, I miss my parents, but they refused to save me from an awful marriage. I'm not sure if I'll ever forgive them for that."

"Were your parents polygamists?" Megan asked.

"No. And while I realize that everyone thinks that most Mormon families do practice polygamy, that is just not the case. Actually, the polygamists are the minority."

"I would never have taken another wife," Zeke vowed. "I'd never want anyone but Becky."

The couple gazed into each other's eyes with such devotion that Glenn felt like an intruder in their presence. "Come on, Megan," he said, "let's go for a little walk before we climb back into that stagecoach."

Megan took his arm and they strolled a short way out into the desert. The wind sent Megan's auburn-colored hair flying. She looked wild and untamed and wonderful to Glenn. He took Megan into his arms and said, "Zeke and Becky are getting married in Reno. How about we make it a double wedding?"

Megan's smile faded. "I don't think so."

Glenn took a deep breath and expelled it slowly. He tried to smile but his face was as brittle as glass and very much in danger of cracking. "Why, in the name of God, not?"

She pulled back and toed the earth. "Glenn, it's just not the right time."

He tried to swallow his exasperation. "Will there *ever* be a 'right time'?"

"Of course! But we've some big challenges ahead of us in California. You have to find this fellow that you are accused of spying with against the Union Pacific Railroad. Once that is resolved, you need to get hired and then help build the Central Pacific over those mountains."

"And while I'm doing all of that, what do you intend to be doing?"

"I . . . I really don't know," she admitted, "but I've been thinking about it a lot. Obviously, I can't operate a tent saloon and follow the Central Pacific's construction crews because the Chinese don't drink liquor and I've heard that they even prefer to cook their own food. Things like dried fish, abalone, seaweed, pork and rice."

"Yes," Glenn said in agreement, "I've heard about their eating habits. They're a far cry from the black coffee and mountains of buffalo meat, beans, potatoes and sourdough bread that the Irish consume."

"So," Megan said, "if I can't serve the Central Pacific's laborers either drinks or food, I'm not sure where that leaves me."

"Why not as my wife?" Glenn asked recklessly. "I'm sure that I can get a job with the Central Pacific. There must be plenty of other engineers and supervisors who are married and have families. They probably live in Sacramento and travel up by the wagonload every Sunday to picnic and visit their husbands."

"I can't see myself doing that," Megan gently explained. "I haven't been dreaming of California all these years with the idea of sitting around waiting to see you on Sundays, as sweet as that may sound."

Megan shook her head and her eyes pleaded for understanding. "Glenn, you *can* understand, can't you?"

"Yes," he heard himself say. "I can understand. In fact, I anticipated this very conversation."

She relaxed and folded her arms across her chest. "If that's the case, did you also anticipate a satisfactory solution to our dilemma?"

"No," Glenn had to admit, "but I do think the answer will come to us when we join the Central Pacific. I have a feeling that it is all going to work out fine."

"I hope so," Megan said with a sigh as she moved back into his arms and laid her head on his shoulder. "I do so want to be near you and find a way to share in the building of this great transcontinental railroad."

"Let's agree to an understanding between us that we'll become engaged when we arrive in Reno and then marry when the Sierras are conquered."

"That would be fine," Megan said as he took her into his arms and they kissed. "That would be *more* than fine."

Glenn would have preferred that they have a double wedding with the young Mormon couple in just a few more days, but he could live with this new and definite understanding they'd just reached. Besides, he was eager to get started working again and knew that tackling the enormously difficult Sierras would require every bit of his concentration. There would not be time for a honeymoon or even living together as man and wife until the job was complete, and that was not a very promising way to start off on a marriage.

By the time their stagecoach was in sight of Reno, the passengers were in very high spirits. After the better part of a week of being packed into the coach together, they had established a special camaraderie. They were almost like a family. There were few secrets between them after so many miles. Everyone's temperament had long since become evident, and most had openly confided about their hopes and their deepest fears.

For example, as their coach crossed the border into Nevada, the passengers had been deeply troubled to learn that the timid and excitable Mildred Appleton was terminally ill with a large tumor. While she could yet travel, her single obsession was to see her son one final time. No doubt she would soon pass away in San Francisco and her husband would never return to the East.

Earl Peamont, the heavyset cloth salesman, soon revealed himself to be rather a kind person who hated selling. Peamont had always yearned to be an expert saddle maker.

"I've a gift with leather," he assured them in a way that told Glenn the man was not bragging. "I love the smell and the feel of leather and I have worked with it all my life. Look, just look at this!"

Peamont had extracted a beautiful hand-tooled and stitched wallet from his coat pocket. Glenn, who also carried such a wallet, could readily see that Peamont's leather work and tooling were far superior. "This is beautiful," he said, meaning it.

"It's nothing," Peamont told them as the wallet was passed around to be admired by everyone. "I've done the same with bridles, purses, and I've even made a half-dozen saddles, although I've still got a lot to learn there."

"Then you should concentrate on working with leather," Megan urged. "I'm sure that you could make beautiful saddles."

"Saddle and harness makers don't earn enough money," Peamont said, taking his wallet back and looking dejected. "Why, I can earn more money on one successful business trip to Salt Lake City, Denver, Portland or St. Louis than I could earn in a year making saddles."

"Yes," Megan said, "but even with the money, you're miserable, aren't you?"

After a moment, Earl nodded. "I *am* miserable. And I hate traveling all the time and living in hotels. I'd like to settle down. Even marry again."

Attempting to lighten the mood, Peamont winked at Megan and then smiled at Becky saying, "If you pretty young ladies weren't already fixed, I'd be sparking you."

Everyone laughed because it was clear that Peamont was far too old and fat to seriously attract either Megan or Becky.

"Mr. Peamont, I suggest," Megan said, "that you buy a shop or just go to work for a good saddle maker as an apprentice. With your talent, in a few years you'll have gained an excellent reputation and you'll be doing just fine."

Peamont was genuinely uplifted by the compliment. "Do you really think so, Miss O'Connell?"

"I am sure of it."

Peamont clenched and unclenched his chubby fists and then he pounded them together and proclaimed, "By George, you're right! I'm going to quit selling cloth and start working leather. I've got enough money squirreled away in the bank to set myself up and live for nearly a year."

"Good luck!" Megan said, and everyone else in the coach echoed that same wish.

"As long as we are talking about tomorrows," Glenn said, turning to regard Zeke Poole, "what will you do to support your new bride?"

"I've always had a knack for making money buying and selling livestock and farming equipment," Zeke answered. "Of course, it will take a while for me to learn the new prices, but after that, I expect that I can make us a good living as a horse trader and dealer of farming implements."

Zeke frowned and said to Glenn, "They *do* farm around Reno, don't they?"

"Yes," Glenn said, "but I understand that farming is much more important over in the San Joaquin Valley of California."

"Is that a fact?"

"I also know that to be true," Megan said, "because I've read a lot about California. They raise everything in that big, fertile central valley. Fruit, citrus, almonds, grains, cattle, sheep, hay and lots of corn."

Zeke looked to Becky. "Perhaps we should continue on to Sacramento."

"I'd like that," she said. "All my life I've listened as the emigrants passing through Salt Lake bragged about what they'd find in California. I'd love to see it."

"Good for you!" Megan exclaimed. "I have the same strong feelings."

"Then it's settled," Zeke declared. "We'll go to California and get married in Sacramento. Becky, are you willing to wait the extra day or two?"

"I can if you can," Becky said shyly, blushing as the passengers listened to this intimate decision-making.

"Any of you ever been to Reno before?" Peamont asked, knowing they had not.

"Well, then," he continued, "before we roll in, let me tell you something about it. The town was originally known as Lake's Crossing, but they renamed it a couple years back after General Jesse Reno, a Union officer, was killed fighting the Paiutes over at South Mountain. It wasn't much of a settlement until the miners struck it rich on the Comstock Lode. The town has been booming ever since. It's a nice place to live, what with the Truckee River runnin' right through its downtown. It's a major distribution center and, if you have any money to speculate in land, you couldn't do much better than to buy in Reno."

"Why is that?" Noel Appleton asked.

"Well, the prices are already rising and they'll shoot up like Chinese skyrockets if the Central Pacific ever manages to beat the Sierras and link Reno with California. There's already talk of joining Reno, Carson City and the Comstock Lode by rail. I tell you, there is no telling how big Reno is going to get if that railroad comes through town."

"I'll do all that I can to see that happens," Glenn said with a smile.

"I hope you do," Peamont said. "I've bought some lots just off Virginia Street and I'm holding onto them expecting to one day make a big profit. Course, I might have to sell 'em off right away if I go into the saddle-making trade."

"Then sell them and establish yourself before the land rush," Megan advised. "Big money and big business bring jobs and prosperity. A well-established saddle, harness and leather goods shop would stand to reap all the benefits."

"I expect that you're right," Peamont said. "Miss, you sound like a good businesswoman. Any interest in working with me and maybe some others?"

"In what capacity?" Megan asked.

"I don't know, but there ought to be some way that you

can help us and yourself as well."

"Maybe there is," Megan said thoughtfully. "It's worth some consideration."

Glenn started to say something to discourage this because he did not want Megan to be living on one side of the Sierra Nevadas while he was helping to build a railroad up the other. But before he could object to this plan, Peamont leaned out the window and shouted, "Here we are. Welcome to Reno!"

The city was not nearly as large as Salt Lake. It rested in the eastern Sierra foothills. The country to the east was all sage but on the west, great mountains towered, many still snowcapped.

"Look at them," Glenn whispered, gazing off toward the huge and imposing Sierra Nevada mountain range. "No wonder so many critics both in Washington and out here believe that they can't be crowned with a mantle of steel."

Megan followed his eyes, leaning close, her breath sweet and warm on his cheek. "You can do it, my darling," she whispered. "If anyone can help put the rails over those mountains, it's you."

Her words made Glenn feel almost heady with confidence, but the sight of those mountains was a great leveler of his emotions. Looking at them now, Glenn could scarcely imagine anyone building a railroad either up or down their steep, towering flanks. Maybe, Glenn thought, the grade was gentler on the western side. It really had to be if there was any hope of conquest.

When they pulled into the stagecoach station, they were in for a very rude surprise. A town marshal grabbed the young Mormons the moment they disembarked.

"Hey!" Zeke shouted. "What is going on!"

The marshal, a stocky and powerful man in his late

twenties, drew his six-gun and said, "You'll just come along and don't give me any trouble, Mr. Poole. We got a telegram warning us to expect you by stage."

"What's the charge!"

"Kidnapping, of course."

"No!" Becky cried, attempting to break free and rush into Zeke's arms. "I came with him of my own free will!"

"Miss York, how old are you?" the marshal asked after handcuffing Zeke.

Becky, eyes brimming with tears, choked and said, "Eighteen. Almost nineteen."

"Miss, allow me to introduce myself as Marshal Abner Call."

He reached into his back pocket and pulled out a rumpled telegram. "Now this here telegram from the marshal at Salt Lake City says that you are just fifteen years old. That means that you are a minor and that you must be returned to your parents and that this young man has committed the crime of kidnapping."

"Now wait a minute!" Glenn said, pushing in between. "This is just ridiculous! Marshal Call, anyone can see that Miss York is older than fifteen."

"Who the hell are you?" the marshal demanded, steely eyes locking on Glenn.

"Glenn Gilchrist. I'm an engineer and their friend."

"You are in my way and I'll have to ask you to remove yourself at once or face arrest."

"What!" Glenn couldn't believe his ears. "Marshal," he protested, "this young couple is going to get married. They're in love and responsible enough to elope."

"It's a kidnapping in the eyes of the Utah law," Call said stubbornly. "Anyway, that's for Utah to decide."

"But they'll be found guilty!" Megan protested. "There

won't be any justice in Salt Lake City for this young couple."

"That's not my problem. My problem is to see that they are safely returned to Salt Lake City, and for that I am going to be paid."

"Then that's it," Glenn said. "This is just a way to pick up some extra money, isn't that true?"

Call's face turned red. "You better mind your tongue, stranger. I won't put up with any of your back talk."

"Marshal Call," Megan pleaded, "we're not trying to cause you trouble. It's just that there is no reason in the world to make an arrest."

"Who are you?" Call demanded to know.

"Megan O'Connell and I can vouch for this couple."

"Well, that's real nice to hear, honey," the marshal said, eyes dropping to Megan's bosom as he smiled. "Why don't we talk about it over dinner?"

Megan couldn't help herself. Her hand streaked up and slapped the marshal in the face, rocking his head back.

"Gawdammit!" Call shouted. "You had no reason to hit me!"

"Yes, I did," Megan said, voice shaking with fury. "But you've no right to arrest this young couple."

Marshal Call was livid and his pride had been publicly wounded. He touched his cheek and then growled at both Megan and Glenn, "You both stay outta my sight. If you interfere anymore with the law, I'll throw you in jail!"

"Marshal," Peamont said, shoving between them. "You know me, Earl Peamont?"

"Yeah, I know you, peddler," the marshal said, dismissing him with a contemptuous glance. "Now get out of here and don't waste any more of my time."

Glenn's fist balled at his side as Zeke and a weeping Becky were hauled off to the jail. Megan grabbed his good arm and held him in check, saying, "We can't help them if we're in jail, now can we?"

"No," Glenn admitted, "we cannot. We'll stay in Reno until we get them out of this mess. All right?"

"Of course," Megan said, her expression wintery as she watched the lawman and the Utah lovers disappear around a corner. "I wouldn't dream of doing it any other way."

CHAPTER
7

Glenn, Megan and Earl Peamont sat waiting in the impressive law office of Sloan, Davis & Janson. After a full hour had crawled by, Earl Peamont jumped up and went over to the young law clerk who had taken their names and asked them to wait.

"This is a matter of some importance," Peamont insisted. "I told you that when we arrived. How much longer will we have to wait to see a lawyer?"

The law clerk was a thin young man with a definite air of superiority. "Sir, I've already explained that, without an appointment, you must exercise patience."

Patience was not in Peamont's vocabulary. "But we don't even care which of the three lawyers we consult! Seems like at least one of them ought to be able to meet with us."

"I think," the clerk said, nervously glancing over his shoulder, "that Mr. Janson might be persuaded to meet with you shortly."

"I hope so."

"Sir, do you and your friends realize that our fee for an initial consultation is twenty-five dollars an hour, payable in advance?"

"That's outrageous!" Peamont exclaimed. "That's a month's wages for some men!"

The clerk's eyes grew frosty. "We are a very successful law firm, Mr. Peamont. There are other firms with lesser talent and lesser fees."

He tapped a pencil up and down on a pad of paper, cocked one eyebrow and said, "Perhaps you and your friends don't need the best legal representation available in Reno?"

Glenn went over to calm Peamont. "Earl, we *do* need the best. That's why we have no choice but to be patient and wait."

The clerk threw a quick smile at Glenn. "A wise decision, sir. The law moves with slow deliberation and it cannot be rushed. I'm sure that Mr. Janson will see you shortly."

"He'd better," Peamont groused as he turned and stomped over to sit beside Megan.

Another thirty minutes passed before a slightly rumpled and very silver-haired old gentleman in his sixties tottered out of a private office with a gold nameplate reading ARNOLD L. SLOAN affixed to the door. Sloan's brow was furrowed in concentration. "Hubert, what time is my luncheon appointment?"

"Twelve-thirty," Hubert said without looking up.

"Ah yes, of course!"

The lawyer nodded and had turned to retreat back into his office when Megan cleared her throat loud enough to attract his attention.

The attorney glanced back with surprise at her and her friends. "Hubert, who are these good people?"

"They're waiting to see Mr. Janson, sir."

"Regarding?"

The clerk looked like a man greatly inconvenienced. "I simply don't know, Mr. Sloan. But they didn't have an appointment and I knew that you would not be available and that Mr. Davis is preparing for a court date this afternoon. That leaves only Mr. Janson."

"Janson is home with a gastric disorder and he probably won't return for several days."

"Several days?" Hubert blinked.

"That's right," Sloan said with disgust. "He has a terrible case of diarrhea. I told him not to eat that spicy Mexican food again."

Megan came to her feet. "Mr. Sloan?"

He smiled benevolently. "And who, dear lovely lady, are you?"

Megan knew in an instant that the old attorney appreciated an attractive woman and saw no reason why that should be an obstacle to helping their young Mormon friends. She introduced herself, then Glenn and finally Earl Peamont.

"And what is the nature of your business?" Sloan asked.

"Perhaps we should discuss this in private," Megan suggested.

"Why, yes," Sloan said vaguely, "That might be appropriate."

He took Megan's arm and guided her inside, leaving Glenn and Peamont to tag along behind. Sloan's office was large and beautifully appointed. His desk was enormous and made of solid mahogany. Diplomas and civic citations adorned his walls along with a pair of crossed Indian lances.

"Like them?" Sloan asked, noting Glenn's interest in the stone-tipped lances.

"Yes, they're quite fascinating."

"Aren't they, though," Sloan said, selecting a smoking pipe and tamping in fresh tobacco which he immediately fired. "And what makes them more fascinating is that those lances belonged to a couple of Paiutes who were killed during a very bloody skirmish that I participated in years ago."

"How about that," Peamont said, looking impressed. "Did you personally kill the Indians who owned those lances, Mr. Sloan?"

"I can't be sure," the attorney admitted. "It was a hard battle and both sides suffered heavy losses."

"What happened?"

"The Paiute Indians had gone on the warpath and pillaged a stage station killing three men and a woman. The entire territory went into a panic and there was a call to arms. We formed a loose and rowdy company and marched north toward Pyramid Lake. I was one of the officers and there was a great deal of drinking among the volunteers. It was not a very orderly group. The entire expedition had the flavor of being a . . . well, a lark."

"You went north to fight Indians and it seemed like a lark?"

"Not to me," Sloan assured them, "but to some of the others, yes, I should say so. At any rate, there was no discipline or military preparation. Not like in the Mexican War when I was an officer. And the result was pretty catastrophic. We blundered smack into a Paiute ambush and many of us were killed in a single withering hail of arrows, lances and bullets. Only the luckiest among us survived."

Sloan's eyes tightened at the corners. "So you see, those Indian weapons are not trophies, Mr. Peamont. They are reminders of the white man's folly when he tries to subjugate innocent people with reckless force."

"Innocent people?" Peamont asked. "I thought you said that the Indians wiped out a stage station."

"As it turned out, the Paiute had nothing to do with the killings at that stage station. The vile acts were perpetrated by a band of cutthroats, one of whom was shot and confessed with his dying breath."

"I see," Peamont said. "So all that killing was just a mistake."

"Yes," Sloan answered, "and a very sad one indeed. Those lances remind me that, before one should act, one must gather all the facts and do so with calm deliberation. Now, my friends, what are the facts behind your visit?"

"Mr. Sloan," Glenn began, "we are in need of some expert legal advice regarding a kidnap and arrest."

"Now that might be interesting," Sloan said, sucking on his pipe as he took to his big chair behind his office desk. "But have you paid my initial consultation fee yet?"

Glenn shook his head.

Sloan grinned around his pipe stem. "It's twenty-five dollars an hour . . . with a two-hour minimum."

"But it won't take anything like two hours to explain the problem," Glenn argued. "It won't take even ten minutes."

"I'll be the judge of that," Sloan said. "But first, you must produce your exhibit of good faith in the form of fifty dollars cash."

Glenn looked at Peamont and the heavyset man shook his head.

"Glenn," Megan said, "perhaps we should go find *another* law firm after all."

"I agree." Glenn was irritated as he turned to escort Megan out the door.

"Wait a minute!" Sloan called, jumping up from his chair, spilling the burning ashes from his pipe across his desk and then smothering them with his coat sleeve. "Listen, if you can give me the facts in ten minutes or less, I'll tell you whether or not I can be of service at no charge. Is that fair?"

"It's fair," Glenn said as they returned to face the lawyer. "Megan, why don't you tell Mr. Sloan what happened today at the stage station?"

"All right," Megan said. "Mr. Sloan, we've just arrived from Salt Lake City where we were joined by a young girl who was being forced to marry a much older man that she did not love. The young man that she *does* love hid her in a trunk on the stage and thus managed to smuggle her out of Salt Lake City. We discovered this girl at stage stop, where the happy young couple joined us with the full intention of being married today here in Reno."

"Good, good," Sloan said, wiping the cinders off his coat sleeve and repacking his pipe. "I salute their courage and resourcefulness."

"We did too," Megan said, "but now your Marshal Abner Call has arrested them!"

Sloan lit his pipe. "Both the boy and the girl were arrested?"

"Yes," Megan answered. "Apparently, Marshal Call received a telegram from the authorities in Salt Lake City stating the girl was forcibly kidnapped."

"But you said . . ."

"She *wasn't* kidnapped," Megan said angrily. "The poor dear came of her own free will. We explained that but your marshal refuses to listen. It is his full intention to see that the couple are returned to Salt Lake City."

Sloan puffed rapidly. "So, we have a romantic situation here. A young man and woman who are in love, and a Mormon elder whose vanity, I'm convinced, has been deeply wounded. I am quite sure that such a man is primarily concerned with saving face."

"All right," Glenn conceded, "but how does that help us resolve this awful situation?"

"Well," Sloan said, "if the Mormon suitor were here, we could figure out some way to assuage his pride and get him to drop his charges of kidnapping."

"But the man is *not* here," Megan said impatiently.

"Yes," Sloan mused, "that is true."

Megan leaned forward. "Mr. Sloan, can you do anything to stop the young couple from being returned to Utah?"

Sloan shifted uneasily in his large leather office chair and puffed for a few moments in reflection before he asked, "How old is she?"

"Eighteen," Megan said.

"Almost nineteen," Peamont quickly added.

"And she has proof of this?"

Megan shook her head. "I . . . I don't think so. You see, the poor thing was hidden in a trunk and she brought few personal belongings."

"Yes, yes of course," Sloan said, his chin bobbing up and down. "And to make matters worse, every personal record of those faithful to the Mormon Church is sealed in the vaults of the Mormon Temple. The Mormon people are zealots about genealogy, you know. They would never release anything of that nature to anyone outside their faith."

"Are you saying that we are stuck unless Miss Rebecca York can prove that she is not a minor?" Glenn asked.

"Not only that," Sloan said, "but her lover can and will be charged with kidnapping."

Sloan steepled his long, pale fingers. "I'm sorry to tell you this, but the kidnapping of a minor is a very, very serious offense. The young man you seek to aid will probably be imprisoned for years."

"Isn't there *something* that can be done to help them!" Megan exclaimed. "This is all wrong."

"I don't mean to upset you further," Sloan said, "but

what if the girl really is a minor? It's very difficult to tell the age of a girl and—"

"She's *not* a girl!" Megan snapped. "She's a young woman and she is at least eighteen."

"And I presume the young man is older?"

"Yes!"

Megan lowered her voice and took a deep, steadying breath. "I'm sorry, Mr. Sloan. I didn't mean to raise my voice. It's just that it appears that there is no way to help this couple and prevent a terrible injustice."

"No," the attorney said with genuine regret, "sadly, it appears that there is not."

Glenn couldn't accept that. "Mr. Sloan," he suggested, "could you speak to Marshal Call on our behalf and ask him to lose that damned telegram?"

Sloan chuckled around the stem of his pipe, spilling more ashes, which he brushed into a silver ashtray. "I'm sorry, but Marshal Call is what you would describe as pigheaded, not entirely a bad trait for a lawman. He would never 'lose' the telegram and the more you attempt to dissuade him from carrying out what he now perceives as being his lawful duty, the more determined he will become."

"Then there's no hope," Glenn pronounced. "All we can do is sit by and watch this travesty unfold with certain knowledge that two young lives will be torn apart, their hearts forever broken."

"Young hearts do mend," Sloan said quietly. "We've all had our little heartaches, haven't we?"

That irritated Megan. "That's the most ridiculous thing I've ever heard, Mr. Sloan! We're not talking about two childhood sweethearts. We're talking about a very fine young man who is going to be sent to prison and a lovely young woman being forced to marry some old goat who is probably well into his sixties!"

"*I* am in my sixties, dear lady," Sloan cried with indignation, "and I'm not an old goat!"

"And neither are you trying to ruin Miss York's life and happiness!" Megan shot back.

"Please," Glenn said, wanting to calm them both. "There is nothing to be gained by wrangling among ourselves. It's not going to help either Zeke or Becky."

Sloan's fingers drummed his desk top. "That's their names?"

"Yes," Glenn said.

Sloan came to his feet and began to pace back and forth, obviously agitated. Finally, the attorney stopped and removed his pipe from his mouth. "There is one way, but you must swear that I never suggested it."

Glenn looked at Megan, then at Peamont before he nodded and said, "Of course."

"Free them," Sloan said bluntly.

"What!"

"They will have to be escorted back to Utah by Marshal Call's deputy. He is a dull-witted man named Eli Harlan. The marshal would not tolerate someone with any brains or ambition so Mr. Harlan is his perfect assistant. Outsmart the deputy and free your friends."

"You're telling us to . . ."

"I'm telling you nothing," Sloan said quickly.

Glenn felt Megan's hand squeeze his arm tightly and knew she was game, but the cloth salesman began to sweat profusely as he wagged his double chins back and forth.

"Uh-uh," he said. "Not a chance."

"Your ten minutes are up," Sloan said.

Once outside in the street, Megan and Glenn both had to grab and haul Peamont to a standstill.

"Let go of me!" he protested.

"All right," Glenn said, releasing the man. "But I don't see how you can walk away from this and have any conscience."

"A salesman can't have a conscience," Peamont said. "It would cost him too much money. All he must care about is profit and survival."

"I don't believe that for a moment," Megan said. "Nor do I believe that you are going to put this thing out of your mind. You can't just walk out on us now."

"It's done!" Peamont exclaimed. "You heard the lawyer. There is nothing *legal* that we can do to prevent them from returning Zeke and Becky to Utah."

"Very well," Megan said frostily. "If that is your decision, then good-bye and good luck."

Peamont sighed deeply. "You're really going to do it, aren't you."

"Yes," Glenn said. "We just don't know where or how."

Peamont scowled. "Perhaps it would help you to know that the eastbound stage makes a short detour through the Comstock Lode to pick up additional passengers. That's where you should free those Mormon kids."

"Thank you."

"That's all I can say or do," Peamont assured them. "Now, good-bye!"

"Good-bye, Earl," Megan said, "and good luck with your new profession."

Peamont nodded stiffly and then hurried away.

"What now?" Megan asked.

"We accompany Deputy Harlan, Zeke and Becky up to Virginia City on the stage while we plot to free them."

"Don't you think that is a little too obvious and will put the deputy on guard?"

Glenn had to agree. "We'll find another way up to

Virginia City and we'll try to do this without even show-
ing our faces to Deputy Harlan."

"It's to our great advantage that he doesn't even know
what we look like," Megan said, linking her arm through
Glenn's as they headed down the street.

"Megan, where are we going?" he asked.

"To buy horses, of course. Once we free Zeke and
Becky, you don't think we'll have time to escape afoot
over those huge Sierra Nevada Mountains, do you?"

"No."

"And we certainly don't want to be charged with horse
stealing on top of Mormon stealing, do we?" she asked
with a mischievous wink.

"Most certainly not!"

"Then we must buy saddle horses and reach the
Comstock Lode in plenty of time to think up a way
to free our young Mormon friends."

"Any idea how we are to do this?" Glenn asked.

"No. You?"

"No."

"We'll think of something," Megan promised. "After all,
Mr. Sloan did say that Deputy Harlan was dull-witted."

"Yes," Glenn agreed. "Let's just hope the man isn't also
trigger-happy."

"I hadn't thought of that," Megan said as they hurried
along Virginia Street.

CHAPTER
8

Glenn and Megan bought four saddle horses and headed south and toward Virginia City, less than twenty miles away. They had both heard stories about the fabled Comstock Lode and, in particular, Virginia City. Neither of them, however, were prepared for the size of the huge mining town perched against the slope of Sun Mountain.

The Comstock Lode had been discovered in 1859, ten years after the great California gold rush which had been ignited by the discovery of gold by James Marshal at Sutter's Creek. California's Forty-Niner gold rush had brought thousands of argonauts streaming westward and they had forever changed the face of America's western frontier. And when California's placer gold had finally been picked clean, the Comstock Lode was discovered. Miners by the tens of thousands who had been enduring tough times in California wasted no time in racing over the Sierras for a second chance at striking it rich in the barren Nevada Territory.

But unlike the California gold rush, where any prospector with luck and a three-dollar gold pan could strike it rich, the wealth of the Comstock Lode was buried deep beneath the surface. Men who had long prided themselves as individuals who worked for no one soon realized that they did not have the skill, knowledge, resources or equipment to work independently on the Comstock Lode. They had been forced from the lush California forests into a far less hospitable country where only the very strongest managed to survive. And instead of panning for gold in the icy California streams and deep, powerful rivers such as the Stanislaus, the Merced and the American, they now had to burrow far underground and become hard-rock miners.

The Comstock Lode mines were hundreds of feet deep and men were expected to plunge into the belly of the earth clinging to wire cages suspended by mine cables. They worked more than a thousand feet underground in steamy shafts eerily illuminated by kerosene lamps, always wondering if they would be the next to be buried alive in an unending series of mine disasters.

"Look at it, Megan!" Glenn exclaimed as they rode their horses into Virginia City and saw the great mines and smelters belching smoke into the clear, thin air.

"It's huge," Megan said. "Bigger than Omaha."

"Far bigger," Glenn agreed. "And I've heard that, if all the tunnels and shafts under Virginia City were connected in one long, uninterrupted line, they would reach all the way to San Francisco."

"I can believe that," Megan said. "Look at the size of those mine tailings."

The tailings were the mountains of waste rock which had been carved out of the shafts and tunnels and then processed for their gold and silver. In addition to the immense tailings, there were thousands of smaller tailings that looked like giant molehills. Each was a mute testimony to the futile struggles of individual miners who had attempted to dig and bore their own shafts by hand. Inevitably failing to strike paydirt close to the surface, one by one these individual miners had abandoned their claims. They had gone to work for the big operators such as the fabulously wealthy Ophir, Belcher and Consolidated Virginia mines whose stock was traded on markets around the world.

"I've never seen anything like this in my life," Glenn said, gazing out at the huge metropolis clinging to the slopes of Sun Mountain. "Now I can believe that liveryman who sold us these horses when he claimed that there are at least ten thousand people working up here in Virginia City and Gold Hill."

They rode their horses up into Virginia City leading a second pair which they intended for Zeke and Becky. The man who had sold them the horses had told them that the stage station was located on B Street, which was one block above the main thoroughfare.

"The Bucket of Blood Saloon?" Megan said, shaking her head in disbelief as they rode up busy C Street, gawking at all the crowded shops and saloons that were doing a huge business. "What an inviting name."

Glenn had to smile at that and, when they passed the Silver Dollar Saloon, he reined their horses up a steep cross street and they climbed up to B Street.

"There's the stage station," Glenn said. "That's where we've got to figure out something."

"If nothing else," Megan said, "we can always pull a gun on Deputy Harlan and take his prisoners by force."

"I don't think that's a very good idea," Glenn said. "We'll be in enough trouble as it is without also risking a shootout."

"Perhaps you're right," Megan said.

They rode on past the stage station about a half block and then dismounted and tied their horses between a livery and a blacksmith's shop.

"Can I help you?" the owner of the livery said, coming out to greet them.

He was in his forties, a weathered but friendly looking sort who hobbled and required the use of a cane. A small black-and-white spotted dog trotted along at his heels tail-wagging a friendly greeting.

"No, thanks," Glenn told the man. "We're just passing through. Hope you don't mind us tying our horses here."

"As a matter of fact, I do," the liveryman said, his smile slipping. "I don't want to sound unfriendly, but these are my hitching posts and I like to keep them available for my paying customers. Otherwise, they just get pulled down by strangers' horses and then I got to replace 'em without any pay."

"Here," Glenn said, digging into his pockets and removing four bits. "How about us renting them for a few hours."

"Well," the man said, "I guess so. But it'll cost more than this. A dollar will do. You see, things are real expensive up here in Virginia City."

"Yeah," Glenn said, giving the man more money, "I can see that already."

"You can water your horses over there," the liveryman said, pocketing Glenn's coins. "I ain't trying to be a bloodsucker or anything. Water up here is also real expensive, yet I'm throwing it in for free."

"Thanks," Megan said with a smile. "Is the stage generally on time?"

"Yep! Comes in about three o'clock every afternoon and is rarely more'n five minutes early or late." He removed a pocket watch from his vest. "Gonna be here in an hour and twenty minutes. You waitin' for someone on that stage?"

"No," Glenn replied. "We were just wondering."

"Well, anyway," the liveryman said. "You can't leave them fine horses tied up out here all night. If you want, I'll board them for you at a dollar a head, comes with good alfalfa hay and two pounds of oats each. Can't beat that price up here on the Comstock."

"We'll think about it," Glenn said, wishing the man would go away and leave them alone to think out a plan to rescue Zeke and Becky.

"I also inspect the shoes on your horses for a dime a foot," the liveryman said. "If you got any loose shoes that come off up here, your horse is bound to go lame. It's all these rocks. You ever see such a rocky place in your entire life?"

"I don't think I have," Glenn said absently.

The man nodded his head up and down. "Well, I'll be over at the stable if you decide to board those fine horses. Come along, Squirt."

The little black-and-white dog beat the rocky earth with a nearly hairless tail and then trotted along happily after the liveryman.

Glenn waited until the man and his dog were out of sight and then he said, "Megan, what do you want to do now?"

"Let's try not to look too conspicuous."

Glenn wasn't at all sure how to do that but he nodded and when Megan took his arm, they strolled past the Knights of Pythias and then the Miners Union Hall. On their return trip a while later, they stopped to admire the immense Piper's Opera House.

"I've heard of this place!" Megan said with real excitement. "They've had some very famous entertainers play here. People like Edwin Booth."

"You don't say."

"I do say," Megan replied. "And look, the door is open. Can we take a peek inside?"

"I don't see why not."

They stepped up to the front door of the imposing two-story structure and peered inside at a cavernous auditorium. Wooden chairs were stacked along one wall, but it was the magnificent stage that caught and held the eye.

"Can you feel them?" Megan asked, walking out onto the floor.

"Feel what?"

"Springs. This floor rests on springs."

"You're kidding!"

"No," Megan said, jumping up and down a couple of times. "I can't feel them but I read that, when the Comstock Lode miners have a big shindig, they get to dancing and stomping and this entire floor begins to rock."

"Well, I'll be darned," Glenn said with genuine amazement. "From an engineering standpoint, I'd sure like to see how they put springs under a floor this size."

They walked across the hardwood floor to the stage, their footsteps echoing loudly in the empty cavern. Glenn didn't know about Megan, but he could almost feel the ghosts of great thespians who had played this famous hall.

"Can I help you?" a deep and very well-modulated voice asked from the wings of the stage.

"Uh . . . no," Glenn said, "we were just curious. Where are you, anyway?"

A very short man of middle age appeared wearing a waistcoat, tie and tails. Eyes fixed on Megan alone, he doffed his shiny black top hat, bowed and then smiled displaying teeth as white as ivory. "My dear, are you perchance a devotee of the stage? Perchance even a great actress come to pay your tributes and respect to this famed edifice?"

"No," Megan said with a half smile. "I was raised under hard circumstances and then left New York with my former husband to work on the transcontinental railroad. But I do admire anyone who can perform well on stage."

"I see." The little man walked to the exact center of the stage and smiled, then took a bow. "Dear, lovely lady, you must know that you have the grace, charm and natural beauty of an actress."

Megan blushed.

The little man did a quick dance step and then he froze and fixed his eyes on Megan again. "Can you sing . . . or dance?"

Megan shook her head. "I'm sorry, but no."

"Have you ever even *tried* to act or sing?"

"I've been too busy trying to make a living."

The little man threw back his head and laughed, his voice projecting so loudly that Glenn swore the stage curtains shivered.

"Well," the little man said, making an expansive and very theatrical gesture. "If I played a song, would you give me the pleasure of your voice?"

Megan took a step back. "No, no, thank you."

The little man pretended not to hear. He marched over to a beautiful grand piano and removed his white gloves, carefully folding them and placing them on the piano bench.

"Do you know the words to 'Sweet Betsy from Pike'?" he asked, fingers fluttering over the keys.

"At least the first couple of stanzas, but . . ."

Without a word, the little man began to play, and when Megan remained silent, shouted, "Come on now, lovely lady, don't be shy! I have played before queens! This renowned house has heard the voices of angels! Do not disappoint me!"

Despite the seriousness of their business, Glenn could not help but laugh and tap his toe to the music. The acoustics in the auditorium were wonderful and music swirled about to overwhelm and uplift them.

Megan began to sing.

> Oh don't you remember sweet Betsy from Pike,
> Who cross'd the big mountains with her lover Ike,
> With two yoke of cattle, a large yellow dog,
> A tall Shanghai rooster and one spotted hog.
>
> Singing too-ral lal loo-ral lal loo-ral lal la
> Singing too-ral lal loo-ral lal loo-ral lal la,
> Sing too-ral lal loo-ral, Sing too-ral lal la,
> Singing too-ral lal loo-ral lal loo-ral lal la!

Megan stopped singing and began to laugh. "See, I told you that I couldn't sing."

"Nonsense!" the little man protested, jumping up from the piano and bounding back to the center of the stage.

He clasp his hands together and cried, "You have a lovely voice! It's just . . . just in need of some cultivation. Like a flower bed with a few little weeds that need attending to. I could give you singing lessons, young lady. With your face, that beautiful auburn hair and those gorgeous green eyes, I could make you rich and famous!"

Megan continued to laugh, but Glenn could see that the little man was entirely serious. He took Megan's arm and turned her toward the door.

"Thanks, but no, thanks!" he called back over his shoulder as they headed back out the front door.

The little man's laughter died. His voice thundered after them. "Go ahead then and waste that youthful beauty!

Have his miserable children! Squander that wonderful figure between soiled bedsheets and grow old in graceless anonymity, never once to taste the sweet intoxicant of fame!"

As they hurried out of Piper's Opera House, the little man began to play again, only this time the music had a harsh and angry sound. Megan paused and turned back to gaze into the hall and watch the strange little man on the huge stage. With a deep sigh, she shook her head.

"What?" Glenn asked.

"He was serious, wasn't he?"

"Oh, yes, quite."

"My, my," Megan said. "I wonder if he really could have taught me how to sing."

"I think you already have a nice voice," Glenn said. "And I think he was batty."

"Perhaps," she replied, "but he certainly did have a commanding stage presence, didn't he."

Glenn did not respond to the question for he had found the little man very disturbing. They strolled on past the Storey County Courthouse, a huge and imposing rock and brick-face structure with its blindfolded statue of Justice looking down at them from over the main entrance. When they came to a bench resting under a shady tree, Glenn took a seat.

"Well, Megan," he said, "have you thought of a way to free Zeke and Becky yet?"

"No. Have you?"

"I'm afraid not."

"I did think of something," Megan said. "It occurred to me that I might manage to distract Deputy Harlan."

"How do you propose to do that?"

"I don't know, but I'm sure that I can think of some kind of distraction."

Glenn was about to say something when he heard a shout and then turned to see the stagecoach swing around a corner and charge into view.

"It's now or never," Glenn said, taking Megan's arm and steering her along the boardwalk toward the stage station, where the horses would be changed and where some passengers would disembark while others boarded for eastbound destinations.

"Look!" Megan whispered. "It's Mr. Peamont! He's on that stage too!"

"I should have known his conscience wouldn't allow him to turn his back on Zeke and Becky," Glenn said.

"There they are," Megan whispered, watching as a handcuffed Zeke and Becky were ordered out of the coach by Deputy Eli Harlan.

Harlan was a very large, unkempt man with wild black hair and brutish facial features. Glenn had a very distinct impression that the deputy was not happy with this assignment. Harlan ordered his two young prisoners to move over to a hitching rail, where he handcuffed them securely before turning to go into the station.

The sight of Becky and Zeke handcuffed attracted a lot of attention and Glenn figured that was going to make it even more difficult to free the pair.

"Let's watch Mr. Peamont," Megan said. "I'm sure he's up to something."

Earl Peamont followed the deputy inside the station, rapidly talking to the hulking lawman. Glenn saw the cloth salesman reach into his pocket and offer the deputy a pull on his silver flask. Harlan readily accepted.

"I'll bet anything that Peamont is after the key to those handcuffs," Megan said.

"Well, even if he gets it, how are we going to steal Zeke and Becky out of here with everyone staring?"

"I'll create a diversion," Megan said, starting toward the stage station.

"Now wait a minute!" Glenn pleaded, hurrying after her. "If Peamont doesn't get the key . . ."

"Then I will," Megan vowed.

Glenn figured that there was nothing to do but to follow after Megan and play whatever hand of cards they were dealt. Zeke and Becky were huddled close, whispering to each other, and Glenn was sure that they were talking about escape.

"Don't lose hope," Glenn said in a low tone as he stopped near the couple and pretended to pick something up that he had dropped.

They both looked up and flashed him a hopeful smile, Zeke whispering, "Mr. Peamont is after the key."

"We'll get it," Glenn promised under his breath as he straightened and walked into the stage station.

Eli Harlan was surrounded by Megan and Peamont. The cloth salesman was telling a joke but Eli didn't appear to be listening because he only had eyes for Megan, who pressed close with a brazen smile on her lips. Glenn didn't know what Megan was saying and he didn't want to know. Suddenly, Peamont detached himself from the others and started for the door. Glenn intercepted the man and Peamont pressed a key into his hand.

"I've done my part," the portly man hissed. "Now it's up to you and Megan."

"Start a fight," Glenn ordered.

"Huh?"

In reply, Glenn shouted, "Dammit, you thief!" Then, before the poor man could react, Glenn shoved Peamont into another passenger. They collided and the man slugged Peamont, who doubled up his chubby fists and went on the attack.

In an instant men were brawling, and when poor Peamont was thrown through the front window of the stage station, the people outside forgot all about Zeke and Becky. Glenn rushed over to them and unlocked their handcuffs.

"Come on!" he whispered. "Run!"

They sprinted away hearing the sound of more glass shattering. Glenn desperately wished to go back for Megan but knew that would be exceedingly unwise. So he led the young couple down to C Street, where they melted into the crowds.

"All right," he said, catching his breath. "We walk a block and then return to B Street where we've got horses waiting."

"But what about Miss O'Connell and Mr. Peamont!" Becky exclaimed. "We can't just leave them."

"Megan will help Earl to our horses," Glenn said. "Someone will have to ride double because there are five of us and we've only bought four horses."

"Becky and I are the lightest," Zeke quickly offered. "We'll ride double."

"Good enough," Glenn said, leading the couple up the street and then circling up the steep hill to the stable.

Megan and Peamont were already saddled and waiting. Peamont was covered with blood and looked terrible, but when he saw Glenn and the Mormons he yelled, "Come on! Let's go!"

Glenn did not need further encouragement. He quickly mounted his horse and when Zeke and Becky were also on horseback, he said, "Megan, what happened to Deputy Harlan?"

"I pistol-whipped him."

"What!"

"He was rolling around on the floor fighting," she explained. "He didn't know what hit him."

"But didn't someone try to apprehend you!"

"No. That awful Reno deputy was beating everyone up. When I pulled his pistol and used it on his thick skull, they all cheered!"

"Oh, for crying out loud," Glenn said as they guided their horses through the heavy traffic and headed for Gold Canyon, which would lead them down the back way to Carson City and then to California.

CHAPTER
9

Glenn reined his horse to a standstill beside California's rushing American River and gazed down the western slopes of the Sierras. "There it is, my friends, the Central Pacific Railroad hard at work."

They all stared at the immense construction army inching up through the heavy pine forests. It was obvious that the Central Pacific Railroad was engaged in an epic struggle to overcome the mountains. Far to the east, they could see the end-of-track supply locomotives huff-huffing smoke into the azure blue sky. But miles ahead of the locomotives, thousands of the Chinese workers were clearly identifiable because of their cone-shaped straw hats. They were busily moving millions of tons of dirt and rock in order to level out the proposed grade, thereby filling in deep gorges. From his vantage point up the mountain, Glenn could also see that the Central Pacific was being forced to make huge, sweeping loops back and forth across the mountain in order to keep the grade from becoming too steep for a locomotive to climb. And closer to the summit, the Chinese were clearing an immense swath through the forests and using much of the timber to span yawning gullies and gorges with immense trestles.

"How many Chinese do you think are working down there right now?" Zeke asked, shaking his head.

"I'd say at least four or five thousand," Glenn replied. "They don't even have wheelbarrows but are moving dirt with handcarts and buckets."

"They're like ants crawling all over a piece of candy," Megan said. "They're in constant motion."

Glenn watched as dozens of small pockets of Chinese worked to remove huge stumps from the roadbed. They attacked the stumps furiously with axes, picks and shovels. But in some cases, they were actually blowing the stumps apart with kegs of black powder. No wonder, Glenn thought, this project was such a nightmare and the Central Pacific had made so little progress.

"Earl, how far have they come from Sacramento?" Glenn asked.

The former cloth salesman scowled. "I don't know. I'm no good at judging distances."

"Give me your best guess," Glenn urged.

"Well, they've passed Cisco, which is fifty miles due east from Sacramento. They're out of the foothill country now and so I'd judge that they've come sixty miles."

Glenn twisted around in his saddle. They had arrived at this point by skirting the north shore of Lake Tahoe, thus missing Donner Summit. "Any idea how far it is yet to Donner Summit?"

"If I had to guess, I'd say fifty more miles, but they'll be far tougher than these first sixty."

"I expect that they'll be the toughest miles any railroad has ever covered," Glenn said.

"What I can't understand," Megan said, pointing to a huge cliff that plunged almost directly down to the American River, "is how they're going to get past that."

Glenn had the same question. "Earl, do you have any idea?"

"Nope," the man said, shaking his head. "It's called

Cape Horn and I've never even seen it before now. You see, the old stage and freight line runs to the north circling around this point. I can't understand why the railroad is following the American River."

"They'll have a good reason," Glenn said. "This route was discovered by a brilliant young surveyor named Theodore Judah. He's the one whose mathematical calculations and survey work proved that locomotives could use these mountain grades he proposed."

"But you told me he died a few years ago," Megan said.

"Yes," Glenn said, "and under very sad circumstances."

"Did you know him personally?" Becky asked.

"Not really," Glenn admitted. "I was in my sophomore year at college studying engineering when Mr. Judah came to talk to our school about his vision of a transcontinental railroad. Remember, only ten years ago, the idea seemed impossible because of the distance and the huge western mountain ranges."

Glenn's blue eyes squinted at the corners as he gazed down at the scene below which he knew Theodore Judah had given his life to help bring to reality. "I remember that talk very clearly because it had such a powerful effect on my emotions. Judah spoke with eloquence and passion. It was then that I knew I wanted to be a part of this transcontinental dream. If Judah had any fault, it was that he was too idealistic. He wanted to build the best railroad possible over the Sierras. One that would last for centuries."

"But his partners," Megan said, "had other ideas."

"Right. You see, the United States Congress, when it passed the Pacific Railroad Act of 1862, thanks to Theodore Judah's constant and impassioned lobbying efforts, allocated forty-eight thousand dollars a mile to the railroad for building over the Sierras. Seeing a way to increase their income, his partners conveniently decided to move the Sierra Nevadas about twenty miles farther west so that they'd get the extra congressional subsidy rather than the regular twenty-six thousand dollars a mile that was provided for building on the flats."

"How could they possibly move an entire mountain range?" Peamont exclaimed.

"Well," Glenn said with a wry smile, "you must keep in mind that very few members of the United States Congress have been west, much less all the way to California. Therefore, all that was required was for the partners to find an accommodating surveyor to fudge on his calculations and place the mountains farther westward. They naturally asked Judah to remake the survey and geological maps of California, but he refused. I think that was the beginning of the troubles he had with Crocker and his friends."

"Are you sure that you want to become involved with these men?" Megan asked. "They sound just as shady as Thomas Durant."

Glenn chuckled. "The Union Pacific has also played with the numbers and calculations to their advantage in respect to the Laramie and, soon, the Wasatch Mountains. In both cases, the directors of these railroads are risk-taking capitalists who have wagered everything they own on this great venture. Sure, they're trying to squeeze every dollar they can out of Congress. But they've also cut costs to the bone and become extremely inventive in finding ways to lay track as cheaply as possible."

"Tracks laid over railroad ties that will probably rot in a few years and all have to be replaced," Peamont said. "I've heard what's going on."

"Yes," Glenn said, "they'll have to be replaced, but by then the vision will become a reality and Congress will gladly pay the piper in order to keep the transcontinental railroad in operation. You see, the problem is very clear to me as we look at what is happening down there at that Central Pacific construction site."

"And that is?" Megan asked as Glenn shook his head in wonder at the great effort taking place in the forests below.

"And that is that forty-eight thousand dollars a mile isn't nearly enough money to build a railroad bed and lay track in these mountains. Why, the cost of the rails themselves having been shipped all the way around Cape Horn from the foundries along the East Coast must be astronomical."

"Well," Megan said, "as you well know, I followed the Union Pacific tracks all the way from Omaha into the Wyoming Territory, but I never saw so many men at work as I see right now. It's as if the Central Pacific has hired half the men of China."

Glenn laughed. "It's true that we're watching a huge army. But I don't see how else Crocker or his Chief of Construction, James Harvey Strobridge, could attack this mountain."

"I don't think they've made ten miles since I was through here last summer," Peamont said with a shake of his head. "And I doubt that they'll go much farther. This river gorge gets steeper and steeper."

"We'll see," Glenn told them. "If I can get hired as a surveyor or engineer, for the first time ever I'll have access to the maps that Judah himself drew. I expect his measurements and calculations to be extremely accurate and that's why I believe these mountains can be beaten by the Central Pacific."

Glenn had to pull his eyes away from the work that was going on far below. He turned to his friends and said, "I guess we all have to make some decisions right about now. What is everyone else planning to do?"

Megan smiled. "I've decided to go on to Sacramento and look that town over while you see if you can gain employment on the railroad. It's only one more day's ride."

"That's probably the most sensible idea," Glenn said after a long moment's reflection. "You can leave a message where I can find you at the Central Pacific headquarters. What about you, Earl?"

The salesman scratched his two-day stubble of beard. He had lost weight during this hard ride from the Comstock Lode and Glenn knew that Peamont was worried about his uncertain future.

"I can't go back to Reno," Peamont said. "Marshal Call will put two and two together and realize that I played a hand in helping Zeke and Becky escape his deputy."

"We're very sorry about that," Zeke said quickly. "We didn't mean for anyone to suffer on our account."

"That's all right," Peamont said. "I expect that I'll try and find work on this railroad. Maybe they need someone to make leather goods or . . . hell, I'll even repair harnesses until I can sort out my future."

"Good," Glenn said. "I'm sure that the Central Pacific can offer you work."

He looked to the two young Mormons riding double. "And I assume that you will also ride on down to Sacramento and start a good life for yourselves?"

"I'm the son of a farmer," Zeke said. "It's all that I know how to do. All I ever wanted to do. Maybe I can get a start someplace, save and buy a little of that good San Joaquin Valley farmland that you said grows just about anything."

"I'll bet you can figure out something," Glenn told the young man, feeling a sense of pride that they had rescued this couple from the very sad fate which would have befallen them on their forced return to Salt Lake City.

"Glenn, I'd like you to be my best man and I'd like for you, Mr. Peamont, to be my second-best man," Zeke blurted out. "And Miss O'Connell, Becky would like you to be her maid of honor. Do you suppose we could find a minister before we all split up? I mean, if it isn't askin' too much."

Glenn smiled, and Peamont looked pleased as well.

"Megan?" Becky said. "I haven't known you long but . . . well, I feel like you're my big sister and I really would be happy if you'd be with me when Zeke and I are married."

"Of course," Megan said. "I would have been crushed if you hadn't asked me to attend your wedding."

"It won't be much but the words," Zeke said. "I don't have money enough to buy a proper wedding ring, but . . ."

"It'll be fine," Peamont told the young man. "There are things more important than money."

"There are?" Megan asked with a mischievous wink.

Everyone laughed and then Peamont said, "I'm sure that we can find a minister someplace between here and Sacramento who will perform the blessed ceremony."

"I sure hope so," Zeke said. "It's been kind of hard, not knowing for so long if we were ever going to become man and wife."

"Well," Glenn said, "you are and that will be one of our first orders of business. Who knows, perhaps Miss O'Connell will even take a notion to change her mind and make it a double wedding."

Becky clapped her hands together. "That would be oh, so special!"

But Megan shook her head with a sad smile. "It's just

not the time for us, Becky. But don't worry, when it happens you'll be right at the top of our invitation list."

Glenn looked back down the mountainside and tried to mask his acute disappointment. He knew that Megan was correct about the timing, but dammit, any time would be fine with him. He'd find a way to keep her close if he were fortunate enough to get work on this railroad.

"Let's go," Glenn said to them as he nudged the flanks of his horse with the heels of his boots. "I expect we can find the construction headquarters before nightfall. Not only am I anxious to meet Mr. Crocker and Mr. Strobridge, but I'm more than a little eager to find and confront this Harry Loudermilk that I am supposed to have spied for in behalf of the Central Pacific Railroad."

Megan reached out and touched Glenn's arm. "But you won't lose your temper and try to fight the man, will you?"

"Not with this arm still on the mend," Glenn said, flexing the fingers of his left hand. He'd abandoned the sling and was using the arm now, but it still ached. "Still, I intend to get a signed statement from Loudermilk that I was never involved in any kind of spy ring. And I want to send a copy of that statement to Thomas Durant himself so that I can clear my good name without any lingering questions or doubts."

"I want to be with you when you confront this man," Megan said. "Just in case he possesses a violent nature."

"And what would you do if he was violent?" Glenn asked, genuinely curious.

"You well know I have long been in the habit of carrying a derringer," Megan said simply. "And I'd make sure that you were not hurt."

Glenn was touched by these words, and if he had been standing before Megan instead of mounted on a damned horse, he would have taken the Irish girl in his arms and kissed her. As it was, all he could do was nod his silent thanks.

"Let's ride on down and join the party," he said.

They rode down the mountain following the American River, and when the Chinese saw them coming they paused only for a moment to stare and then continued their work. As Glenn and his party rode in among the army of diligent workers, he marveled at the strength of these small, busy people.

"I bet you they don't average a hundred pounds each," Glenn said in a quiet voice. "But look at the size of the rocks they're digging up and carting away."

"They're sort of shy, aren't they," Megan said, noticing how the Chinese refused to meet her eyes.

Peamont rode up beside them. "I was in Sacramento when the Irish went on strike and Crocker sent men to San Francisco to recruit these little buggers. You should have heard the outrage! The existing crews were so mad that they walked off the job. Said that they wouldn't work within sight of the Chinese, much less side by side with 'em."

"So what did Crocker say to that?" Glenn asked.

"Crocker said that he'd keep the Chinese working out of sight of the others. That lasted about a week, and then he put the Chinese crews in competition with the regulars."

Peamont chuckled. "I guess there was quite a rivalry. The Chinese weren't as strong, but they took almost no breaks except for their hot tea. At the end of the day, they always seemed to get the most work done."

"That was quite a gamble," Megan said.

"It was, and it wasn't," Peamont said. "The Comstock miners had formed a strong union and were getting four dollars a day."

"That's an awfully high wage," Megan said.

"Yes it is," Peamont said. "More than I've made at times these past couple years. Anyway, the Central Pacific could only pay half that, so Crocker had no choice but to try out the Chinese. He said he needed ten thousand laborers, not the eight hundred misfits that he was having trouble employing."

"I'll bet those words made some of his laborers mad," Zeke said.

"You bet it did," Peamont agreed. "The misfits that Crocker was using threatened to kill off every Chinaman that hired onto the payroll. But the Chinese didn't understand. All they wanted was jobs, and they just kept coming over from San Francisco until damn near all of the men were out here working for the Central Pacific. I heard that Crocker and his partners then took to recruiting them directly out of China."

"That's about what we'd heard while I was working on the Union Pacific," Glenn said. "I heard that he has more than five thousand on the payroll."

"And that number is supposed to double," Peamont said.

When they came to the lead locomotive, the engineer waved at them and Glenn saw a half-dozen big camp tents. It appeared that some were being used as offices, others as sleeping accommodations, supply depots and mess halls. Compared to the huge rolling camp that he had become accustomed to with the Union Pacific, this looked rather small and unimpressive.

"Say," Glenn called to a young man who appeared from one of the tents and was furiously scribbling in a notebook, "can you tell me where we can find Mr. Crocker and Mr. Strobridge?"

The young man paused. "Mr. Crocker is inside that third

tent down the line. The big one with the gray patch sewn on the front. Mr. Strobridge is out on the construction site like always."

"Thanks!"

The young man started to move away, but then he stopped and turned. "Maybe I'd better warn you right now that Mr. Crocker is in a pretty foul mood these days."

"Why?"

"Cape Horn," the man said, gesturing up toward the huge cliff. "The engineers are shaking their heads about how we're going to get past 'er."

"Mr. Judah must have addressed that difficulty."

"Yeah, but nobody here can decipher his maps and calculations. The engineers are saying it just can't be done."

"They're wrong," Glenn said.

"No offense, stranger, but how would you know?"

"Long story," Glenn replied as he moved on down the line toward Crocker's tent.

A few moments later, Glenn passed his reins to Zeke and stood outside Crocker's tent listening to the man swearing in anger. Turning back toward the others, Glenn said, "Maybe I'd better go in alone."

"No," Megan said, taking his arm, "I think I had better go in with you."

So they stepped inside the large, canvas tent. Glenn had never seen Charles Crocker before, but he had heard a good many descriptions about the man and was able to spot him immediately among the men in the tent. Crocker was very large with chin whiskers, a heavy brow and piercing brown eyes. He was younger and far more vital-looking than Glenn had expected, perhaps in his late thirties or early forties, and probably weighed about 250 pounds. He had the look of a man who would not hesitate to use his fists if a blistering tongue-lashing failed.

"Mr. Crocker?" Glenn said, removing his hat. "I'd like to have a word with you?"

Crocker turned away from a table of surveyors' maps and glared at the intrusion. "If you're looking for work, you're in the wrong damned tent!"

Crocker seemed to notice Megan for the first time and his voice softened. "And who the devil are you, Miss?"

"Megan. Megan O'Connell."

"Well, Miss O'Connell, I'd enjoy talking with you but right now we're having a meeting. So, if you'll excuse us."

"Sir," Glenn persisted, "I'm an experienced engineer and surveyor. I've just been fired by no less that the UP president, Thomas Durant. He says I was spying for you folks."

Crocker had been about to say something, but now his jaw sagged and then he threw back his head and gave forth with what Glenn could only describe as a horse laugh.

"Ha! That's rich! We're spying on them! What for, so we can hear about all the miles and government dollars they're gobbling up while we're fighting for every inch we can climb?"

"I was supposed to have been conspiring with a man named Harry Loudermilk. Do you know him?"

"Hell, yes! Harry is my labor contractor. He's in San Francisco right now contracting for more Chinamen."

"Will he be coming back soon?"

"As soon as he's hired another thousand men." Crocker scowled. "Listen, I don't know what all this ridiculous spying business is and I don't have time to talk about it now. Later, okay? Right now, we've got one hell of a tough decision to make about Cape Horn."

"Sure," Glenn said. "But I knew Mr. Judah and I've studied some of his work. I even remember him talking to our class of engineers about what has to be done to transverse Cape Horn."

Crocker's expression changed from one of mild annoyance to real interest. "From what my surveyors and engineers tell me, we've somehow managed to lose some of Mr. Judah's most important measurements and calculations. That's the bind we're in right now. But if you'd like to step over here and take a look at what we do have, then feel free, Mr. . . ."

"Gilchrist. Glenn Gilchrist." Glenn moved over to the table and focused on the maps, none of which he had ever seen before. But there was no mistaking Judah's work; he could have picked it out among that of hundreds of surveyors.

Glenn listened while one of Crocker's surveyors patiently described the highlights of the maps and then pointed out where Judah had said Cape Horn could be transversed.

"The trouble is," the man said, "we're not sure if the rock will bear the weight of a locomotive, even if we can cut a roadbed across the face of it. Those are some of Mr. Judah's calculations that seem to be missing."

"Some of us theorize that these crucial calculations may have been deliberately taken," a stern-faced man said.

Glenn frowned. "For what purpose?"

"Isn't it obvious?" the man said. "What if we do succeed in making a cut and laying track across the face of Cape Horn? Then, on the day that the first locomotive makes the climb, its huge weight buckles the foundation rock and whole works drops hundreds of feet into the American River. Can you imagine where we'll be then?"

"Yes," Glenn said. "I'm sure that there will be plenty of newspaper reporters."

"There will be," Crocker said. "It would not only be a disaster in terms of human life and the loss of property, but also a major setback in Congress. Mr. Huntington has assured us that we can't afford such a debacle. We have to be absolutely sure that the rock bearing the crosscut will support our rolling stock."

"What's the average slope of that rock face?" Glenn asked.

"It begins and ends at only a little over fifty degrees but averages seventy-five degrees."

"Yes, and its almost vertical in most of the center section," Glenn mused.

"Exactly," an engineer said.

"I couldn't help but notice that you have started the cut at both sides. How did you propose to work that cliff when it becomes vertical?"

"We're not even sure of that," Crocker admitted. "That's part of what we're trying to decide right now. The American drillers and blasters aren't willing to work the rock face but the Chinese are. In fact, they seem damned eager."

"How would they do it?" Glenn asked bluntly.

Crocker reached for a cigar. "They want to weave big reed baskets and then be lowered down the cliff's face. They say they can drill blast holes from those wicker baskets, stuff them with black powder and soon blast us a cut wide enough to lay track across."

"Do you think they can?" Glenn asked, framing the vision of Cape Horn in his mind and trying to judge the soundness of this desperate plan.

"I don't know," Crocker admitted. "But we've come too far to change course now. I think that I'm just going to let them have a try. One of the problems is that we have a difference of opinion. We've resurveyed the face of Cape

Horn twice and we're still not sure of what is the best line to take."

"That's a big problem," Glenn said quietly.

"Of course it is!" Crocker snapped. "I can't have the Chinese blasting away foundation rock."

Glenn pulled his eyes away from the maps. "Mr. Crocker, I don't pretend to be any smarter than your colleagues but sometimes a fresh perspective can be illuminating. With your permission, I'd like to survey that wall tomorrow and study what you do have of Mr. Judah's maps and Cape Horn calculations."

"Do it!" Crocker ordered. "And I'll expect a report on your findings tomorrow evening right here in this tent. Agreed?"

"Agreed."

Crocker bowed slightly to Megan. "Are you his wife?"

"No, sir."

"Good," Crocker said as he exited the tent.

Glenn looked at the other young men and stated his claim so that they would all understand. "Miss O'Connell is my fiancée."

"That's a pity," one of the men said before he led his friends out the door.

Megan glanced at the table covered with surveyors' maps. "All those lines and numbers might as well be the Greek alphabet as far as I'm concerned. Glenn, I sure hope that your faith in Mr. Judah is justified."

"It is. And by this time tomorrow evening, I fully expect to have won myself an important job."

"But what about your promise to Zeke and Becky? They want to get married right away, not wait around here."

"I hadn't thought about that," Glenn admitted.

"Well," Megan said, "I have. We'll wait a day and then we're going on down the mountain to find a minister."

"Perhaps there's one right here."

"I doubt it," Megan replied. "Not after seeing and listening to Mr. Crocker's profanity."

Glenn had to smile. "He is pretty tough, isn't he."

"This is a very tough job," Megan said, kissing Glenn on the cheek. "And I'm glad that you're going to be here to help beat Cape Horn and whatever engineering obstacles this mountain is going to throw at the Central Pacific."

"Don't get ahead of yourself," Glenn said with a smile. "I'm not on their payroll yet."

"Yes, but you will be. I saw the admiring looks that the other men were exchanging while you talked. I could tell they were as impressed with you as Mr. Crocker."

Glenn sighed. "Let's just hope that they are still impressed after I make my recommendations on how to beat Cape Horn."

"You may be worried, but I'm not," Megan said. "Now, look at your maps while I go outside and explain things to our friends."

"Sure," Glenn said, feeling drawn back to the work laid out before him on the table. He quickly lost himself in the maps and Judah's accompanying mathematical calculations. Glenn was so absorbed in them that he didn't even realize until long after dark that Megan hadn't returned.

CHAPTER
10

"Come on," Megan told her friends, "we might as well try to find accommodations for ourselves."

"What about Glenn?" Zeke asked.

"He's already absorbed in maps and engineering things," Megan answered, gazing around the huge construction camp in search of food or shelter. "He'll join us later."

Megan, having long been around the construction camps of the Union Pacific, realized that there were many similarities in this end-of-the-line construction site despite the fact that this camp was teeming with Chinese. Back on the Union Pacific, the Irishmen and ex-Civil War soldiers that formed the bulk of that railroad's tough work crews had tended to congregate around their huge triple-decker rolling bunkhouses. These were the special sleeping cars designed with narrow bunks which could accommodate hundreds of workers and protect them from the icy winter blasts that swept across the Northern Plains.

The Union Pacific also had immense dining cars filled with long wooden tables and benches. Megan had never forgotten the first time she'd seen the laborers fed and had been utterly appalled by the efficiency with which each meal had been delivered. The workmen had been served in fifteen-minute shifts and their food was always ladled or spooned onto metal plates nailed down tight on

the scarred wooden tables. The workers had been given
all the food they could wolf down during their hurried
time allotment and then, at a signal, were rushed outside
while kitchen workers jumped into the dining cars and
pitched buckets of boiling water across the tables and
plates, washing everything down in seconds in a frantic
preparation for the next shift of famished laborers.

But here, Megan saw no huge dining cars or towering
bunkhouses. Instead, she noticed that there were hundreds
of small camps and in each, a single Chinaman appeared
to be cooking and preparing the evening meals.

The shrill but familiar sound of a steam engine's whistle
blasted three times and its echo boomed around in the
gullies and the gulches. Megan watched as the Chinese
stopped and then slowly began to stack their tools or else
dump the last of their buckets filled with dirt before they
started to chatter and head for their campfires. They talked
extremely fast and seemed like happy people, laughing,
a few of the younger ones even engaging in horseplay.
Megan hadn't been aware that she possessed any pre-
conceptions about the Chinese, but they were far more
likeable than she had imagined from the gossip she'd
heard on the UP line.

"I expect it's quite different from what you are accustomed to seeing, Miss O'Connell."

Megan turned to the voice and saw a very tall, slender and handsome young man, one who had drawn her
attention inside the surveyors' tent. Now, he was smiling
down at her, his dark eyes reflecting a hint of amusement.
He was dressed in a brown suit and a gray, flat-brimmed
Stetson adorned with an eagle's feather and a headband
with silver conchos. His boots were polished and he was
clean-shaven, unlike most of the men who had been in
the tent.

"Yes, very different," Megan agreed.

"Allow me to introduce myself," the young man said, removing his hat. "My name is Ford Hayward. I am Mr. Crocker's personal assistant and rather a jack-of-all-trades."

When he extended his hand, Megan took and was enveloped by it. The man's hands were extraordinarily large but soft. "My pleasure, Mr. Hayward."

Megan introduced her friends and then added, "Mr. Peamont is very much hoping to secure a position with this railroad."

Hayward's attention slid to Peamont. "We are in short supply of almost every talent you can name. And so what skills do you bring to us, Mr. Peamont?"

"I'm a . . . a leather worker," Peamont said, stumbling over the word.

"Are you sure?" Hayward asked almost jokingly. "I don't mean to offend, but you seem rather unsure of your profession."

Peamont drew himself up and cleared his throat. "I am sure of what I can do, Mr. Hayward."

Hayward extended his hand and when they shook, Crocker's handsome assistant remarked, "Your hands are rather soft for a leather worker, Mr. Peamont."

Peamont retracted his hand and shoved both hands into his coat pockets. "I might as well explain," he said. "The fact of the matter is that I've been a representative in the clothing industry."

"I see. You've been a traveling salesman."

"Yes, and I've done rather well by myself. In fact, I even own some property in Reno, among other investments."

"Good for you."

"Yes," Peamont said, seeming to gain confidence, "but

I am fifty-eight years old now and I am ready for a change. What I really enjoy and can do is leather work. And, if I do say so myself, my leather tooling is—"

"I'm afraid that we can't use those skills, important as they are," Hayward interrupted with a regrettable shake of his head. "You see, Mr. Peamont, the leather goods that we need are very utilitarian. We already employ two or three cobblers and harness makers as we use a lot of mules and horses on this work site when the weather permits. Occasionally we need work that surpasses the level of their ability—some kind of unusual leather rigging is a good example—but then we simply order it from Sacramento or even San Francisco."

"I see," Peamont answered, looking dejected.

"However, since you were a seller of goods," Hayward quickly added, "I'm sure you possess excellent negotiating skills."

"Negotiating skills?"

"Of course! You are a merchant and have demonstrated your ability at commerce. We *do* employ buyers, Mr. Peamont. People who can win this railroad the best prices available on everything from beef to blasting powder. Are you interested?"

Peamont frowned. "I don't know. I hadn't thought about that sort of thing."

"I assure you that a buyer would earn a great deal more than a cobbler or harness maker."

"Really?"

"At least three times over."

"My, my," Peamont said.

"My suggestion would be to apply for employment as a buyer—and I'd be willing to recommend you for that position. And then," Hayward added, "stick with it until this great race is over. Bank the extra money and then you'll have a very substantial sum to tide you over in your old age or even to support you while your new career gains hold."

"That's very good advice," Zeke said. "I'd do it, Mr. Peamont."

Hayward looked at the young man. "And what are your plans?"

"After we are married," Zeke said, "Becky and I are going down to the San Joaquin Valley and take up farming."

"The farmland down there is quite expensive."

"It is?" Zeke's smile faded.

"Yes. You see, twenty years ago, before the California gold rush, the good farming and grazing land was held in title by great Spanish grants. Then Mexico took over and the Spanish land grants were broken into smaller farms and ranchos. Cattle, grain, hides . . . all of that was very cheap, or so I'm told. But when gold was discovered at Sutter's Mill and thousands of miners rushed to strike it rich, the value of farmland soared along with the value of their produce. California now supplies most of the food that goes to feed the booming Comstock Lode and, of course, our own efforts."

"I see," Zeke muttered. "Yes, I understand this. It was the same for us in Utah when the Forty-Niners came through. Demand always raises prices."

"And right now," Hayward said, "prices for food have never been higher. If I were you, I would strongly consider becoming an independent wholesaler or retailer of food."

"How would that work?" Megan asked.

"Buy food commodities and sell them to us," Hayward said simply. "Just like Mr. Peamont might buy steel or timber."

"It sounds good," Zeke agreed, "but it takes capital to buy goods for resale. I'm afraid that's the one thing I don't have at this time."

"Maybe you could borrow the money," Hayward suggested.

"Who would loan anything to a couple of Mormon fugitives?" Becky blurted out before realizing she had said way too much.

There was a moment of strained silence before Hayward broke the tension by saying, "I'm going to forget that I even heard that, miss."

"Thanks," Zeke said.

"I can loan you some money," Megan told the young man.

Zeke looked at Crocker's assistant. "Could I get any kind of a contract with the Central Pacific Railroad with a modest investment?"

"Sure," Hayward said. "You wouldn't be able to buy cattle or anything on that scale—initially, but you certainly could buy hay for our livestock and certain inexpensive staples like flour for our cooks."

"Do the Chinese eat flour?" Megan asked. "I thought they all ate rice, fish and things from their own culture."

"They do," Hayward admitted, "but we do employ nearly a thousand American workers ranging from our Superintendent of Construction, Mr. Strobridge, all the way down to our freighters and mule skinners. And I'll guarantee you they eat nothing but meat and potatoes and drink coffee or whiskey."

"I couldn't buy whiskey or hard spirits," Zeke said quickly. "It would be against my personal beliefs."

"Don't worry about that," Hayward joked. "There are legions of men who have no qualms whatsoever about buying whiskey, rum and beer. The problem is getting them to deliver rather than consume it!"

Hayward laughed at his own joke, and Megan decided that he was a genuinely nice and very helpful man. "Is there someplace that we can stay tonight?" she asked.

"Of course," he said. "We try to accommodate visitors, mostly politicians who drive Mr. Crocker and Mr. Strobridge mad when I'm unable to deflect their stupid questions."

"I promise you, sir, that we won't ask any of those."

"Call me Ford," he said, offering her his arm. "And I'll escort you all over to our guest tents and see that you are well provided for until you make your plans to leave."

Megan ignored the arm and took up her reins. "We'll also need a place to tie our horses."

"We can turn them in with our own livestock and they'll be well fed and tended," Ford promised.

"You seem to be able to handle everything," Megan told the man as they led their horses over toward a huge corral filled mostly with oxen and mules.

"Like I said, Miss O'Connell, I'm a jack-of-all-trades. I'm expert at nothing but I do manage to help keep things running."

"We're lucky to have met you," Zeke said, grinning broadly. "Really lucky."

"Luck," Ford said, looking straight into Megan's green eyes, "had very little to do with it."

Zeke and the others missed that look, but it caused Megan's cheeks to redden and she realized that Ford was right. This had nothing to do with luck and everything to do with his powerful physical attraction for her.

Ford showed them the guest tents, one for the women and another for the men. They were far nicer than Megan had expected, with solid wooden floors which she made reference to.

"You're probably used to the fact that wood is a rare commodity on the Great Plains," Ford explained. "I understand that wood for railroad ties and trestles is a very expensive item for the Union Pacific. But here in the Sierras, we have more wood than we know what to do with. So we use it to fuel our locomotives instead of the coal that is used by the Union Pacific."

"Ah," Megan said. "And that would explain the bigger, wider smokestacks I noticed on the locomotives."

"That's right. The UP's would look funny to us, like skinny cigars, while ours probably look oversized and maybe even ridiculous to you. Megan?"

His tone had changed and she stepped back outside the tent. "Yes?"

"I would be honored if I could escort you and your friends to dinner in a half hour."

"We accept," she said, knowing the others would be as hungry as herself. "And will Glenn also be there?"

"He might," Ford said with a wink. "Then again, he might not. Mr. Crocker has given him quite a challenge. One I expect he will meet?"

"I'm sure that he will," Megan said. "We are to be married, you know."

"Yes," Ford said. "I do recall he told us that you were his fiancée. Any date for the wedding?"

"No."

"Well, your fiancé is going to be very, very busy for the next year or two. Just as I will be until we beat these mountains and prove to everyone that the Central Pacific is not going to fail."

"You sound confident."

"I am. I believe in Mr. Crocker and Mr. Strobridge. If

you are around them for even a short while you'll quickly realize that they are totally dedicated to the success of this venture."

Ford started to turn, but then stopped and looked at Megan. "I sense that you are quite a determined woman in your own right, Miss O'Connell. Would that be an accurate assessment?"

"It would."

"And I'm guessing you have also been successful." He smiled disarmingly. "I mean, it's not that big a guess since you've already mentioned that you have the funds to back the young Mormon gentleman. That tells me a great deal."

"Don't read too much into anything," Megan said. "I come from poor but hearty stock. Nothing has ever come especially easy for me but I seem to work through obstacles."

"You *are* a very determined woman!"

Megan smiled and excused herself. She was very tired and dirty due to their long horseback ride over from Virginia City. They had ridden hard and constantly looked over their shoulders, afraid that a posse or some such thing would be chasing them and the young Mormon couple. But of course that hadn't happened. From just the few minutes she had observed Marshal Abner Call, however, Megan had judged the lawman to be every bit as determined as herself. Furthermore, the Reno attorney, Arnold Sloan, had confirmed her opinion of the local marshal. What all of this meant was that it was unlikely that Call would just forgive and forget. Rather, he would be constantly looking for news of his escapees and when he found out their whereabouts, he would most certainly act swiftly and with force.

•   •   •

Glenn did not appear for supper but Megan had all the attention she needed. She had bathed and changed from her riding habit into a pale blue dress which was wrinkled but clean. Her hair was still a little damp from being washed but it was brushed. Altogether, she and Becky looked quite clean and respectable. And judging from the looks they were receiving, even attractive.

"Where does Mr. Crocker eat?" Megan asked, looking around the huge table as the Central Pacific's officers and supervisors were being served.

Ford leaned closer than was necessary. "Neither he nor Mr. Strobridge usually eat with the rest of us unless it has been a very, very good day. And frankly, Megan, we haven't had any of those for a good long while."

"I see," Megan said. "And I take it the railroad is far behind schedule?"

An official named Homer Wilford overheard the question and jumped right into the conversation. "Miss O'Connell, we are actually on schedule. When we began this project, we told the Congress of these United States that it would take seven years to build over the Sierras. And so far, in less than two years, we've come halfway. The trouble is, the hardest half is still in front of us."

"You can say that again," another of Crocker's staff added. "We're going to have to bore six tunnels before we punch through onto the eastern slope of these mountains. Why, right now we're about to complete our five-hundred-eight-foot Grizzly Hill Tunnel just a few miles to the east and that will allow us to fight our way through these forests until we reach Cisco."

"That's a town?"

"No," Ford said, "it's just a stage stop. You'd have had dinner there if you'd come over on the stagecoach from Reno. Which reminds me to ask. Why didn't you finish up by stage if you began that way in Salt Lake City?"

Megan pretended to examine her plate and then fork a piece of venison. Thankfully, Peamont fielded the question. "We wanted to see Lake Tahoe and take a more leisurely pace, Ford. If you'd have come across the Great Basin in a stage all the way from Salt Lake City, you'd understand perfectly."

Ford paused for a moment, then said, "Yes, I see your point."

Megan *knew* what the man was thinking, that he was remembering Becky's ill-advised remark that they were fugitives. But Ford had the grace and the presence not to pursue the issue.

"Mr. Peamont. Mr. Poole. I understand," Wilford said, "that you are seeking positions as buyers for our railroad."

"That's right," Peamont admitted.

"I hope that you are successful in that endeavor," Wilford remarked pleasantly. "And I hope that you ladies will have the occasion to visit us often. Many of us have wives, you know. They live in Sacramento and often come to visit on Sundays. We have picnics, weather permitting, and a great deal of fun."

Megan looked at Becky. "I'm sure that we would love to attend if the opportunity allows."

"Yes," Becky said, leaning close to her young man. "But everything is happening so fast that we aren't sure of anything anymore, are we, Megan?"

The girl's remark caused a chuckle among those near enough to have overheard it. There was more conversation about Cape Horn that Megan dismissed. Her own thoughts turned to what she was going to do herself. Without quite realizing it, Megan discovered that she felt quite comfortable among these railroad builders. As an end-of-track

saloon operator, she knew that she had inherited a love
for the railroad and a sense of the camaraderie that was
part of the epic undertaking. The idea of retiring to some
mundane business in Sacramento suddenly offered little
appeal. This surprised her. She was in California, but
she was not in the sense that these mountains and heavy
forests could just as easily have been the northernmost
Rockies or the Laramie Mountains. And while the warm
valleys that waited only a day's ride beyond were inviting,
they could wait.

This railroad was opportunity. It was excitement and
challenge and yes, even the romance of danger. Glenn
wouldn't want her to admit that, but it was true. He would
rather she settle in comfortably in Sacramento and become
his Sunday wife, joining all the others.

Not yet, Megan thought. Please, not yet.

"More wine?" Ford asked, reaching for a bottle of
California sherry.

"Yes," Megan said, feeling the effects of the previous
two glasses and not really caring. "Why not?"

"Why not indeed?" Ford said, smiling wolfishly as he
refilled her glass.

CHAPTER
11

Charles Crocker pushed into the tent, his commanding presence alone silencing the assemblage of engineers and surveyors. He picked Glenn out and said, "Mr. Gilchrist, this is my construction boss, Jim Strobridge. Have you figured the angle of the cut for Cape Horn and the load factors its rock will support?"

"I have," Glenn said, shaking hands with the stern-face Strobridge and spreading out the maps and the calculations that he had been working on for the past twenty-four hours. "I did my survey work independently, but it only verified what Mr. Judah had already confirmed."

"And that is?" Strobridge asked.

"And that is that a sixteen-to-twenty-foot cut across the face of Cape Horn will most certainly bear the tonnage of your locomotives and supply trains."

Glenn bent over the maps and the others crowded around to gaze at his survey marks and figures. In a concise manner, he explained his mathematical calculations and how he had deduced the angle of the cut and the factors necessary to determine the bearing weight of the roadbed.

"There are, of course," Glenn said, after nearly forty minutes of explanation, "fissures that spiderweb across the face of Cape Horn and they will certainly have to be watched, but they do not appear to be deep enough to be a cause for concern."

"How do you know that?" Strobridge demanded. "That rock face is better than two thousand feet tall."

"Two thousand and sixty," Glenn corrected. "And while there is no way to precisely measure the depth of the fissures, the rock is sure to be solid granite underneath the exposed shale. My experience in the Laramie Mountains tells me that the fissures will not be a concern. I estimate that they do not run at a depth of more than three feet through the surface shale. That's not a factor considering the cut itself will be much deeper."

"And the grade out of the Long Ravine?" Crocker asked, chewing rapidly on an unlit cigar. "Can our locomotives pull it *and* our heavy supply cars and later passenger cars?"

"Yes," Glenn said decisively. "The grade is exactly as Judah calculated and entirely feasible for even your heaviest and most powerful double-header 4-6-0 locomotives."

"And how," Ford Hayward asked, "do you suggest that the cut be made? Remember, at the center of that mass of rock, the Chinese will be dangling more than a thousand feet over the American River. It would be a scary proposition, to put it mildly."

"More than fourteen hundred feet," Glenn corrected. "And yes, most men would lose their nerve working suspended over that dizzying height."

"But not Crocker's Pets," Strobridge interrupted, using the common term for the Chinese. "If they claim they can work at that height, they'll do it and have a damned good time in the process."

"Let's not fool ourselves," Crocker warned. "There are bound to be accidents and some Chinese will die. The river's mist lifts over the top of Cape Horn and the reed baskets could soften and break or shred apart."

"There's no choice," Strobridge said pointedly. "Charles, we either give the Chinese their chance, or we pack up our tents and go back down to Sacramento with our tails tucked between our legs."

"Never," Crocker growled. "We've come too far and spent way too damn much government money. Besides, we're nearly through the Grizzly Tunnel."

"Then it's decided?" Ford said, turning along with everyone else to Crocker, who had the final decision.

"Yes," Crocker said. "Mr. Strobridge, first thing tomorrow morning I want you to tell the Chinese to start weaving those baskets. But you can also tell them that we would prefer that they use our stronger canvas or even cowhide slings."

"They'd refuse to use 'em," Strobridge said. "You know how stubborn those people are once they get an idea into their heads. They trust only what they've made themselves just like they'll only eat what they've cooked themselves."

"Yeah," Crocker said. "Damn but they are independent little sonofabitches! All right, but tell them we need to get started right away. And . . . and tell them that I'll give the ones who are willing to drill and blast extra pay for the time they're in the baskets."

"They'll like that," Strobridge said. "But we need to also tell them that the ones who fall to their deaths will be returned to China."

"All right," Crocker agreed, "go ahead and promise them that I'll send their remains back on the first available boat to China."

"Good enough," Strobridge said. "The fact of the matter is that I suspect they've already started weaving their wicker baskets. They seemed pretty excited about the idea."

"They don't know the word *fear*, do they?" Ford said.

"No," Crocker said with grudging pride. "They sure as hell do not."

After most of the men had left, Crocker pulled Glenn aside along with his construction boss. They were all about the same height, but Crocker was by far the most imposing. He said, "Jim, young Mr. Gilchrist seems sure that our man Loudermilk is involved in spying on the Union Pacific."

Strobridge was a lantern-jawed man with sharp, protruding features. He was reputed to be a slave driver and a very hard man. Now, he turned to Glenn and said, "Why the hell would we want to 'spy' on the Union Pacific? Them bastards have a walk in the park compared to what we have to fight up here."

"I was fired by no less than Mr. Thomas Durant himself," Glenn explained. "He had a letter sent from Loudermilk to a man named Peter Arlington III. Arlington claimed to be the son of a wealthy Boston newspaper owner and that he was doing a story on the Union Pacific. He—"

"He's a liar," Strobridge snapped. "Arlington gave us the same song and dance but we checked out his credentials and discovered that he was lying. We threw him off the line and warned him never to come back."

"I see," Glenn said. "We should have done the same, but Mr. Durant is always trying to gain favorable publicity. So we took Arlington's bait and it wasn't until he was killed by Comanche that we found out he was a fraud."

"If the Indians killed him," Crocker said, "then good riddance. He was a dandy, and he rang false in my mind right from the start."

"Could it be possible that he and your man in San Francisco, Harry Loudermilk, were in cahoots?"

"Sure," Crocker said, scowling. "But to what end? I mean, what was there to be gained by spying?"

"Excuse me, Mr. Crocker," Glenn said, "but the Eastern newspapers are eager to make this transcontinental race headline news. And since most of their subscribers are rooting for the Union Pacific, they would welcome good news about the UP's progress and bad news about yours."

"Then they must be laughing themselves sick," Strobridge growled, "because we have had little else but unfavorable news."

"Too bad that you were fired by those fools on the UP," Crocker snapped. "But I'm hiring you on as of right now. You'll like working for me a hell of a lot better than working for that weasel Durant."

"I'm grateful for the job," Glenn said, "but I'd still like to confront Loudermilk and get him to confess that he was up to some chicanery with Arlington. I'd like to clear my good name."

Crocker actually laughed. "Mr. Gilchrist," he said, "by the time that we finish beatin' these gawddamn Sierras, ain't none of us going to have a 'good name.' So have your little showdown with Harry, but it won't mean anything."

Glenn was a little offended. "I beg your pardon, sir, but my family—"

"Is in New England and has money, I'll wager," Strobridge interrupted. "The thing you need to understand is that no one gives a damn about family name out here in the West. I'm telling you that it doesn't matter if your father was a horse thief or a minister. All that a Westerner is judged by is what he can do, not what his ancestors did."

"I see," Glenn said a little stiffly.

"No," Strobridge said, "I don't believe that you do. But if you work for Charley and me for a while, you'll soon catch on. The only thing we care about is results. That's the way that we all operate and the way that I'll expect you to operate as well. Understood?"

"I believe so."

"Good," Strobridge said. "You'll do fine here and we're happy to have you on the payroll. What were Durant and those robbers paying you?"

"A hundred and twenty dollars a month."

"Then that's what I'll pay you," Crocker decided out loud. "And if you help us beat Cape Horn then I'll raise that to two hundred a month."

"That's very generous."

"You'll earn every penny of it on this line," Strobridge vowed. "This job will make you think you were on vacation while you worked for the Union Pacific."

"I expect that Cape Horn is only the first of many challenges."

"It is," Crocker said, and then he turned to Strobridge. "Jim, our new Chief Surveyor has a fiancée. Prettiest woman I've seen in a long, long time."

Glenn didn't know if he should feel flattered or offended. He chose flattered. "Thank you, sir."

"Don't thank me," Crocker said. "It's the truth. Where is she going to stay while you're helping us beat our way up to Donner Pass?"

"I don't know," Glenn said. "We haven't really discussed it."

"Well," Crocker said, "get it discussed and decided and let's get this Cape Horn behind us. You know, we've got at least six tunnels to bore including the one under the summit of Donner Pass."

"Yes, I saw that in Judah's maps. The Summit Tunnel is some sixteen hundred feet long. It might take years."

"The way we are going, it probably will take years," Strobridge groused. "And all the while, the damned UP is gobbling up prairie and government money like ducks after bread laid upon still water. Somehow, we've just *got* to find a way to get over the top and down the other side of this mountain so we can make the last few hundred miles a real race."

"He's right," Crocker said. "At forty-eight thousand dollars a mile we're losing our ass up here, and it's going to get a lot worse before it gets better. In addition to everything else, we're praying for a mild winter."

"I'm sure that would help," Glenn said.

"Damn right it would but," Crocker said, "with our luck, we'll probably get another like the one that trapped the Donner Party some twenty years ago."

"Let's hope not," Glenn said. "And now, if you'll excuse me, I need to talk to Miss O'Connell."

"You ought to just sweep her up, drag her off to the nearest preacher and marry the girl."

"I'd like to," Glenn confessed, "but she's not the kind that takes to being ordered about."

"Have you tried it on her?" Strobridge asked point-blank.

"I have," Glenn said, holding up his left arm, "and she broke this arm, which still isn't completely healed."

"Sonofabitch," Strobridge breathed, looking very impressed, "now that is a woman I want to meet!"

Crocker burst into guffaws and then Glenn confessed that he'd been kidding, at least about Megan breaking his arm. Afterward, he left the tent and went to find Megan. He would tell her the good news about getting a job and then they'd sit down and make some hard decisions about what Megan wanted to do next.

When he found Megan, she was with Ford Hayward and they were having a lively and obviously enjoyable conversation. Ford looked up when he saw Glenn approaching and said, "Hello, Glenn. I was just telling Miss O'Connell what a good job you did in that tent and how Mr. Crocker was going to offer you a job for sure."

"I would have liked to have told her myself," Glenn said, realizing that he sounded testy.

Megan had been sitting beside Ford on a log outside the women's tent, but now she came and threw her arms around his neck and said, "I'm very proud and happy for you, although not a bit surprised. Congratulations!"

Glenn forced a smile. "And now we need to talk about us. That is, if Mr. Hayward will excuse us?"

Crocker's tall young assistant nodded and came to his feet. "Of course," he said. "I have duties to perform and look forward to working with you, Glenn."

"Likewise," Glenn said, trying to muster up sincerity.

But apparently he did not do that good a job because, when they were alone, Megan said, "Don't you like Ford?"

"He's fine," Glenn answered. "But I'm not interested in talking about him. I want to talk about *us*."

"Yes, you said that."

"Well? What's our plan?"

Megan took his hand and they began to stroll toward the broad American River with the imposing face of Cape Horn looming almost overhead. "Glenn," she said finally, "I really want to be nearer to this railroad than Sacramento."

"Good!"

"I want to somehow be a part of it."

"Marry me and I'll make you a big part of it."

She ignored his comment. "Ford says that we ought to be able to figure out some way that I can both stay close and make a nice income."

Glenn pulled up short. "You've already discussed this with Ford?"

"Well, of course! He's practically guaranteed that Mr. Peamont and Zeke will be employed. Why wouldn't I seek to explore my own possibilities with him?"

"Because he's a stranger!"

Megan stiffened. "And you're jealous!"

"It's just that I want to be the one that helps you, not a stranger."

Megan's eyes flashed. "I don't think there is any point in discussing this matter further. I am perfectly capable of handling my own destiny, thank you."

"Then do it!" Glenn said hotly. "Because I'm fed up with trying to win your hand while you consider every other option but marriage."

"We're not really even engaged!" Megan stormed. "You never gave me a ring. And you are the one that had to come to work on this railroad, irrespective of what I wanted. It was far more important for you to clear your sterling reputation than it was to win my hand anyway!"

"That is not true!"

"It is true!" Megan shouted as she turned around and marched off.

"Damn," Glenn swore to himself as he stomped off in the other direction. "Damn!"

CHAPTER
12

"Glenn?"

Glenn looked up from his survey maps to see Earl Peamont. The man was smiling. "I'm going on my first buying trip for the railroad tomorrow."

"That's good news. And what about Zeke?"

"He's going too. We're all heading down the mountain and they've promised we'll find a preacher in Auburn for the Mormon kids. Wish you were coming."

"I do too," Glenn said, "but I've already explained to Zeke why I can't get away and be his best man. You're just going to have to stand in for me, Earl."

"Oh, I'm honored to do that," the heavyset man assured him. "But I'm wondering if there isn't some way that you and Megan could get back on track together."

"I don't think so. What we really seem to need is time apart to think things out."

"She wants to be a buyer for the railroad just like Zeke and me, but Mr. Crocker wasn't too keen on the idea. He said she ought to marry you and live in Sacramento with the other wives who come up to visit on Sundays. I guess they send up a special train and make quite an occasion out of it."

"Yeah," Glenn said glumly, "that's what I've been told."

Peamont stepped forward, his brow furrowed with concern. "I'm sorry that things didn't work out better between you."

"I haven't given up on marrying Megan," Glenn said. "It's just that I've decided not to push her in that direction any longer. If she's ever ready, then maybe I'll still be too."

"That's the stuff!" Peamont stuck out his hand. "Good luck. We'll be back in a couple of weeks. I'm buying canvas and cloth along with a bunch of other things on the docks in San Francisco. Zeke is going to be buying hay, grain and dried fruit, mostly down in the San Joaquin Valley, so you'll be seeing him more often than me."

Glenn shook the man's hand. He had grown rather fond of Peamont and would always remember him as someone who had acted with courage when he was needed in Virginia City to help free the two Mormons and avert a terrible wrong.

When Peamont left, Glenn found that he could not really concentrate on the survey maps that were spread all over a large table before him. Restless and disturbed by his fight with Megan, he went outside and watched as his friends mounted their horses and prepared to leave.

"Why don't you at least go over and tell her good-bye," Ford Hayward suggested with a mocking smile.

Glenn angrily turned to face the man. "Why the hell don't you?"

"All right." Ford chuckled. "I shall."

Glenn turned and went back into the tent. He marched around the table three times and then he headed back outside and saw Megan and Ford talking. Megan's eyes lifted and, for a moment, Glenn felt his heart skip a beat, but then Megan looked back down at Ford.

"Oh, the devil with it!" Glenn swore under his breath as he marched up the canyon past the trains and into the construction that was going on along the American River.

Strobridge was prowling the roadbed, shouting orders to the workmen. Since very few of the Chinese understood English, a harried Chinese translator dogged his footsteps, interpreting his orders as fast as they were shouted. The translator possessed a very high, nasal voice and the habit of gesticulating wildly. How the man could listen, translate and shout all at the same time was a mystery to Glenn, but he was apparently quite effective because hundreds of Chinese jumped every time Strobridge barked an order. Strobridge saw Glenn and nodded, suddenly craning his head back.

"Look up there!" Strobridge shouted, pointing upward.

An army of Chinese stopped in their tracks and stared at the lofty summit of Cape Horn.

"No, no!" Strobridge yelled at his translator. "Not them! I was speaking to Mr. Gilchrist!"

The translator's shrill translation sent the Chinese workmen scurrying about again, leaving Glenn the only one still gazing upward. "Jim, what the devil am I supposed to be looking at?"

"They're going to lower two baskets this morning over the top of Cape Horn. You need to be able to signal to them where to start drilling the blast holes."

Glenn hadn't expected this to happen so soon. "Be right back," he yelled, taking off on at a run.

"Where the hell are you going!"

"To get my transit and my maps!"

He was able to return on time with the things he needed, and when the brave Chinese were slowly lowered down in their large wicker baskets, even Strobridge was holding his breath. Crocker was there too, neck craned as the two Chinese slowly floated down the face of Cape Horn while Glenn took his last crucial measurements.

"Hold it!" he shouted up at the face of Cape Horn. "That's far enough!"

But over the roar of the American River, Glenn could not possibly be heard by the two brave Chinese suspended high above. Realizing that, Strobridge drew a pistol from his coat pocket and fired it into the sky. The retort slammed back and forth against rock walls and the two dangling Chinese, both tightly gripping their baskets and no more than twenty feet apart, froze. Glenn was sure they were wondering if their wicker baskets would separate and send them plummeting to a watery grave far, far below.

The two Chinamen remained immovable for less than thirty seconds while the wind gently brushed their baskets back and forth along the face of the cliff. At last they slowly bent over and picked up their drills and hammers. In perfect unison, like puppets working on the same string, they struck the drills, and Glenn saw the men and the baskets quiver as small pieces of rock fragment exploded off the cliff's imposing surface.

"It's solid granite where they're working," Strobridge muttered to himself. "I told 'em to drill holes three inches deep and pack them with powder."

Crocker nodded. "Let's make damn sure that those men are dragged way above the explosions when the drill holes are finished and the powder and fuses are set."

"Yep," Strobridge growled. "They're fearless but they don't have a wish to die."

"Right," Crocker said. "And besides, it costs a fortune to ship 'em back to China for burial."

Everyone returned to work for the next hour, or at least tried to ignore the two tiny specks dangling more than a thousand feet up the face of the cliff as they hammered with the precision of matched metronomes. Every few minutes as Glenn consulted his maps and transit, he would stop and stare at the two Chinamen with wonder. From his vantage point on the floor of the canyon, the Chinese appeared to be the size of ants on a bathroom wall.

When the hammers finally stopped ringing, everyone looked up again and saw the Chinese retract their drills from the granite and then pack their blast holes with powder.

"Mr. Gilchrist, do you have any idea how much rock will be displaced?" Crocker asked.

"I expect at least a ton."

"Look, they're setting the fuses," Strobridge said to no one in particular. "I warned them again and again to set both fuses extra long."

Glenn realized he was holding his breath when the Chinese lit the fuses and then jerked hard on their ropes in signal that they were to be raised. Almost at once, Glenn saw the tiny figures on top of Cape Horn appear to grab the ropes and quickly haul the two baskets up the cliff while the drillers held on tight, both staring down at the sputtering fuses.

The Chinese drillers were not pulled over the lip of the cliff but instead were left dangling a few feet below it. When the blasts finally erupted, they were less than twenty seconds apart and seemed rather puny, little more than loud bangs. But when huge plates of the granite dislodged and cascaded down to plunge into the river far below, it was a sight that was worth remembering. Great geysers of water burst into the air and the American River roiled like a storm-tossed ocean.

"Good God!" Crocker exclaimed with admiration. "Give those two drillers *triple* pay, not double!"

"Not a good idea," Strobridge said. "In fact, I didn't even offer 'em double pay."

"What!" Crocker cried. "Didn't you just see what they did up there!"

"Sure," Strobridge coolly replied. "But you know as well as I do that the Chinese love fireworks. Why, they've been setting off rockets long before we ever thought of using the simplest weapons. I tell you, Charles, those Chinamen are going to be fighting over who gets the job of drillin' and blastin' on Cape Horn. Mark my word, they'd think you were crazy to pay 'em double for what they consider to be great fun. And if you start doing that sort of thing, well. . . . you'd be setting a real expensive precedent."

"You mean they'd start expecting us to pay them double for certain jobs that they thought we thought were dangerous?"

"Exactly," Strobridge said. "So my translator told those two that it was an honor to be chosen to work out of those wicker baskets."

"Humph!" Crocker grunted. "An honor, huh?"

"Yes, sir!" Strobridge smiled. "And from what I heard, the Chinese were practically fighting among themselves for the job. They gambled for the honor and we just saw the two lucky winners up there."

"Give more of 'em the honor," Crocker decided. "As many as you feel will be safe and not blow each other to pieces."

"I figure that five working from their baskets at the same time would be about right," Strobridge said. "Glenn and I talked it over late last night and he figures the same."

"That's fine," Crocker said. "Glenn, with five of them drilling and blasting, how long might you think it will take to get that cut made across Cape Horn?"

"Two weeks," Glenn replied. "Barring some disaster, the drillers will get better and better as the cut progresses along Cape Horn. I expect that they'll move an astonishing amount of rock in a very short time."

Crocker was pleased. "That's excellent news! The Grizzly Tunnel is almost finished. Jim, let's start the next tunnel and the next. I want our camp and supply train to be standing just below Donner Pass when the first snow flies. We'll tackle the Summit Tunnel this winter."

"Yes, sir," Strobridge replied. "I've already sent men and equipment up there."

"How many are you pulling off this site?"

"Thirteen hundred," Strobridge said. "We'll split them up at the next two tunnels and have them drilling and blasting in both directions. We'll be knocking at the back door of Donner Pass before winter. Only thing is, I doubt that door is going to be easy to open."

"No," Crocker said, "but there hasn't been anything easy yet so why should the Summit Tunnel be the exception? Glenn, maybe you ought to go up there and work on those tunnel sites for a few weeks, just to make sure that our boys have figured them right."

"I'll be happy to do that," Glenn said. "When shall I leave?"

"Give it a couple of days," Crocker decided, "until we all feel sure about the correctness of this cut."

That was fine with Glenn. He was itching to get to work because the harder and more intensely he labored, the easier it would be to forget about Megan.

Crocker returned his gaze to the two baskets that were in the process of being lowered back down the rock face so that more holes could be drilled and more rock dropped. Crocker shook his head and muttered, "Some honor," as he pivoted about and hurried back to their construction camp.

Several miles down the canyon, Megan pulled her horse up shortly and said to her friends, "Did you hear that?"

"What?"

"That explosion," Megan said. "It was quite unlike any I ever heard before on the Union Pacific when they used blasting powder."

"How do you—"

"There! There it is again."

"I heard it now," Peamont said.

Both Zeke and Becky vowed they had heard it too. They all twisted around in their saddles to gaze back up the canyon, and that was when they saw the tiny specks of humanity bravely working from their baskets.

"They did it!" Megan said. "They've already started blasting away at the face of Cape Horn."

"Maybe we should have stayed to watch the excitement," Peamont offered.

"No," Megan said, suspecting that the man just wanted to try and reunite her and Glenn so they could at least settle their differences. "We've a minister to find and a wedding to perform, right?"

"That's right," Zeke said, grinning at his bride-to-be as she blushed with joy.

Dear Lord, Megan thought, *why can't Glenn and I be so much in love and so happy?*

Auburn was a busy little mining town that had boomed during the Forty-Niner gold rush, then wilted as the rush died and now was resurrected because of the Central Pacific

Railroad's construction. It had become the county seat for Placer County and its steep, hilly streets were lined with colorful old public buildings, homes and saloons. The Kaiser Brewery was back in operation after being closed for several years and was advertising nickel-a-glass beer, while a banner across High Street proclaimed that St. Luke's church was holding a dance that night.

"I'm sure we could find a minister there," Megan said, pointing out the church to her friends.

"Yes," Becky said. "But a justice of the peace would be better."

"Why don't we go to the Placer County Courthouse?" Peamont suggested, pointing to a sign that instructed them to ride up a steep hill. "I'm sure that they can perform the marriage or at least tell us who can."

"Good idea," Megan said.

They found the imposing county courthouse, which had a sign telling everyone that it had been constructed from public donations during the gold rush and, in keeping with the public spirit of the donations, had incorporated marble mined from the Colfax area, granite from nearby Rocklin and slate from Slatington, and that the bricks that composed the exterior had been fired in Auburn itself.

"And look!" Megan said, pointing to a small sign tacked to the wall. "It says that they perform marriage ceremonies at the courthouse for just two dollars."

They tied their horses and hurried inside. Ten minutes later, they were standing before a smiling justice of the peace while Zeke and Becky prepared to recite marriage vows. There were no frills but just before the ceremony, a little old lady with a large yellow, white dress and white shoes rushed out of the wings to hug the newlyweds and present them with a beautiful bouquet of flowers. Becky wept and young Zeke tried to look mature and assured as he recited his vows, but Megan could see that he was very nervous.

Fortunately, Earl Peamont had found and bought a gold wedding band. "It ain't much," he said in the way of an apology, "and I expect you'll get this girl a nicer one when you get your first railroad paycheck."

"I will," Zeke promised, "and I'll give this one back to you."

"Naw, you can sell it and buy yourselves something," Peamont said. "The fella I bought it from said that his wife gave it to him but she died of smallpox about a year later. He didn't want it anymore."

"Then neither do I," Becky said, chin lifting. "I mean no disrespect, Mr. Peamont, but I am a little superstitious about such things and I'd rather not wear any ring than one associated with sorrow."

"I understand," Peamont said as Zeke handed the ring back to him. "I truly do."

Megan had a ring given to her by her grandmother and whose real value was sentimental. "Here," she said, giving it to Zeke. "It belonged to my grandmother and she lived to the age of ninety-three without any sickness. She was married to my grandfather for fifty-seven years and theirs was a marriage made in heaven."

Becky took the ring, eyes shiny with tears. "Then I'll not need another."

The wedding was over in a few minutes, and then everyone realized that they didn't know where to go for a celebration.

"Go to the Bonanza House," the little old lady urged. "My brother owns it and it's the nicest place in Auburn. The prices are reasonable and I promise that you'll be happy with the rooms and the dinner."

"Then let's give it a try," Megan suggested. Since everyone thought that a splendid idea, they went outside, mounted their horses and rode off to celebrate at the Bonanza House.

They were given the best table in the dining room while the nicest room in the little hotel was made ready for the newlyweds. Megan had brought over a thousand dollars in cash from Wyoming, but Earl had less than one hundred. Still, the man proved himself to be generous and insisted on paying for the room, while Megan paid for their dinner of roast duck smothered with a delicious sweet almond sauce. Peamont ordered champagne and four glasses.

"All right, but just a sip," Becky conceded.

"A sip? Ha!" Peamont cried. "This is *good* champagne! You'll want much more than a sip."

And they did. The newlyweds drank full glasses as they repeatedly toasted the Central Pacific Railroad and the start of their new lives in California. Megan, despite her sadness at leaving Glenn under such troubling circumstances, enjoyed herself immensely. The dinner was every bit as good as promised and the young couple from Utah were almost giddy with happiness. But after they blushingly excused themselves and left the table to enjoy their first real night alone and together, Megan could not help but feel let down.

"What's the matter?" Peamont asked. "You look like we've just suffered a death instead of a marriage. Is it Glenn?"

"Yes," Megan said. "And it was my fault we fought. All my fault."

"All you need to do is to climb on one of the supply trains and ride on back up there and apologize."

"I know, but I can't," Megan told him. "I need to find my own way first."

"I see," Peamont replied, not looking as if he saw her reasoning at all. "Well, have you decided what you are going to do?"

"No. I need a little time to explore possibilities."

"Sacramento is the best place to do that," Peamont said. "We can be there by tomorrow at noon and—"

"I don't think so," Megan interrupted. "I want to stay here in Auburn for a while and just rest and think. But thanks for the offer."

"You're welcome," he said. "Another bottle of champagne?"

Megan shook her head. "I'm going upstairs to my room and go to bed early."

"Good idea," Peamont said in an almost fatherly manner. "It's my experience that things always look much brighter in the morning."

Megan leaned forward. "And what about you?"

"I'm not sleepy yet," Peamont told her. "I'm going to find a good saloon and game of poker. Have a few more drinks and try my luck at the cards."

"If you lose all your money you can borrow some of mine before you leave tomorrow morning."

"You're a peach," he said, winking. "And if I were younger, slimmer and better-looking, I'd be—"

"Good night," Megan told him with a smile as she rose to leave.

Earl Peamont sighed and then he said, "Good night, Miss O'Connell."

"Excuse me, miss!"

Megan turned to see an attractive and well-dressed man in his mid-twenties. He was of average height with curious brown eyes, a wide, friendly grin and a dimple in the center of his square chin. His face was clean-shaven, and his hair was parted down the middle, thick, brown and wavy.

"Yes?" she asked.

"I . . . I don't wish to be bold, miss. But there is a dance tonight at the church and I saw that you just rode in with that older fella and I thought you might enjoy the entertainment."

"I'm sorry," Megan said. "We've been riding hard for two days and I'm very tired. But it's nice of you to ask."

The man took a step closer. "Really, we could go for only an hour or two and I can assure you that you'd easily be the prettiest woman at the dance."

Megan looked down at her wrinkled and soiled dress which she'd tried to clean before the wedding but without much success. And her hair was badly in need of washing. "I'm afraid that I really don't look very pretty."

"You know the old saying, 'Beauty is in the eye of the beholder.' "

He winked. "I don't think I've introduced myself. My name is Mitch Townsend and, in addition to my regular clients, I do most of the county's legal work. Maybe you even saw my office just down the street."

"No," she told him, "I missed that. And, if I do say so, you look rather young to be a lawyer."

"I started studying the law early in life. You see, my father was a judge. He had a fine career and did very well for himself in mining law during the height of the gold rush."

"So you followed in his footsteps."

"That's right," Townsend said. "My father made the law seem exciting and I had a love for it right from the start. But later, I learned that lawyers are a lot like undertakers—we're only used as a last resort."

Megan had to grin until Mitch said, "My father, bless his heart, died this spring."

"I'm sorry."

"Me too." The man cleared his throat and forced a smile. "But he died in his sleep and at peace with the world. That's not easy to do when you practice the law as long as he did."

Mitch reached into his pocket and extracted a business card printed on expensive card stock. "I don't often have a reason to hand these things out. Everyone in Placer County knows me, but you look like someone that I'd like to know better."

"Did it ever occur to you that I might be married?" Megan asked with amusement.

"Nope. You're not wearing a wedding ring and the man who escorted you into this hotel was too old to be your husband."

"You're very observant."

"Easy to be when the subject is beautiful."

Megan felt her cheeks warm at this bold compliment. "Good night, Mr. Townsend. And I hope you enjoy the dance."

"Oh, I don't usually dance," he said.

Megan was confused. "Then why . . ."

"I play the fiddle and enjoy watching others dance. But if you were to change your mind and come with me this evening, I'd put down the fiddle and give the dancing my best try. I sure wish you'd give the people of Auburn a treat."

Megan's resistance dissolved under the great warmth of his smile. "Maybe just a couple of dances," she relented.

He beamed. "Wonderful! Shall I come back in a little while or are you ready now?"

"I'm ready now," she told him. "As ready as I'm going to get."

Mitch Townsend offered Megan his arm saying, "This just goes to prove that sometimes a fella just gets lucky."

They strolled out of the Bonanza House and down the street into the soft warm evening. "I hope that there is someone else who can fiddle in your place."

"Me too," he said earnestly. "If I have to do it, the bachelors of this town will swarm and I'll have lost you for the evening."

"I'll tell them . . . well," Megan said, "I don't know what I'll tell them. You're a lawyer, I'll leave the talking to you."

"Thanks," he said, "I'll think of something to keep them barbarous young devils away from you."

Megan breathed deeply of the sweet, pine-scented air. She suddenly felt very light and expectant. And why not? Megan had not been to a dance in such a long time and a little good, clean fun might be just what was needed.

CHAPTER

13

Mitch Townsend was a very popular man, judging from the warm and enthusiastic greeting he received when they entered the hall at St. Luke's church. Men and women alike hurried over to greet him and Megan was completely overlooked for a few moments because nearly everyone was asking Mitch why he hadn't brought his fiddle.

"I'm taking the night off!" he announced. "You've got enough fiddlers here without needing me."

This news was not well received. "Listen, everyone, I brought a beautiful guest instead tonight!" Mitch shouted, holding up his hands. "I want you to meet . . ."

Suddenly, Mitch blushed with embarrassment. "Good heavens, my dear, I don't even know your name!"

The hall erupted with laughter and catcalls. It took several minutes to quiet the boisterous crowd. Megan cleared her throat. "My name is Megan O'Connell," she announced, loud enough to be heard by all. "I just arrived in town today and I'm delighted to be here."

"Not as delighted as we are to see you!" a strapping young man shouted. "And if Mitch ain't lassoed your heart yet, I'd like the first dance!"

This request resulted in more laughter, partly because Megan's cheeks turned crimson.

"I'm sorry!" Mitch shouted. "But Miss O'Connell has promised me *every* dance tonight!"

A storm of protest from the young bachelors forced Mitch to compromise. "All right, every *other* dance. But she can't stay for very long so I'm taking all of my turns first!"

Someone struck up the music and Megan saw that there were three fiddlers already in the church hall. As they began to play a lively tune an old man with suspenders, a red flannel shirt and a jug of spirits sang, "When Mother Drank All Dad's Rye Whiskey."

It was a hilarious song and the old man soon had everyone laughing and singing. The first chorus went like this:

So bring out the rye and kiss dear Mother good-bye,
And listen dear laddies, now don't you cry
'Cause Daddy's gonna send her off to Singapore
Where she'll drink tea and never get drunk no more!

Megan laughed until tears ran down her cheeks. And as soon as that song was finished, the fiddlers struck up a polka.

"Here we go!" Mitch shouted, taking her into his arms.

Megan had danced the polka back East as a girl many times and so she had no difficulty keeping up with her partner. Around and around the huge hall they twirled, faster and faster, it seemed, until the room began to spin and finally the music stopped, leaving everyone excited and breathless.

"Maybe we ought to sit the next one out," Megan said as the fiddlers struck up a reel.

"All right, would you like some refreshments?"

Megan had already spotted the table filled with punch bowls, cookies and cakes.

"I am thirsty."

"Then let's have something to drink."

There were a lot of young people crowded around the punch bowls and Mitch had to clear the way to get them liquid refreshments.

"These have something extra in them," he warned. "But if you want the regular . . ."

Megan tasted her punch. It did have a strong kick but was delicious. "It's wonderful," she told him. "I might even want more."

"So do I," he said as he put his arm around her slender waist.

No sooner did Megan empty her glass then another was offered to her and then another. In between, she danced with a succession of eager young men.

"Mitch is gonna play pretty soon now," one of them promised. "He's real special on a fiddle and he can't hardly keep his hands offa one when there's dancing."

Megan was out of breath from her strenuous exertion on the floor. But so was every other lady. As in most western towns, the women were outnumbered about five to one by the men and they were expected to dance every dance.

"Megan, my darlin', this one is for you!" Mitch called across the dance floor as he put his bow to his borrowed fiddle and cut loose with a wild Irish jig. That was when the hall really began to come alive and men threw back their heads and howled.

"Let's dance another one!" the young man pleaded.

"No," Megan said, eyes glued on Mitch, "let's watch."

Mitch had removed his suit coat, loosened his tie and bent one leg to lean forward over his instrument. And now, as his bow began to skitter across the strings of the fiddle, the music really came alive. Everyone stopped dancing and began to clap and stomp their feet faster and faster in time with the music. One by one, the other fiddlers quit playing to admire Mitch's artistry.

Megan had listened to fiddlers before but never one like Mitch Townsend. His music charged the hall until it crackled with energy and swept everyone into a joyous frenzy. Mitch's right hand was a blur as he bent over the fiddle. As the music grew faster and faster, Megan realized that she was holding her breath. There was so much power radiating out of the man that she expected Mitch to shatter into a million fragments, like a fiery comet striking the face of the moon. And then it ended as suddenly as the music had begun when Mitch slumped over his instrument, chest heaving with exhaustion.

Megan was shaken to her innermost core. She took a deep breath and expelled it slowly, her mouth dry, her eyes wet. Mitch lifted his head and smiled softly to her and began to play something almost magical as his eyes burned with strange and lovely lights.

Megan placed her glass down on the table and was forced to steady herself. Everyone and everything except Mitch and his song vanished and they were alone in this crowded church hall. An exquisite melody sent shivers racing up and down Megan's spine. The violin spoke of love and tragedy and angels and heaven. Its music was ethereal. Large, salty tears rolled down Megan's cheeks. No one, not even the small children, seemed to breathe until the music drifted into an eternity of silence.

"I told you he could play special," the earnest young man said at last.

But Megan didn't hear the man for she was rushing across the room to throw her arms around Mitch and cry, "You were wonderful! Glorious!"

He was pale and trembling. It was as if he had undergone some powerful spiritual experience.

"I could use some fresh air," he finally whispered in her ear. "Music possesses me."

"Come along," she urged softly as she led him out a side door into the warm, pine-scented night air. "We can sit, or we can go for a walk."

"I'd rather walk," he told her, using a silk handkerchief to mop his face dry.

"Are you sure you're up to it?"

"Yes."

They hiked up Union Street past the *Placer Herald* newspaper office. "I'd think I'd like to show you the lights of our town at night," he finally said. "If you're up to a little climb."

"Are you?"

"Yes," he said, leading her up a steep side street that was bordered by huge and elaborate Victorian homes.

"This is quite a neighborhood," she remarked, already winded. "It must be where all the rich people live."

"We get along quite nicely," he agreed. "My house is just up the way and there is a breathtaking view from my front porch."

"I'm already out of breath," she told him, and it was true. "What is the elevation here?"

"It's only about twelve hundred feet."

"Seems higher."

A few moments later, Mitch came to a stop and looked up at a huge two-story Victorian mansion which glimmered under the light of a big melon moon. "Rather ostentatious, isn't it?"

Megan just stared. The house was white with soft blue trim. Large and graceful, it boasted a wide veranda that stretched all the way across the front of the mansion. The windows were made of leaded glass and a front porch lamp illuminated the intricate scrolling and carved wooden shutters and porch posts. There was a small balcony off the second story where delicate climbing roses now blossomed in profusion. The front yard was stunning, with gardens, a marble walkway and a huge spreading oak.

"This is yours?" Megan asked.

"It was my father and mother's," he explained. "My mother died four years ago and my father never really recovered from the loss. In some ways, it was a blessing when he passed away this spring from a broken heart."

"And you've no other family?"

"I do," he confessed, "and I might as well tell you right now that my only brother was hanged in 1854 for killing three men in a barroom brawl."

"Self-defense?"

"My father argued that it was, but there were too many witnesses that said Randy shot the last two men in cold blood. One of them in the back."

"I'm sorry."

"My brother was wild and out of control when he was drinking," Mitch explained, shaking his head. "He was quite a lot older than me and fell in with a bad crowd early on in his life. Randy and my father were always at odds. I think that Randy just wanted to show Father that he could do something that my father could not—namely, physically intimidate men. I always found him scary although he never laid a hand on me. Randy's trial caused quite a stir and the newspaper made a very big deal of it because of my father. It was the only stain on his entire legal career and it hurt him very deeply."

"I have a sister named Aileen," Megan said. "She and I are not very much alike either."

"How so?"

"She's far gentler and much more of a lady."

"And you are neither?"

"Did I look gentle or lady-like out on the dance floor?"

He took her into his arms and kissed her lips, then whispered, "You feel and taste like a lady to me, Megan."

She was caught by surprise and every instinct told Megan to push him away, but she found that she could not. Her head was spinning either from the punch, the altitude or his kiss, and quite possibly the potent combination of all three.

"Megan, come on up to my house and I'll fix you something else to drink while we enjoy the view together."

"I can't," she whispered, knowing that she should turn around, but Mitch was already walking up to the house and mounting the stairs. Megan felt compelled to follow.

"Just have a seat on the porch and relax for a moment until I come back with refreshments," he called over his shoulder.

Megan took a seat in a lounge chair that was incredibly comfortable. She stared over a low porch railing out across the lights of the town and thought the view was nothing short of magnificent.

He was back in minutes setting a tray, crystal pitcher and glasses on a marble table. Taking a seat close beside her, Mitch filled the glasses and handed her one. Then, filling his own glass, he raised it to the golden moon and said, "To Megan O'Connell and to Mitch Townsend. Strangers no more."

She smiled. "That's a curious toast."

"You won't think so very long."

Megan tasted her drink and it was sweet and very delicious. "What is this?"

"It is rum and a special mix of tropical fruits that I use to blend something that I call The Miracle."

"The Miracle?"

"Yes," he said with a chuckle, "Mitch's Miracle. Drink a couple of these and you feel miraculous no matter how rotten the day."

"I feel pretty fine already, thank you."

"So do I," he told her. Leaning over, he kissed her again, very gently and with a slow passion that caused Megan's heart to race.

She needed some breathing room. "Where did you learn to play music with such grace and inspiration?"

Taking a deep breath, he replied, "My mother's dream was that Randy become a violinist and play all over Europe. When he became a thug and brawler instead, she focused all her energy on me. I hated playing until I was about twelve years old; then a great Spanish violinist named Pablo Reyes came to San Francisco. My parents took me there and I fell in love with the violin and music."

"Just like that?"

He snapped his fingers. "Yes, just like that. I saw, for the very first time, what magic a violin could create. What unbridled passion it could inspire."

"Did you meet the Spaniard?"

"Oh yes, Mother made sure of that," Mitch said. "She probably paid him handsomely to spend an hour with me. Tragically, Reyes went down on his return voyage home during a great storm off Cape Horn, as did so many of the Forty-Niners. I was so young and impressionable and I felt that I should carry on the artistry of Pablo Reyes. Give something of his talent to the world. Fill a void left by his shining brilliance. He was just becoming well known, you know."

"I'm sorry that he was lost," Megan said, "but that's a very ambitious commitment for a twelve-year-old boy."

"I am a very ambitious man," he admitted. "And so I began to take violin instruction. I was obsessed and quickly excelled beyond the ability of my teachers. When I was fifteen, I was sent to live with relatives in Boston even though I thought I would also be lost at sea."

"You mean like Reyes?"

"In a way. You see, Reyes had become my ghost, my spiritual inspiration. I half believed that, if I died before I became worthy, I would stand before Pablo Reyes on Judgment Day and be eternally damned by my failure."

Megan expelled a deep breath. "And to think that, when I was young, all I dreamed about was food. We were poor and often hungry. And you dreamed of Pablo Reyes."

"Your hunger was more real than my ghost, and far healthier. Anyway, back East I studied under a succession of gifted teachers. I was a prodigy and could have played concerts in Europe, but then my mother died and I rushed home to Auburn. For two years, I wouldn't play at all."

Megan let the silence stretch out before she finally asked, "And why did that change?"

He shrugged and closed his eyes. "I came to understand that music is a gift, a joy created by one's soul. When the gift is great, music transforms the human heart. It can send one's spirit heaven-bound or hurl it into the dungeons of Hell. I also came to believe, I am ashamed to say, that great music creates its own selfish power."

"Power?"

"Sure!" He tried to laugh. "Megan, if you can change another's mood and feelings, isn't that power?"

Megan tasted more of her drink, thinking about the powerful waves of emotion that his music had evoked in her heart. "I wouldn't disagree," she said, "but that is a very unusual way of looking at such a gift."

"I'm an unusual man," he said without a trace of arrogance. "And you're an unusual woman. Why don't we go upstairs and make unusual love?"

Megan gulped. "You don't believe in wasting any time, do you, Mitch?"

"We're already starting to fall in love. Why fight the inevitable?"

Megan pushed to her feet. Her head was spinning again and she took a faltering step. She hadn't thought that she had drunk that much of Mitch's Miracle or the punch before that, but . . .

He was picking her up and kicking open the door! She looked back over his shoulder and saw the moonlight streaming in through the open door and thought only that he should not leave it hanging wide open. But by the time that thought slowly unfolded they were up the stairs and he was lowering her onto a bright blue bedspread.

"No," she whispered, her head rolling back and forth on his pillow. "This *isn't* what I wanted."

"You don't know what you want, my darling," he said quietly. "But I'm about to show you. Trust me."

Megan watched as he moved over to the upstairs window, found his violin and then began to play. Mitch curled over the violin as he had before, giving her the definite impression that he was pouring his very essence into the music. He played softly, every note stretched and filled with yearning.

"Oh," she sighed, closing her eyes and letting herself be transported into a state of euphoria. His music changed so subtly that she was not at first even aware of the power and intense desire it created. She lay still, and when the music finally ended and he came to her, Megan was aflame with desire unlike any she had ever felt for any man.

Their lovemaking was a continuum of his music. He took her with great tenderness, with intimate words and intimate touches that seared her with divine ecstacy. But before long, Megan was consumed with an insatiable passion. She could not get enough of the man! And deep, deep within, spinning off the last fraying remnants of her reason, Megan O'Connell believed that in this spiritual and physical union, they were not really of this world.

CHAPTER 14

Glenn had never become so focused on *anything* as he was Cape Horn. Every waking hour for the past week he had stared at that great outcropping of granite rock. He had studied it at daybreak when the sunrise brought its magnificent face into the light of day, and marveled at how cloud shadows had sailed like dark eagles across its now-scarred profile. At sunset, Cape Horn glowed like a shrine, and when the drilling and the blasting were finally over for the day, night shrouded its face and Cape Horn brooded in angry darkness.

It was funny, Glenn thought, how, if you watched a physical thing long enough, it took on human characteristics. Cape Horn had become to him the rugged, ruined face of an old ship captain standing at the bow of his vessel, gazing into the endless expanse of green ocean and frothy wave. The captain's face was being blasted away, first the left cheek, then the proud bridge of the nose, all horribly mutilated. Now, they were scoring the captain's right eye, tearing it from his proud, weathered face.

No wonder, Glenn thought, *the captain glares at us with such pure, unwavering hatred and defiance. He is already half-blinded, and today we obliterate his right eyebrow.*

Glenn realized that his reflections on the lifelike aura of Cape Horn probably reflected the turmoil of his own troubled mind. Perhaps it had something to do with his bitterness over the way he and Megan had parted. Perhaps it was also that he had some twisted feelings regarding his dismissal from the Union Pacific. Or perhaps it had something to do with Harry Loudermilk, the Central Pacific labor contractor. No matter. Glenn decided that the only way to exorcise his demons was to work hard and fast. To defeat the captain and then to race ahead to the next engineering challenge. Allowing Cape Horn to take on the persona of a proud sea captain was not in and of itself a dangerous thing, but Glenn would not have confessed his imaginings, especially to such practical and hard-driving men as Crocker or Strobridge. So he kept quiet as he watched the daily disfiguration. And each day he vowed not to study the captain's face at sunrise and at sunset, but he found the temptation much too powerful to resist.

"I'll be glad when we beat him," Glenn said one evening as he and Strobridge watched the sunset burn the captain's face.

"Beat who?" Strobridge asked.

Glenn paused. "I *meant*," he corrected, "beat Cape Horn."

"Sure," Strobridge said, "damned great ugly piece of rock! Sometimes I almost think of it as a living thing opposing our will."

Glenn blinked. "You do?"

"Yeah," Strobridge confessed a little sheepishly, "but that's crazy. Still, I will be glad to put that big, ugly brute behind us."

"Me too," Glenn said, feeling better to know that he was not alone in allowing the captain to work his spell.

The following day began with heavy, lead-bellied clouds lumbering in from the west. By noon, the wind had grown strong and it was whipping the pines. High up near Donner

Pass where the snow still capped the tallest mountain peaks, gusts of wind sent it rooster-tailing into the dark, boiling cauldron of stormy sky.

"We're in for a cold, hard rain," Strobridge said, pulling the collar of his coat up. "It's going to be a long, miserable day to work."

Even as the man spoke, Glenn saw the first splashes of rain strike the rocks. In another moment, it pelted the eyes, cutting in low under hat brims. The Chinese were especially vulnerable and they quickly removed their conical-shaped straw hats and handed them to one of their own, who stacked them until he had twenty or more and then raced into the trees to hide them out of the force of the wind. Now, the Chinese worked bareheaded and the plaits of long, braided hair that they wore at the back of their heads—Glenn had learned they were called queues—wagged like the black tails of dogs. But the Chinese did not slacken their work pace. If anything, they worked even faster.

"I'm worried about those drillers up there in the baskets," Glenn told the construction boss. "I'm afraid that they might be tossed about hard enough to be injured."

"Oh," Strobridge said, "they'll be all right. I expect that it'll be a little tougher packing the drill holes with powder and keeping the fuses lit if this rain really begins to pour, but other than that not much else is going to change."

Glenn wanted to be as sanguine as Strobridge but, as the intensity of the rain and wind increased, he could see that the baskets were beginning to swing and that the Chinese drillers were having an increasingly difficult time maintaining their positions. Glenn could not even imagine how terrifying it would be to hang almost two thousand feet above the American River in a driving rain while your wicker basket was being tossed about like a piece of bark on a raging river.

"I don't know," he said. "I think maybe we ought to . . ."

"Holy Jezus!" Strobridge cried into the storm. "The bottom of a basket has broken through!"

Everyone below seemed to have heard the startled oath despite the deep growl of heavy thunder. Glenn raised his hand and shielded his eyes from the rain to see that one of the baskets really had broken open at the bottom. Miraculously, its occupant had grabbed for the edge of the basket even as most of his body had fallen through. And now, as the other drillers gaped in horror, the poor Chinaman was madly trying to haul himself up to grab the rope so that he could be hauled up to safety.

But the rain conspired against the driller and the broken reeds of the soggy basket kept unraveling. Glenn thought he heard a scream as the man suddenly dropped. His body fell more than a hundred feet to strike a glancing blow to the captain's prominent chin. No human being could have survived that impact and a groan of anguish escaped Glenn's lips as the body began to cartwheel over and over, caroming off the upper torso of the unforgiving captain to vanish into the boiling river.

"Pull up all the baskets!" Strobridge roared.

But his words were whipped away by the wind and the rain. The other drillers stared down at the body, which was tossed to the surface of the river only to be sucked back under its churning current.

"Pull up all the baskets!" Strobridge shouted over and over, gesturing madly with his hands.

Because of his background in physics, Glenn immediately understood the urgency in Strobridge's voice. The reeds used to weave the Chinese baskets had quickly become soaked and had lost their tensile strength. They would *all* be breaking or unraveling in the next few moments under the force of this fierce summer rainstorm.

Glenn also began to gesture wildly but the baskets did not move and, through the blasts of wind-driven rain, he was staggered to see that several of the Chinese were actually going back to work!

"Those stupid sonsabitches!" Strobridge cried helplessly. "They must . . ."

But Glenn wasn't listening. He was charging over to a horse and using his knife to hack away the harness that bound it to a wagon. A moment later, he was whipping the animal into the fierce downpour and racing up a long, winding trail.

As he raced up the mountain clinging to the bare back of the heavy-legged wagon horse, Glenn caught glimpses of the face of Cape Horn. It was being pelted by sheets of hard rain. The wind was rising and the pines were thrashing wildly at each other. His horse, unused to a man on its back, kept slipping and balking and finally, when the beast skidded and almost tumbled over the side of the mountain, Glenn abandoned it altogether and raced the last few hundred feet up to the top of Cape Horn on foot.

By now, the Chinese on top had interpreted Strobridge's wild gesturing not to mean that they should keep working, but that they should pull up all the baskets before others disintegrated. But gusts of wind were playing havoc with the driving sheets of icy rain to make things extremely difficult. At a point less than two hundred yards below the summit, Glenn rounded a curve, stopped and gasped for air, then realized that another of the baskets had opened at the bottom.

He had lost his hat somewhere, and the cold rain was nearly blinding until he shielded his eyes with his hand

and stared out to see a Chinaman lying on a thin wrinkle of rock that lined the captain's craggy face. The ledge was some sixty or seventy feet beyond the main cut. There was no doubt that the Chinaman was badly injured. Glenn could see that his eyes were closed and his body was twitching fitfully. And even as he watched, a powerful gust of wind almost sent the Chinaman spiraling to his death. Thunder clapped over Donner Pass and a wicked fork of lightning turned the sea captain's face a sickly, fish-belly white.

"Hold on!" Glenn cried, tearing off his boots and then scrambling out on the cut.

He had already walked the cut where the tracks would soon be driven. Usually, however, it had been at the end of each day in order to do his survey work and judge the strength of the rock and its ability to support a railroad. But never had he ventured out on the exposed face of Cape Horn during a dangerous thunderstorm.

Glenn tried to hurry but the wind was a demon, buffeting him in all directions as it tried to knock him over the ledge and to his death far below. Glenn slowed and grabbed rock as a particularly vicious gust seemed to snake along the captain's face and push him outward. He waited until the powerful force lessened, then he groped onward. A bolt of lightning stabbed into the captain's temple and a shimmering rainbow of sparkling granite fragments pasted the furious sky.

Glenn felt something smash him in the face and almost carry him over the side. He tried to bat it away until he realized that it was the remnants of the second broken basket. There wasn't much left of it, just some tattered reeds knotted to a thick hemp rope. Glenn ducked the swinging mass of rope and reed and started forward, but then he stopped, turned and grabbed the rope. Jerking it up and down fiercely, he waited an instant, then felt the rope being jerked as if in signal from up above. Glenn leaned back against the face of Cape Horn. Heavy rivulets of water were cascading down from above, but he could see the faces of Chinese through the rain.

Gesturing wildly, Glenn tried to make the Chinese high above him understand that he would use the rope in an attempt to rescue the injured Chinaman. When a waving hand finally appeared, Glenn prayed that he and the fellows above were of one mind and purpose. Tearing the useless reeds away, he somehow managed to tie the rope around his chest. It wasn't easy. He was shivering violently and his fingers were numb with cold. But once Glenn had the rope secured, he felt much safer and plowed forward to the very end of the cut.

"Hang on!" he shouted, forgetting that the injured driller could neither hear nor even see him. In fact, the man might even be dead. Glenn took a deep breath and pushed forward onto the narrow ledge that would carry him just beyond to the badly injured Chinaman.

He lost his footing almost immediately and tumbled into space. For a horrifying few moments, the merciless wind battered him against the rock walls. Momentarily dazed, Glenn clung to the rope and was slowly raised back to the ledge. He regained his footing and inched forward. Twice, he would have gone over the side if the Chinese above had not suddenly taken up the rope's slack. Glenn passed under a gutter of rain pouring through a crevasse that drove him to his knees. Half blinded, he crawled the last few yard to the fallen driller.

The man was just barely conscious and Glenn doubted that he would be able to withstand being moved to safety. It was very probable that the driller had sustained massive internal injuries, possibly even brain damage.

"We're getting the hell off the captain's face!" Glenn exclaimed, dragging the Chinaman into a sitting position, then attempting to unknot the rope around his chest so that he could tie it around them both.

But the knot resisted his best efforts. It was pulled so tight and Glenn's fingers were so stiff from the cold that he could not begin to untie the damned thing. Giving up that idea, Glenn simply hugged the Chinaman and tried to loop the rope under the man's armpits.

He gave three hard jerks and felt himself being dragged erect. His heart was in his mouth when his feet left the ground and his lips drew back from his teeth in a grimace as he and the driller were slowly hoisted up the face of Cape Horn. Fortunately, the driller was slight and Glenn's broken arm had sufficiently healed so that he was able to use it as he and the driller were dragged upward. Perhaps the worst part of the ordeal was that the infernal wind kept scraping them back and forth across the captain's face. Twice, their upward progress was obstructed by an outcropping of rock, but Glenn was able to kick his way clear. By the time he was hauled finally over the ledge, he was sure that the driller was dead.

The Chinese mobbed Glenn. A cup of bitter and scalding tea was pressed to his numb lips, burning them. He did not care. Over and over the Chinamen kept thanking him and he kept asking about the fate of the driller he'd held while being winched up the face of Cape Horn.

None of their excited talk made any sense to Glenn as he was carried into the trees and laid beside a roaring fire tucked back under an immense outcrop of boulders. Every square inch of dry ground was filled with Chinese, all of them staring at him with expressions that Glenn could not even begin to decipher.

And finally, one graceful Chinese appeared and spoke with remarkably good English. "I am Ah Toy. You are brave friend, Mister Gilchrist."

Glenn gaped and cocked his head a little to one side. "You're . . . a woman?"

She bowed her head in silent assent.

Glenn kept staring, unsure if he was more amazed that he was still alive or that he was speaking to a beautiful woman. Ah Toy was several inches taller than the average Chinese and her features were a curious mix of European and Asian. Her eyes were oval and her face heart-shaped and much fuller than that of the typical Chinese. Even her hair was different for, although it was definitely black, it possessed a ruby-red cast which shone in the firelight light.

Ah Toy poured him more hot tea. It tasted delicious. The bonfire nearby began to thaw his flesh and he noticed that everyone's clothes were steaming. They air should have been thick with foul body odor but the Chinese smelled clean, and that reminded Glenn how they faithfully bathed every evening after work no matter how inclement the weather or impossible the camp conditions.

"What are you . . . a woman . . . doing here?"

She smiled at him but did not answer his question.

"How come you speak English?"

"Sea captain teach me. Mister Loudermilk teach even more."

"Harry Loudermilk!"

She nodded, her eyes widening with surprise at his violent reaction.

"What the deuce has he got to do with your being here?"

"Mister Loudermilk sometimes my boss man."

"You work for him?"

Ah Toy smiled, her teeth as white as Sierra snow. It was impossible to judge her age, but she looked to be about twenty. Glenn noticed that her hands, when she brought the cup of tea to Glenn's lips again, were exquisite. She reminded Glenn of a priceless and delicate China doll and she smelled sweetly of jasmine.

Glenn greatly desired to ask Ah Toy much more about what she was doing on the Central Pacific's construction site, and especially about Harry Loudermilk, but suddenly the Chinese began to sing and wail. And without having to ask, he knew that not one, but two of their drillers had died this terrible day.

CHAPTER
15

Much to his annoyance, Glenn came down with a hacking cough and fever. His nose ran and his eyes watered. He spat phlegm and was ordered to his tent bed before he contracted a full case of pneumonia.

"You should have let one of the Chinese attempt to reach that fallen driller," Strobridge said sternly. "You're much too valuable to be risking your life for a coolie."

Glenn had heard the term "coolie" used before and it had always left a bad taste in his mouth. Even more troubling was the implication that a coolie was not worth risking one's life to save.

"He was seriously injured," Glenn said. "I didn't take the time to consider his color."

"Listen," Strobridge said, pulling up a chair beside Glenn's bed and leaning forward, elbows resting on knees, "Mr. Crocker and I have as much respect for the Chinese as anyone, but they are cheap labor and easily replaced."

"Yes, but . . ."

"Hear me out," Strobridge persisted. "The Chinese work like demons but they don't have any love either for us or our country. You don't see them trying to learn our language or our ways, do you?"

Glenn thought of the girl, Ah Toy, who spoke excellent English, but he held his silence.

Strobridge continued. "In fact, Glenn, if the truth be known, they consider themselves *our* superiors."

"No."

"It's true!" Strobridge exclaimed. "They bow and hop to it when Mr. Crocker or I crack the whip but they're just posturing to please us while, behind our backs, they're feeling like we're really inferior beings."

"I never got a sense of the Chinese feeling like that," Glenn said.

"That's because you only see what *they* want you to see," Strobridge insisted. "Let me tell you something about their background so that you have a clearer understanding of their personalities. Back in China they were almost all farmers and were recruited out of the Cantonese districts of Sinong and Sinwai. I guess when they don't get a good rainy season, a lot of them starve to death. Anyway, it's easy for our Chinese labor contractors over there to sign them up them by the hundreds and advance them the ship's passage money—usually about twenty-five dollars. And once they arrive in San Francisco, they're indentured to us and a portion of their wages are sent back overseas to the Chinese labor contractors."

"Then what is Loudermilk's role in San Francisco?"

"He screens the ones strong enough to work out here. He arranges their transportation to Sacramento and helps with their food and other needs. He speaks a little Chinese, enough to do the job. In short he brokers the labor for us in San Francisco."

"What happens when a Chinaman comes over but Loudermilk doesn't hire him to work on the Central Pacific?"

"I don't know," Strobridge admitted. "And I don't even want to know because that has nothing to do with this job."

"I've heard that many die during the ocean passage."

"Yeah," Strobridge said. "But again, that's beyond our control. Some are luckier than others. Some ship's captains are decent men and some gather the coolies up in the ports of Canton and treat them like cattle. I've heard stories about how they're packed into the hold of ships and forced to stew in their own excrement for weeks on end. We don't get into that. We just hire those that are willing and able to work, and it's understood that they'll be treated fairly."

"And what will become of them when the job is done?"

"I don't know," Strobridge admitted. "And for that matter, what will become of *us*?"

"It's not the same," Glenn insisted. "We can always find another western railroad to build."

"So will the Chinese. I'm convinced that there are no better survivors on the face of the earth. Look at how they take care of each other."

"I see what you mean," Glenn said, nodding in agreement. "They don't fight among themselves like the Irish did on the Union Pacific Railroad construction crews."

"Oh," Strobridge corrected, "they fight, all right. I guess you've never heard of a Chinese tong war."

"What's a tong?"

"I'm not sure but I think it's some kind of secret Chinese society based on where they lived in their homeland. They're always warring over territory and rights over in San Francisco's Chinatown. So far, we've had no trouble up here with the tongs, but we worry about them. Their wars are extremely bloody affairs."

"Do you think most of these people on our payroll will return to China or to San Francisco's Chinatown?"

"I think that the vast majority will sail back to their homeland," Strobridge replied without hesitation. "When their job is done with us, they'll have saved enough of their wages to retire as young and very wealthy men."

"And what," Glenn asked, "about Chinese women?"

"Mainly, they stay home," Strobridge said. "But I won't lie to you. A hell of a lot of young Chinese girls are sold by their parents and sent to San Francisco, where they become slaves, usually to wealthy old Chinese, but sometimes to respectable whites as mistresses."

"What about women coming here?" Glenn asked bluntly.

"You mean *here*, on this construction job?"

"That's right."

Strobridge's eyes narrowed. "Listen," he said, "when we learned that the Chinese built their little ceremonial joss houses where they smoked opium, Mr. Crocker squashed that foolishness right away. But otherwise, the Chinese are pretty much allowed to govern themselves. They don't cause us problems and we don't cause them problems. We let them do whatever they choose to do when they are on their own time."

Strobridge paused and studied Glenn's face thoughtfully. "Are you suggesting that they have sneaked young prostitutes into their camps?"

"No," Glenn said quickly.

Strobridge scowled. "Listen, as far as I am concerned, if they have girls in their camps for pleasure, that's their own business. As long as they're not fighting over them and killing each other, we don't care."

Glenn hadn't even thought about the fact that Ah Toy might be a prostitute. And something told him that it was better not to bring up the young woman's presence. Even so, he could not forget the way she had looked and how she had spoken. He was sure that she was not a prostitute, but not at all sure what her exact role might be. The fact that she spoke excellent English was certainly a valuable asset, and he had little doubt that it was a talent that her countrymen would use to their advantage. But beyond that, well, Ah Toy was a mystery woman.

"Don't worry about the Chinese, Glenn. Just start feeling better and get back to work."

"I will," he promised. "How is the cut across Cape Horn progressing?"

"Well, we've almost finished and are preparing the roadbed for track to be laid next week. As you would expect, our main work has already moved up the mountain as we bore more tunnels."

"Damn," Glenn swore, "I wish that I was up there helping."

"You will be soon."

"Did you ever find the body of the first man who dropped from his basket?"

"No," Strobridge said. "We sent a couple Chinese up the American to work both riverbanks. We were hoping that the body would wash up, but it didn't. We are, however, sending the man you rescued back to China for burial."

Strobridge climbed to his feet. He drew a cigar from his pocket and offered another to Glenn, then retracted it quickly saying, "Probably wouldn't be good for your breathing right now. Mind if I light up?"

"Of course not."

Strobridge lighted the cigar, squinted through the blue smoke and asked, "How is your fiancée Miss O'Connell?"

"I don't know."

"Well, you will this Sunday. We received word that she's coming to visit. She must have learned that you were badly injured."

"Dammit!" Glenn raged before he was overcome by a fit of violent coughing.

"Easy!" Strobridge ordered, looking shocked and surprised. "What the hell is the matter with you? I know you two had a little spat, but she's going to rush up here and be all teary-eyed and you'll patch things up."

Strobridge winked. "Take it from me, Glenn, nothing makes a woman forgive and forget faster than seeing her man sick in bed—and you being a big hero to boot!"

Glenn didn't want Megan to see him sick in bed. Furthermore, the very last thing he wanted was to make her feel compelled to come to visit him out of sympathy. But it was clear that Strobridge's intentions were kind and the man was well meaning.

"When do you expect Megan to arrive?" he asked.

"Sunday. She'll be coming up on the train with the other wives on Sunday." Strobridge winked. "Hell, if you play it right and we have a preacher on hand, maybe . . ."

"No!" Glenn lowered his voice, concerned that he had hurt the big construction superintendent's feelings. "I'm sorry."

Ruffled, Strobridge marched over to the door of the tent. "She's going to be here and you're going to patch things up, by gawd! And that is an order!"

That evening one of the engineers brought Glenn a plate of beef, cooked cabbage and potatoes but Glenn found that he had little appetite. "Just place it on the table," he requested. "Maybe I'll feel hungry later."

"You got to keep up your appetite," the young surveyor, named Charles Pitkin, said. "You haven't been eating much the last couple of days."

"I'll eat when I'm hungry."

"Fever still with you?"

Glenn nodded. "Sometimes I feel so hot that I'd like

to climb on a horse, ride up to Donner Pass, and throw myself naked into the snow."

Pitkin chuckled. "Now that would be a sight! If the Chinese saw you do that, they'd think you'd gone plumb crazy."

"I suppose they would," Glenn agreed. "But this damned fever hangs on and on. One day I feel pretty good, the next day I'm on fire."

"Maybe you'll feel better tomorrow," Pitkin said hopefully. "But you should eat to keep up your strength even if you don't feel very good."

"I'll try," Glenn replied, closing his eyes.

"I'll see you in the morning," Pitkin said after a long silence. "Crocker is sending a bunch of us up the hill to work on those tunnels."

"I wish that I were going with you," Glenn whispered.

"Yeah, and I almost wish that I was in your place."

Glenn opened his eyes. "In heaven's name, why?"

"Because everyone here knows that your fiancée is coming up to visit with the other ladies this Sunday. You sure are one lucky dog."

Glenn offered no comment. A few minutes later, he was alone, the aroma of beef, cooked cabbage and potatoes strong and unpleasant in his nostrils.

He must have drifted off into a feverish sleep because the next thing Glenn knew, he felt a cool, gentle hand resting on his forehead and smelled jasmine.

Glenn's eyes popped open and the China doll's image swam serenely before him. "Ah Toy?"

"Shhh," she whispered. "You are unwell."

"I'm going to get better," he told her, his words hollow and lacking conviction.

"Please drink," she said, a large cup of some dark liquid

magically appearing in her graceful hands.

"I'm sorry," he apologized, "but I don't like the taste of your tea."

"*Special* tea," she promised. "Make you feel better. Drive away devils that make fever."

"There are no devils left in me," Glenn said, trying to make a little joke. "They've all been baked out."

Ah Toy did not laugh, or even smile. "Drink," she said quite firmly as she raised the cup to his lips.

Glenn had the feeling that Ah Toy would have pried open his mouth if he had refused. He drank.

"Agghhh!" he choked. "This stuff is even worse than what you gave me up on the top of Cape Horn!"

"Drink it all and I promise you feel much better tomorrow."

"Or I'll be dead," he replied, choking down the vile liquid. "What is in this awful stuff?"

"No want to know."

"Aggghhh!" The drink made his eyes water and it threatened to boil up out of his gut as Glenn fought the reflex until beads of sweat coated his body. The idea of vomiting in front of Ah Toy was extremely repugnant.

"Very good," she said, inspecting the cup in the faint candlelight beside his bed. "You get much better now."

"I thought I would get better anyway."

She placed her hand gently against his cheek. It felt so light and cool that Glenn shivered. She said, "You get sicker and maybe die without ancient Chinese medicine."

Glenn supposed that he ought to have made light of that macabre prophecy but he hadn't the heart to do so.

"I go now," she said. "Come back with more medicine tomorrow night."

"Please stay a little while," he said, gently enveloping her hand in his own. "I really would enjoy your company."

"But I must not be seen here."

"I know, but just take a moment and tell me about yourself, Ah Toy."

There was a long silence. Finally, she whispered, "What you want to know for?"

"I just do," he said. "I want to know a great deal more about you."

Her tone of voice was dutiful. "My father was a English seaman, a captain. My mother was of royalty but when she became with his child, she was held in disgrace. Driven from her kingdom, she died when I was ten."

"Did you say, 'Driven from her kingdom'?"

"Her family was very rich and powerful in Canton," Ah Toy explained. "But when she disgraced them, she was banished. She die later and I become street orphan."

"What happened to your real father, the Englishman?"

"He sailed away and never returned."

"I'm sorry."

"Live on streets until I was eleven years old, then become mistress of powerful slave trader. Name Lee Ming Fong. Very bad to Ah Toy. Then one day I meet American sea captain. He bring me to San Francisco."

"Aren't you leaving a lot out? How come the slave trader let you go?"

"After three years, I already too old. Lee Ming Fong want little girl again. He plan to sell me for much money but I steal his money and run away. Lee Ming Fong kill if find so I come to America. I meet Mr. Loudermilk. I become his mistress but he have many China girls and I no like him."

"Why?" Glenn asked, keeping the bitterness and hatred from his voice.

"No good, that man. Hurt China girls! Cheat and take poor Chinaman's monies."

Glenn wanted to ask her a great deal more about Harry Loudermilk but Ah Toy pushed on, determined to finish her story and be gone. "I come to this place and work for my people. Everything okay now."

Glenn could not help but wonder if this girl who had already been mistress to two older men had not turned to prostitution in order to support herself in the Chinese camps. As if she could read his mind, Ah Toy said, "I take railroad pay and make sure white bosses paid bills."

"Loudermilk?"

She nodded. "And money for gamble."

It was extremely important to Glenn that he clearly understand Ah Toy's exact role in the Chinese construction camp. "Let me understand this clearly, Ah Toy. You pay off gambling debts and then settle their bills every payday? Is that correct?"

Again, she nodded.

"Anything else?"

"No," she said, chin lifting higher and obsidian eyes gleaming in the candle light. "Ah Toy go now. Come back tomorrow night."

When she gently pulled away, Glenn knew that he could not hold her a second longer. And now that he knew her dark and sordid past, Glenn felt even more tenderness for her than he had before. "Ah Toy?"

She stopped, crouched near the flap of his tent as she prepared to spring into the night and escape back into the forest where her people waited.

"Do you have any relatives in America?"

"No. Only China and they forget Ah Toy."

"I won't ever forget you," Glenn blurted out, knowing he sounded like a little schoolboy with his first crush, but not really caring.

Ah Toy might have smiled then. He could not be sure because she was a flicker of light escaping into darkness. He called out softly to her. "Good night!"

But the soiled China doll was already gone.

CHAPTER
16

"Megan, will you marry me?"

She reached out and touched Mitch's handsome face. "But I've only known you a few weeks."

He rolled over and propped himself up on one elbow. "And how long—exactly—do we have to know each other before you'll marry me?"

Megan climbed out of bed and pulled on a silk bathrobe. She could feel his eyes warming her skin. She knew that he would have enjoyed her leaving the bathrobe open in the front, but modesty prevailed.

"Megan?" he persisted. "How long? A month? A year? Two years? How long?"

"I can't answer that because I don't know."

"Come here, please."

When she came to him, his fingers brushed through her long, auburn hair and stroked the curve that formed the small of her back.

"On Sunday, you'll tell Glenn about us, won't you?"

She shivered with dread. "I don't want to. God knows that he loves me so."

"How could Glenn do otherwise? But so do I and you can call it selfish if you want, but I'd much rather Glenn's heart be broken than mine. Come back to bed," he urged, heat already creeping in his voice.

196

"I can't."

"All right then, my darling, but what are you going to do?"

Megan raised her hands and dropped them helplessly at her sides. "I'm not quite sure."

"In that case, I think we should go and get married now and put this whole thing to rest. Besides, I expect that your conscience is eating you up inside."

"It is," she confessed, coming to her feet. "I feel like a traitor to Glenn and yet . . . yet I've never been this happy."

"Then marry me tonight! I know that the Reverend Beamon will perform the services in his parlor. We can be man and wife and then you can simply write Glenn a kind note of explanation. Megan, you were merely engaged, not married to Glenn. Engagements are very often broken. Their very purpose is to test the relationship. Quit feeling so guilty!"

"I can't help it. On top of everything else, he's sick with pneumonia."

"So," Mitch said, "you'd deny yourself happiness because of his illness?"

"No," she said quietly, "I wouldn't do that, but our timing is all wrong."

"It will always be wrong," Mitch argued, "because you don't love Glenn Gilchrist and you never will."

"I've actually tried. He's handsome, good, kind and brave. But despite everything . . ."

"You still can't love him," Mitch said, filling in the truth for Megan. "You see, love defies sense and logic. It either happens, or it does not. You can't force it or feel guilty when it is absent. You just have to accept your feelings and act on them. You don't love Glenn, you *do* love me. Am I correct?"

"Yes."

"Then you only have one decision and that is to be honest with Glenn."

She frowned. "How come you're always so damned analytical?"

"I'm an attorney," he said with a half smile. "We're supposed to be all head and no heart, remember?"

"That's absurd," she protested. "You're the most romantic man I've ever known."

He reached for her, a devilish gleam in his eyes. "Climb back in my bed."

"No," she told him gently. "I need to go back to my hotel room and be alone tonight and think."

"And tomorrow," he said, "you need to go see Glenn and bury this thing once and for all."

"I know, but it's going to be one of the most difficult things I've ever had to do."

"Maybe when he sees you so radiant and in love, he'll just know at a glance," Mitch hopefully suggested.

"I doubt it."

Megan dressed quickly. Her whole life had been turned upside down by this man and while she was deliriously happy, she also experienced moments of utter despair when she thought of Glenn. How could she have fallen in love and gone to bed with a man on the very same day she met him! There was no rational explanation for her wanton behavior. No excuse that would explain the way that Mitch Townsend made her feel when he gazed at her, touched her, made love to her.

"What exactly are you going to do?" he asked, climbing out of bed and reaching for his clothes.

"I'm going up to Cape Horn and stay with Glenn until he is well and strong enough to accept my decision."

"I'd like to come with you."

"No," she said, shaking her head. "That would make things even worse."

Mitch pulled on his trousers and reached for his white silk shirt. "I'll be counting the moments until you return."

"I'll be back inside of a week," she promised. "And nothing will change between us."

"All right," he finally said, "but I'm going to drive you up to Cape Horn and collect you when it's time for you to leave."

"Mitch . . ."

He raised his hand. "Megan, I swear that I won't even get out of the wagon. Is that agreeable?"

"Very well," she said, feeling relieved. "We can leave early tomorrow. But I'll expect you to drop me off at the edge of the camp and leave. It has to be that way."

"I give you my word. I won't do anything to interfere. I won't even show my face at the construction camp."

"Thank you."

Mitch slowly buttoned up his shirt and then stuffed it into his trousers. He was five-foot-ten inches tall, and had admitted that he wished he were several inches taller. But the man was beautifully proportioned and possessed an utterly graceful and sensuous way of moving. He was cat-like and his body reminded her of the dashing Joshua Hood, the Union Pacific's chief hunter and scout.

"Will you marry me the very hour we return to Auburn next week, Megan?"

"Yes."

"But if you change your mind . . ."

"I won't."

"Would you like a big church wedding?"

"No." Megan was emphatic. "I had that long ago back East when I was just an innocent girl. Now, I would very much prefer a simple ceremony by the Reverend Beamon."

He looked relieved. "We can honeymoon in San Francisco or even go over to the Canary Islands. You'd love them! Warm beaches, friendly people."

"Mitch, I can't be just a housewife. I can't just sit here in this wonderful old mansion and be some kind of ornament. I have to *do* something."

"Make babies! Give me tall, strong sons and daughters that look just like you."

Megan tried to laugh. "I want to see the rails meet. I want to be a part of the transcontinental race."

"Why?" he asked, smile fading. "It's a job for men, not women."

"It's *history* in the making!"

His voice hardened. "I won't have a wife who is gallivanting off with the railroad. I'm very sorry, Megan, but you can't have it both ways."

"That's what I keep hearing." Megan hurried across the room and threw herself into his arms. She hugged his neck and felt tears on her cheeks.

"Find me something to do with the railroad so that I can be a part of *both* worlds, Mitch!"

He held her for a long time before he spoke. "I'll try," he said at last. "I know people. Maybe I can think of something that you can do for the Central Pacific and which won't take you away from me very often. Maybe. But if you become with child before the rails meet . . ."

"Then I'll stay here forever with you," she vowed. "I'll happily remain in Auburn and become the wife that you want and deserve. What about my wedding dress and . . ."

"I'll make *all* our wedding arrangements," he promised. "You've got enough to worry about at Cape Horn."

Megan knew that Mitch was right. Leaving him tomorrow was the hardest thing she had done in a long, long time. What if she changed her mind? Was she so confused that she could? And what if *he* changed *his* mind! Dear God, it would serve her right if her heart were broken the way that she was about to break Glenn's. It would be poetic justice. Nothing less than well-deserved pain.

For a moment, Megan's resolve and courage deserted her completely. She took a faltering step back toward him, but he smiled then and said, "Megan, it's going to be all right. In a week, we'll be man and wife."

"Yes," she whispered. "Man and wife."

Megan left then and returned to the Bonanza House. As she passed through the lobby, the hotel clerk, a prying fellow with an aquiline nose that was always sniffing at other people's business, said, "Good evening, Miss O'Connell."

"Good evening," she retorted, hurrying toward the stairs.

"I trust that you are enjoying the company of Mr. Townsend very, very much."

Megan's stride faltered. Her head snapped around and she saw that the desk clerk had a superior look on his smug face. *He knows.*

Blushing and desperately wishing for some words that would wipe that sneer off his ugly face, Megan hurried up the stairs, unlocked her door and then rushed inside to throw herself on her bed and have a good cry.

"Your fever is gone," Ah Toy happily pronounced to Glenn on the third night as she used chopsticks to feed Glenn a huge Oriental feast of steamed rice, dried cuttlefish, mushrooms and stewed seaweed, which tasted like some delicious and wonderful vegetable grown in the warm Sacramento Valley.

"I know, " he said. "And they expect me back on the job bright and early Monday morning."

When Ah Toy said nothing, Glenn added, "Ah Toy, there is a woman . . . my fiancée actually, coming to see me tomorrow."

The chopsticks paused, but only for an instant. "Eat," she said quietly. "Need more strength to work."

Glenn opened his mouth and accepted more of the cuttlefish. He chewed thoughtfully, then looked up at her and said, "Do you understand what the word 'fiancée' means?"

"No."

"It means that I am supposed to marry her someday."

Without looking up, Ah Toy said, "You take wife? Very good, Mr. Gilchrist!"

Glenn tried to hide his disappointment and it took him a moment to say, "You think so, huh?"

"Sure, she feed you better, huh?"

"I doubt that she'll keep stuffing me like a Christmas goose, Ah Toy."

"You no hungry now."

He grabbed the chopsticks, spilling seaweed on himself and not caring. And then, because he was obsessed by her, Glenn kissed the China doll.

Ah Toy felt as if she were made of porcelain. She did not react to either his kiss or his rising passion, not even to pull away. Finally, Glenn pushed her out to arm's length. "Ah Toy, at least look at me!"

She slowly turned those huge, dark eyes toward him and Glenn searched them for her true feelings, but the beautiful orphan girl from China remained inscrutable.

"Ah Toy, what did you think of that kiss?"

She looked down, collected her dishes and retreated out of his reach to say, "I think you better take wife or go to work on Monday, Mister Gilchrist."

Before Glenn could recover enough to react to her pronouncement, Ah Toy fled into the darkness leaving Glenn in a state of misery and confusion with seaweed spilled all over him.

His first reaction to her rejection was anger. After all, Ah Toy had been the property of men who had used her for their pleasure since she was just eleven years old. She had even indentured herself to Glenn's sworn enemy, Harry Loudermilk, who had no doubt also used her for his pleasure. Ah Toy, then, was nothing. But hurt and anger were almost immediately drowned by an overpowering emptiness as a single question kept resounding from within.

If Ah Toy is nothing, then why am I so damned crazy for the mere sight, sound and smell of her?

Glenn couldn't answer his own question, but he knew that he needed to examine it hard before tomorrow when he saw Megan O'Connell.

CHAPTER
17

Mitch drew the fine team of matched sorrel geldings up before the Bonanza House at just after eight o'clock the next morning. He spotted young Jess Allard and motioned him over. "Jess, if you'll watch this buggy until I escort Miss O'Connell out, I'll pay you two bits."

Jess grinned. He was a shy boy who rarely wore shoes or even a shirt, preferring instead to wear baggy overalls and a dirty red bandanna. "Yes, sir!"

Mitch straightened his tie and went inside the hotel. He would take Megan to breakfast in the hotel's restaurant and then they would leave for Cape Horn, a distance that Mitch guessed would be only about twenty miles. They would be there by mid-afternoon and he could visit a client whom he had been needing to see regarding a lawsuit over a mining injury. The client had lost his right arm and most of his left hand and Mitch was hoping that he could win the poor fellow a good settlement to help him support his large family.

Megan was waiting in the lobby, a traveling bag at her side. When Mitch saw her, he could tell at once that she had not slept well and was nervous and upset. Hurrying across the lobby, he sat down beside Megan and took her hands in his own.

"My dear, please forgive me for saying this, but you

look exhausted this morning. Didn't you sleep at all?"

"I don't think so," she allowed. "I really dread facing Glenn and telling him about our plans to marry."

"I could still do it for you."

"Thanks, but no," Megan said quickly. "I'd feel even worse if the news came from you."

"Let's go eat some breakfast and be on our way," Mitch suggested.

"Could we skip breakfast? I have no appetite this morning."

"Very well. We can stop for lunch or something at the little railroad stop called Weimer. I know a very good place to eat and we can be there in just a few hours."

Megan nodded in agreement and they came to their feet. But as they started across the hotel's spacious lobby, the desk clerk said, "Oh, Miss O'Connell?"

Megan stopped, feeling her hackles rise. "Yes?"

"I see that you have a traveling bag," the clerk said with a thin smile. "Does that mean that you are leaving us, perhaps to move in with Mr. Townsend?"

Megan's cheeks burned and she started to say something, but Mitch tightened his grip on her arm and said, "Megan, I'll handle this."

Megan stood and watched as Mitch walked briskly over to the desk, placed his hands on both sides of the guest book and said, "I'm going to suggest to the owners of this establishment that you be fired, Wally."

The clerk's smugness vanished. He drew himself up tall. "And why would you do that, Mr. Townsend?"

"Because you are an insufferable sonofabitch and deserve to have your self-righteous face bashed in."

The words were spoken so softly that Megan almost missed them, but Wally's reaction was quite pronounced. His lips curled down at the corners and he sneered, "If you touch me, I'll sue your ass off!"

It was a long reach over the desk, but Mitch's fingers still managed to dig into Wally's coat and drag the clerk forward. Holding him with his left hand, Mitch slapped the clerk first one way, then the other, spanking his cheeks like a father would the butt of a naughty child. The blows were powerful enough to rock Wally's head back and forth, and a trickle of blood coursed down his jaw to drip off his pointed chin.

"Then sue me," Mitch said quietly. "I always appreciate a good laugh."

Wally broke free and smashed into the rear wall, knocking a picture to the floor. He jumped up with the shattered glass in his fists and screamed, "It's your fault this got broken, Mr. Townsend! You're going to pay for this too!"

Mitch turned his back on the hateful man. Picking up Megan's bag in his left hand and extending the crook of his right arm to her, he said, "Megan, I think we are ready to go now, don't you?"

"Yes," she said, shooting Wally a triumphant smile. "I surely do!"

Outside, Mitch paid Jess and they were soon on their way out of town. The wide freighting road that they followed was packed with wagons and it closely paralleled the Central Pacific's new tracks up the western slope of the Sierras.

After they had traveled for nearly an hour in silence, Megan said, "Will he sue you?"

"I certainly hope he tries."

"Why?"

"Because there is only one other attorney in Auburn worth consideration and my father helped him to pass the bar. I sincerely doubt that Mason Jakes is going to take the case."

"Then you've got things sewn up rather tightly in Auburn, don't you?"

"For the present, yes. But as the town grows, other attorneys will try to become established."

"Does that threaten your own practice?"

"Good heavens, no!" Mitch patted her knee. "There is a shortage of attorneys and has been since all the miners and big money moved over the mountains to the Comstock Lode. I could, for example, make a far more impressive income if I specialized in mining law up in Virginia City."

"Then why don't you?"

"Because I love this town, my home and my friends too much," he said. "And there still isn't a good fiddler in Auburn to replace me."

Megan laughed. "Now that *is* important."

"Besides," Mitch added, "has it occurred to you that we'd never have met if I'd raced over to the Comstock Lode like all my greedy colleagues?"

"No," Megan confessed, "it has not."

"Well, it has to me and it makes me realize that God or the universe or whatever it is that creates a happy destiny has been working hard in my behalf."

Megan hugged him tightly. "You are," she said, "a flattering man."

They had their midday meal in Weimer, and it was packed with freighters and Sunday travelers. Just east of that small railroad community, Megan and Mitch saw a Central Pacific train filled with women and children going up to visit their loved ones at the Cape Horn construction site. The passengers waved gaily and Megan waved back, knowing she would soon be meeting these happy people.

Two miles farther on, Mitch pulled their buggy off the main road and drove them about a half mile up a steep,

logged-out hillside to a small cabin where a bunch of
thin but clean-looking children smiled shyly at them. The
mountain homestead place was hardscrabble, exactly the
kind of place Megan had seen on the prairie, only made
of logs instead of a sod.

"What is this?" Megan asked.

Mitch quickly explained. "These are the Emery children
and their parents are probably inside. Mrs. Emery is not a
very strong woman and her husband is recovering from
a serious mining accident caused when the Sierra Mining
Company tried to save a few dollars by buying faulty
fuses. Because of those fuses, the man lost his right arm
and three of fingers of his left hand. I'm trying to win him
a fair settlement."

"I see," Megan said, smiling and waving at the children.
"How many children are there?"

"Seven," Mitch said, "three boys and four girls."

"Yes," Megan said, "but isn't there something that can
be done in their behalf while this goes to court?"

"I'm doing the best that I can," Mitch assured her. "This
is not the only family that I represent that is having an
awful time making it. I have several others almost as
desperate that I also help support."

Megan knew at once that Mitch was probably the *only*
support that these families were receiving. "You're a very
wonderful man, know that?"

"Ah," he said, "they'll repay me when I win them large
settlements."

"You'll take their settlements?"

"No," he said, pulling the buggy to a standstill before
the cabin, "but our pantry will never want for chickens,
milk, eggs or meat. I can assure you we won't starve,
my dear."

"I see," she said as Mrs. Emery emerged from the cabin.

She was a small and frail-looking woman whose calico dress was so faded that it had no real color. An infant was clutched to her breast and she was shoeless, like her children. Her hair was pulled into a tight bun at the back of her head, and when she spoke, Megan could see that her teeth were very bad.

"Mr. Townsend," she said, bowing and smiling. "Come inside. They's not much I kin offer you, 'ceptin' a chair and some hot water and . . ."

"No thank you," Mitch said, climbing down from the buggy. "Mrs. Emery, I'd like you to meet my bride-to-be, Megan O'Connell."

The poor woman brushed at her hair and tried to smooth her dress in order to look presentable. When Megan was helped down and came to meet her, Mrs. Emery was so painfully shy that it was uncomfortable to watch.

"If I'd knowed we was havin' such fine company," she told them, "maybe we could have got some coffee and . . ."

"That's all right," Megan said. "You have a beautiful family, Mrs. Emery."

The little woman lifted her chin. "Thankee, Miss O'Connell. I try and so does my man, Clinton. But sometimes the Lord tests our will."

"Yes," Megan said, thinking how insincere her agreement must have sounded as she stood in her fine dress, about to be married to a wealthy and handsome young attorney.

"But me and Clinton believe that your Mr. Townsend was sent by our Creator to help us. He's gonna get us some money and maybe we can start over. We'd do a sight better where it's warm down in the valley."

"That's right," Mitch told her. "Once your husband is back on his feet, I know some people in Sacramento that could probably use a general caretaker. Someone to watch over their estate and do light work. I'm sure that it will all work out fine."

"If'n we go down there, the children would need shoes and such before they could go to one of them big schools," the woman said, wringing her bony hands. "Otherwise, they'd be treated unkind and . . ."

"We'll make sure they have new shoes and clothes," Mitch promised. "And you'll all be much happier down there."

"I know. I keep tellin' Clinton that you're going to make a new life for us."

Mitch took the woman's nervous hands. "We're going to try," he promised. "But I told you right from the beginning that the mining company is going to fight us in court. It's going to take time, Mrs. Emery. You just have to believe we'll win and things are going to get much better before this winter."

Tears welled up in her eyes and, when she spoke, Megan could hear a powerful current of panic in her nasal voice. "They *gotta get better*! We'd freeze this next winter up this high. Our ax is lost someplace around the woodpile and . . ."

"I'll bring a new one by on my way back late this afternoon," he said. "Mrs. Emery, I need to see Clinton for a moment. Then Megan and I have to push on up the mountain to the end of the line."

"He's inside," she said. "But he's not doin' so well today."

"All right," Mitch said. "Maybe I can cheer him up a little."

"Oh, you always do, Mr. Townsend! God bless you!"

Mitch had tightened his grip on Megan's arm until it was almost painful, but she wouldn't have complained for the world. Now, he turned to her and said, "Megan do you want to come inside?"

"No," she answered too quickly, "I'll wait out here with Mrs. Emery and the children."

"That might be better," he told her before he went into the cabin.

Megan was aware of the woman staring at her, and she felt so uncomfortable at the envy in Mrs. Emery's face that she turned, knelt and beckoned to a little blond girl of about four.

"That's Emily Sue," the woman said. "She's a little shy, like most of 'em. Come here, Emily Sue!"

The child gulped but obeyed. She stared at Megan with such big blue eyes that Megan had to smile and say, "Would you like a little present?"

Emily Sue nodded her head.

"Ah," Mrs. Emery said, "you'd best not be givin' her anything, Miss O'Connell. The other kids would just think they deserved a treat too."

Megan marched back to the buggy and found her purse. Extracting all the change she carried, Megan handed a quarter to little Emily Sue. The other children saw this and rushed over.

"Now don't you children dare beg money from this fine woman!" their mother shouted.

"It's all right," Megan said, giving the oldest children quarters and the smallest nickels, dimes and pennies until her purse full of change was all gone.

The children were beaming, and Megan was about to ask them their names and get better acquainted when Mitch emerged. His expression was grim and he took her arm, calling back over his shoulder as they jumped into the buggy, "I'll be back through this evening, Mrs. Emery. Just . . . just don't leave Clinton to himself for long!"

Megan only had to take one look at her beloved's face to know that Mitch was very upset. With the children and the woman waving and calling out good-bye to them, Mitch sent their sorrels wheeling around and then hurrying down the steep rutted road.

"What's wrong?" she asked after they had finally connected with the main road and were headed up toward nearby Colfax.

"Clinton's left hand, the one with the missing fingers, I think it's infected with gangrene."

"No!" Megan cried, hand flying to mouth as she stifled an urge to gag.

"Yes." Mitch expelled a deep, ragged breath. "We'll stop here in Colfax and I'll talk to their doctor. But I sure don't care for the man and have little faith in his medical ability. I think he's more of a tooth puller than a trained physician and he's certainly no surgeon."

"Then why . . ."

"Because *someone* needs to attend to Clinton before his blood is poisoned and he can't be saved."

Megan was so upset that she didn't remember the doctor's face, much less his name when they left Colfax. All she was sure of was that the so-called "doctor" had refused to go visit Clinton Emery unless he was paid ten dollars.

"I ain't no damned angel of mercy!" he'd stormed. "I got my own troubles and bills to pay."

"Have you never even heard of the Hippocratic Oath!" Mitch had shouted.

"The what?" the rumpled, mean-spirited physician had retorted.

"Never mind! Just go take care of him and tell me what you think when I stop back by in a few hours!"

Mitch had torn the money from his pockets, flung it at the doctor and stomped out of the office with Megan hurrying along behind. It wasn't until they had driven completely through Colfax and were back into the pines that Mitch calmed down and said, "I'm sorry, Megan."

"For what?"

"For losing my composure." He took her hand and held it tight. "I was hoping that this would be a nice outing for us. A time when we could make plans for our honeymoon."

"I know," she said quietly. "I had thought the same. But this is better."

"Better?" he scoffed loudly. "You've seen all this . . . this sickness and misery and you call this better?"

Megan couldn't help herself. She threw her arms around Mitch's neck and kissed his face again and again, tears streaming down her cheeks.

"I love you even more now," she told him. "I love you so much!"

Mitch slipped his right arm around Megan's waist and drew her close, neither of them noticing the envious looks of the travelers that soon began to pass them by.

CHAPTER
18

Megan climbed down from the buggy and steeled herself to leave Mitch and go face Glenn.

"I still want to come with you," Mitch said quietly, "if you'll let me."

Megan looked off toward the construction camp. "Thanks anyway, but I'll meet you here in one week."

"All right, Megan. But if things go sour or become difficult, you can always speak to Mr. Crocker or some other official and ride a supply train back down to Auburn. Or just send me a telegram and I'll come running. The important thing to remember is that you don't have to stay here a minute longer than you want."

"I know. Good-bye, my love."

Megan hurried away while she was still able. She soon attracted more than the normal share of attention in the construction camp headquarters although the visitors' train had already arrived and there were plenty of other women in attendance for this Sunday gathering.

"Well, hello there!" a voice called out to her.

Megan turned to see Ford Hayward striding in her direction with a huge grin pasted across his face. "Why, Miss O'Connell, I see you've come back to stay with us awhile!"

"Only a few days."

214

His eyebrows arched and he glanced up at the departing wagon. "Say, wasn't that Mitch Townsend, the stuck-up attorney from Auburn?"

Megan bristled defensively. "He's not stuck up as you put it. As a matter of fact, we're going to be married!"

Megan regretted her outburst even before she'd finished speaking. She certainly hadn't planned on telling anyone of her marriage plans before she told Glenn. He deserved to hear this news first, but Ford's remark had really gotten her goat. Now, she was enjoying the shock on his handsome face. He was such an arrogant ass that it did her heart good to see him thrown off balance.

Ford dredged up a weak smile. "Are you serious? You're really marrying Mitch Townsend?"

"That's right," she said as happily as she could under the trying circumstances. "We're to be married a week from today in Auburn."

He removed his fancy hat, the one with the silver conchos, and shook his head. "Have you lost your senses! You've only just met the man!"

"Perhaps, but I already know him well," she said, feeling her cheeks warm as she realized the implication of her words. "Anyway, I'm in love with Mitch—not Glenn—and that's what I've come to tell him."

"He's been sick," Hayward clipped, his expression hardening with disapproval. "This news isn't going to raise his spirits."

"I know, but my news is not going to make him any sicker," she said, looking all around. "Where is Glenn?"

"He's in that fourth tent up the line on your right." Ford reached down and took her little bag. "I'll carry this over to the ladies' guest tent for you."

"Thank you. And Ford . . . well, I'm sorry."

"Why?" he exclaimed, shrugging his shoulders and trying his best to look completely unconcerned. "*I'm* not the one that's being jilted."

That last word stung Megan and, for a moment, she thought that she was going to make a fool of herself. But thankfully, Ford pivoted on his heels and marched down between the officials' tents. Megan breathed a sigh of thanks that she had a few moments to compose herself before facing Glenn.

When she pushed the tent flap aside, Glenn was sitting fully dressed beside his bed reading a book. The interior of the tent was dim, but even so she could see enough of him that she was shocked at how much weight he'd lost just in the short time since they'd parted. My God, she thought, my news is going to kill him!

"Hello, Glenn."

His head snapped up and the book slipped from his fingers. Glenn stared at Megan for a moment. Then he did the worst thing possible, which was to try and make a joke in order to ease their tension.

"Hello, Megan! I was afraid it might take something like pneumonia to get you back up here." He barked a dry laugh that turned into an awful coughing spell.

"Dear heavens, Glenn!" she cried, rushing to him. "You sound just terrible!"

When he finally recovered, he said, "Don't be alarmed, Megan. The doctor says that I'm actually recovering."

She sat on his bunk. "Glenn, I'm sorry."

"No matter. I'm going to be just fine."

"I mean about our fight."

"Did we fight?"

Megan took a deep breath. This was going to be even more difficult than she'd expected. "Glenn, we really need to talk."

Glenn found a handkerchief and blew his nose. His eyes

were sunken in his face and he seemed to have aged ten years since they'd parted.

"So talk," he said, patting her hand in a fatherly manner.

Megan came to her feet and moved over to a table covered with surveyors' maps, putting off what she had come to do. The maps were just as unintelligible now as they'd been the last time she'd been here.

"Do you like working for the Central Pacific?" she asked, hating herself for not being able to come directly to the purpose of her visit.

"Oh, sure. Mr. Crocker and Mr. Strobridge are great to work for. They're tough, but fair."

"I'm glad to hear that." She was struggling to make small talk. "Have you made some good friends yet?"

"A few." Glenn was silent for a moment and then blurted out, "Megan, I . . ."

"I have something to tell you," she rushed in to say, sure that he was going to apologize and plead with her to marry him again. "Glenn, before you say anything, I want you to know that I've fallen in love with another man . . . and I'm going to marry him next week in Auburn."

Megan had prepared herself for anything ranging from tears to pleas to pure rage, but Glenn surprised her with dead silence. He just stared at her for a few seconds and then he closed his eyes.

"Please, Glenn, say something!" she begged, clutching at his hand. "For gawdsakes, cuss me out, I've got it coming! Hate me, hit me! But do or say *something*!"

He opened his eyes and said in the calmest imaginable voice, "I love you, Megan, I'll always love you. But I'm tired of the chase and I'm glad it's over. I wish you the very best of everything that life can bring."

She was stunned! And . . . well, deflated. Megan could

scarcely believe she'd heard him correctly. "You mean that you're not hurt, or angry?"

"Oh, my pride is wounded, sure," he told her matter-of-factly. "And I'd be lying if I said I wasn't hurt. But when you left, I decided that something just wasn't right between us and that it most likely never would be. I mean, you would have married that Dr. Thaddeus Wiseman if your sister hadn't done it first."

"That's true," she said, feeling utterly ridiculous.

Glenn sighed. "So, I guess that there was just something between us that was all wrong."

"There's nothing wrong with you," she said quickly. "I was always the one that had to be free and could not make a commitment."

"That's water under the bridge, Megan. I've had a lot of time to think since I caught pneumonia. And I just came to understand that marriage wasn't meant for us. It is no one's fault that things just wouldn't work."

"You'll find a woman and she'll cherish you for your good looks and wonderful heart," Megan said, meaning it with all of her heart. "And I'd like to stay in this camp a few days and take care of you, if you'll have me."

"As a matter of fact," he said a little sheepishly, "that won't be necessary because I've already got someone who been taking good care of me."

Megan's eyebrows lifted in question. "Who is he?"

Glenn smiled almost shyly. "*She*, and her name is Ah Toy. She's beautiful, kind, and I've gotten so I like to have her around. In fact, I'm trying to think of how to tell Crocker and Strobridge that I need another week of recovery."

He was smiling! Megan couldn't believe it but Glenn actually looked joyful! She squeezed his hand. "I could not be happier for you, Glenn. I sincerely mean that. And you are definitely not well enough to go to work yet."

"I know that," he said, "but I sure wish that I could come to your wedding. How are Zeke and his bride, Becky?"

"They seem positively delirious with happiness," Megan said. "They've moved down to Sacramento and I haven't seen them lately, but I will one of these days."

"And our courageous Mr. Peamont?"

"He came through Auburn and stopped to see me for a few minutes. He was going away on his first buying trip for the railroad."

"Good!" Glenn said, then added, "Megan, would you like to meet Ah Toy?"

"Very much."

"She'll be in this evening, I hope. I mean, she usually comes to feed me all this Chinese food that looks pretty awful but tastes wonderful. And wait until you see how she can handle a pair of chopsticks! It's a mystery to me how she can do it, but she's been feeding me three meals a day since I came down with the fever."

"I can hardly wait to meet the young lady," Megan said, meaning it. "But what does she do here . . . I mean . . . besides feeding you?"

"She is sort of a manager of the payroll for a big group of men from her province in China. Since she doesn't gamble, they trust her to be honest with their wages, to pay off gambling debts fairly and to buy their food and supplies."

"It sounds like she's mostly their buyer and their banker."

"Exactly," Glenn said. "And because she speaks excellent English, Ah Toy is extremely valuable to her people."

"I'd like to meet her."

"That's easy," Glenn said. "If she doesn't come tonight, I know where she and her people are camped and it's not far."

Megan couldn't believe the way this long-dreaded conversation had taken on an air of friendliness and even anticipation. All her fears had been unfounded. And as they talked and caught up on the big changes in each other's lives since arriving in California, Megan thought she had never enjoyed Glenn's company so much now that they didn't have to worry about hurting each other's feelings.

Ten miles back down the mountainside, Mitch Townsend leaned close to Clinton Emery and said, "The doctor I sent up here agrees that your left hand has to be removed or you'll die of gangrene. Clinton, you've no choice."

"If they take off my only hand and last two fingers, I won't be worth nothing to anybody!" Emery trembled violently. "Without a hand, what the hell could I do to help feed my children, Mr. Townsend!"

"You could do lots of things," Mitch said, damning himself for being unable to think of a single thing that a working man like Clinton Emery could do without hands.

When Clinton just kept staring at him like a drowning man waiting for a rope, Mitch stammered, "And if nothing else, Clinton, losing your other hand will make our legal case against the Sierra Mining Company even stronger."

"It will?"

"Sure! Why, any jury in California would be sympathetic enough to award you a small fortune."

Clinton gulped. He was tall, angular and exceedingly thin. His bedclothes were stained and crusted with dried food and the air inside the dim and cramped log cabin was putrid with the stench of his rotting flesh. Clinton's eyes burned with fever, and Mitch wondered if the man could possibly survive until either an out-of-court settlement was reached or they won their case before a Placer County judge and jury.

Mitch's voice took on new urgency. "You *have* to be strong, Clinton. If not for yourself, then for your wife and your children. We can win this thing! We can win you enough money so that you'll never have to work again if you don't want to and you'll never have to worry again about putting food on your family's table."

Clinton squeezed his eyes shut and tears slid down his sunken cheeks. "Mr. Townsend, I appreciate all you've done and are tryin' to do, but I think I'm dying."

That got to Mitch, kicking him right in the gut. It was a moment before he trusted himself to respond. "Listen, I'm returning to Auburn this evening, but I'm bringing a doctor back on the supply train tomorrow. We're abandoning this cabin and I'm finding you a surgeon and a place for your family in Sacramento. I'll give the Sierra Mining Company one week to pay you . . . ten thousand dollars or we're going to trial and I promise you that we'll win twice that much."

Clinton's eyes flew open and his mouth worked for a moment before he managed to gasp, *"Ten thousand dollars!"*

"That's right. And all I want is the satisfaction of seeing you and your family finally getting a decent break in life."

Without thinking, the gangrenous hand, or what remained of it, covered Mitch's hand. It took all of Mitch's willpower not to recoil, but he managed.

"God bless you, Mr. Townsend! God bless you!"

Mitch needed the fresh air badly, and it was almost dark when he stumbled out of the Emery cabin and hurried to his buggy. He called out a farewell to the wife and the children and put his team of horses into a fast trot. When he reached the main road, he turned west, breathing fast and deep and wondering if he could really talk a doctor into coming up here and helping him relocate the Emery family down the mountain near good medical help.

Mitch wasn't a bit sure that Clinton would survive, but he was more determined than ever to nail the Sierra Mining Company's hide to the wall and win a huge settlement. But given his preference, he wanted to settle out of court and very quickly, before his client died.

Mitch was so upset and preoccupied about the plight of the Emery family that he did not see the lone rifleman emerge from behind a big pine tree. The rifleman took very careful aim and fired, deliberately blowing away the ear of one of the sorrels. Blood sprayed over both horses, who panicked and veered wildly off the road. Mitch tried to control them but it was impossible, and then his buggy yawed over the edge off the road toward the gorge that plunged far below.

"No!" Mitch shouted even as the buggy began to roll over and over, crashing through manzanita and heavy brush as it plunged downward.

The two horses died almost instantly, one from a broken neck and the other from internal injuries suffered when the buggy crushed its ribs before coming to a stop nearly a hundred yards below. An avalanche of loose shale half-buried the buggy and the horses, then eased to a grinding halt only a few feet from a towering wooden trestle built by the Central Pacific Railroad the previous winter.

Being unconscious, Mitch did not see the rifleman, who quickly descended from the road above and lost his footing in the shifting shale, almost plunging to his death. But he managed to snag the branch of a little spruce and pull himself up to solid footing, then struggle back to the road above. The rifleman gazed down at the wreckage far, far below and, apparently satisfied, turned and hurried back into the trees.

Mitch awoke to the sound of a heavy supply train as it eased across the great wooden trestle. It was barely daylight and the air was especially cold down in the gorge. He felt numb and that was even more terrifying than being consumed by pain. Mitch rolled his head around and studied the silhouettes of his two dead horses, and then the half-buried wreckage of his buggy. The buggy's wheels had been torn away and its axle was snapped like a matchstick. They were resting in a thick stand of pines. A pair of blue jays were screeching insults down at either Mitch or the lumbering supply train as it crawled across the long wooden trestle high above.

"Help," he croaked. "Help!"

The blue jays screeched even louder and the train rumbled overhead. As the light grew stronger, Mitch could see that the huge trestle pilings actually shivered and bent under the enormous weight of the supply train.

Mitch closed his eyes and must have dozed for several hours, because he did not awaken until a shaft of brilliant sunlight danced across the treetops, then probed until it found his battered face. With the light suddenly flaring in his eyes, Mitch started, then tried to get up, but was horrified to find that his legs were numb and unresponsive.

"No!" he shouted, pushing himself into a sitting position that sent fire coursing through his torso and told him that his ribs were broken. "Oh, God, no!"

Mitch leaned forward ignoring his ribs. He doubled up his fists and beat at his thighs, willing them to feel, to move. But they were like the stumps of dead trees. He collapsed, sobbing with anguish, until the blue jays returned and mocked him in his misery. He cursed them until he remembered the derringer in his coat pocket.

Filled with rage, Mitch raised the derringer with a shaking hand and fired up through the branches toward the sound of the raucous jays. His shot sent the two birds beating into the sky, still mocking him as their voices faded into silence. Mitch rolled over and stared up at the road far, far above. He had no idea how he had survived this terrible wreck, and he doubted that he would ever be found down in this cluster of thick pines.

Shoving the derringer into his pocket, Mitch reached out and grabbed a tree root, then hauled himself toward the slope. Next, he found some manzanita and even though its sharp edges torn his soft palms, he used it to drag his body a full thirty feet. He was gasping and trembling as he spotted a little ponderosa pine not far above. If he could just reach it, he could pull himself up the slope even farther.

"Who," he cried, "did this to me? And why?"

And even as the question reverberated up and down the deep gorge, Mitch knew its answer and choked with rage, "The Sierra Mining Company, they were laying for me!"

CHAPTER
19

"Miss O'Connell! Megan!"

She had been about to get Glenn his breakfast when Ford Hayward rushed into the tent. One glance at his face told Megan that something terrible had happened.

"What is it?"

"I think Mitch Townsend had a bad accident," Ford said, grimly. "His buggy must have tumbled over the side of the road and down into a gorge. It was a miracle that one of the trainmen saw it just after daybreak as they were crossing Trestle Number Six."

Megan jumped to her feet. "Dear God! Is he alive!"

"No one knows," Ford said, "but the news we just received from the engineer says he doubts that anyone could have survived that wreck. The buggy is lying on its back down at the bottom of the gorge with a couple of dead sorrels."

Megan was so shaken that she jumped for the door of the tent, but Ford caught her arm. "We're forming a rescue party. It might not even be Mitch Townsend that went over the cliff."

"But it could be and I'm coming!" Megan stormed. "No one is leaving me behind!"

Glenn struggled to his feet. "I'm coming too."

"No!" Megan shouted as she hurried outside. "You

can't help and I don't want *both* of you dying on me!"

"She's right," Ford said.

"Any idea what happened?" Glenn asked.

"Maybe the horses just spooked and jumped over the side. Who the hell knows?"

"If it's Townsend, stay real close to her, Ford. Make sure that Megan . . ."

But Crocker's assistant was already leaving and Glenn's words died unspoken on lips. Ford ran after Megan and caught up with her as the members of the rescue party prepared to leave. Word had spread rapidly around the camp and there were far more eager volunteers than were actually needed.

"If whoever is down there is still alive, he'll be needing urgent medical attention," Strobridge said. "We'll run whatever is left of him down to Sacramento on the supply train."

Megan nodded. "Any other news that you can tell me?"

"Not much," Strobridge said. "Trestle Number Six is just west of Colfax so it'll be faster to take wagons than to build up steam in a locomotive. The engineer sent a telegram up to me and it just said that there was a wreck down in the gorge but that he couldn't even tell exactly what it was. They couldn't even get close enough to get a good view without men and ropes."

Megan prayed that it was not Mitch. "Let's go!" she urged.

A few minutes later, two buckboards full of rescuers were charging down the mountain.

"You better hang on tight," Ford warned, leaning close to grab her in case a hard jolt sent Megan flying into the air.

Megan clung to the side of the buckboard filled with men, medical supplies and ropes. Strobridge was driving like a maniac. The horses were running full out and the buckboard sloughed around hairpin curves on two wheels.

"Jaysus!" someone cried with alarm. "Slow down, Boss, or we'll all go over the side and have a party in Hell!"

But Strobridge didn't slacken the pace at all. The buckboard, despite being heavily laden, seemed to bound and skip over the rocky road as it raced through the cold morning air. After what seemed like forever, they barreled around the outskirts of Colfax and soon rounded a curve to see the trestle and the supply train. The engineer, the fireman and several other railroad workers had left their empty supply train and were gathered at the edge of the road, all staring and gesturing down into the gorge.

"This ain't going to be easy," Ford said as their buckboard was hauled to a dusty, rattling stop. "That gorge is a good thousand feet deep."

"I won't risk lives going down there if there's no hope for survivors," Strobridge said tight-lipped.

They rushed over to line the edge of the road and stare into the gorge. The empty supply train had pulled across the trestle and was now waiting close by, steam engine huffing and puffing as its engineer and crew hurried over to meet them.

"You can see the wheel tracks where the wagon went over the side, Mr. Strobridge," the engineer said. "And then you can see busted pieces and splinters of the wagon scattered all the way down that rock slide to where it disappears into the pines."

The foreman nodded. He raised his eyes to the supply train. "What kind of a view can you get from the train or the trestle?"

"No better," the engineer said, shaking his head. "We could see a dead horse and a broken wheel and, of course, all that splintered wood and such scattered down the rock slide. But most everything down at the bottom is either covered up by the rock that musta slid over it, or else hidden in that thick stand of pines."

"No movement at all?"

"Nope. And we've been shouting and carrying on up here since we spotted the wreck. Ain't heard nothing back."

"Most likely whoever went over the side was killed along with the horse," the engineer ventured.

"The horse?" Megan repeated.

"Yeah, we can only see one and it's half buried."

Megan turned to Ford. "Didn't you tell us back at the camp that there were a couple of sorrels?"

"No, I didn't," he replied calmly.

Strobridge glanced at Ford and said, "Maybe we could get a better view if we went down a hundred feet or two using the ropes."

"I doubt that it would be worthwhile," Ford quickly countered. "Nothing could have survived that kind of fall. And the engineer said . . ."

"I heard what he said!" Strobridge snapped. He turned and yelled at his men, "I want three hundred feet of rope. Now!"

Megan rushed to Strobridge's side. "But three hundred feet won't get you close enough to see anything! Can't you go down farther?"

"Yeah, I guess I can," Strobridge finally allowed, "but it's not going to be any picnic and I doubt there's much point in any of this."

Megan was practically beside herself with worry. Over and over she kept thinking that Ford really *had* told her that there was a pair of sorrels down at the bottom of this gorge. How could he know that unless . . .

Strobridge didn't notice the stricken expression on her face because he was too busy giving his men orders to lower him down and to keep alert.

"Mr. Strobridge, if that damned shale starts sliding," Ford said, "you could get torn away in an avalanche and there wouldn't be a thing that we could do to save you from up here."

"I know."

"Goddammit, it just isn't worth it!"

"We have to at least give it a try!"

"Why don't you let *me* go down there?" Ford suggested.

"No!" Megan blurted out without thinking.

Both men turned to regard her with curiosity. Megan stammered, "I mean . . . why doesn't one of the workmen go down? They're more accustomed to climbing around on loose rock."

Strobridge was confused by Megan's erratic behavior, but too impatient to waste time trying to figure her out. "Listen," he growled, cinching the rope around his narrow waist, "I'm going down."

And he did. The slope was probably about sixty degrees, and the moment that Strobridge started down his feet sank in the loose shale and it began to shift.

"Come on back!" Ford yelled. "You're going to get yourself killed down there!"

"If this mountainside starts to go, then haul me up like a fish on a line," Strobridge shouted, continuing on down the treacherous slope.

"This is crazy!" Ford raged. "The horses are dead and no one could have survived that wreck."

Megan looked at the man with deep distrust. And while her attention was on Strobridge, she couldn't help but think again, *How did he know there were "sorrel horses"?*

Why not bay horses? And why did he say "horses" when no one from up here or on the trestle has been able to see more than one horse? And how . . . how in the world could Ford possibly know that it was a buggy when the wreckage is mostly buried and can't be seen hidden down in those trees?

The only possible explanation Megan could arrive at was chilling. There was only one way to know the color of the horses and the nature of the wagon: this man had had a hand in causing this so-called accident.

"Is something wrong, Miss O'Connell?" Ford asked.

Megan was startled to discover Ford staring at her and his eyes were sinister.

"I . . . I'm just afraid that it is Mitch," she managed to say. "I'm so afraid that he's dead."

Ford's expression softened. "Maybe it's not, but I'd say that you had better be prepared for the worst, Miss O'Connell. I'm just damned sorry."

"I'm sure," she said, watching Strobridge descend deeper and deeper into the gorge. When he finally reached the end of the rope, he shouted up to add more line, which was immediately fed down.

"He's going all the way to the bottom," Ford said. "I should of guessed it. There's never been anything halfway about Mr. Strobridge."

Megan held her breath and watched as Strobridge skirted a huge stand of manzanita. A moment later, the construction chief shouted, "It's Mitch Townsend and he's still alive!"

"Thank heavens!" Megan sighed, collapsing to her knees and biting her lip to keep from sobbing.

"I'm going down and help him get that fella outa there," one of the men said, tearing off his coat and grabbing the rope.

"Me too," another added.

"Now hold on!" Ford shouted.

But the two men worked for Strobridge and they were already on their way down the mountainside.

Mitch had lost consciousness and had fallen, then slid back down into the manzanita. When Strobridge reached him and lifted his head, he roused and opened his eyes.

"Mr. Strobridge?"

"Yeah, it's me and you're costing us work time."

"Sorry," Mitch whispered.

"Might have to sue your rich ass," Strobridge grunted. He knelt close. "Mitch, how badly are you hurt?"

"Pretty bad, I'm afraid," Mitch panted. "The worst part is that I can't move my . . . why, I've got some feeling back in my legs!"

To prove it, he wagged both his feet although it hurt like blazes.

"That's good but you're still in pretty rough shape. We're going to need to get you back up this mountainside somehow. You think you can handle that?"

"I don't think that I have much choice, do I?"

"Not if you'd like to live," Strobridge said with a wry smile.

"I'd like to live very much," Mitch told the big man. "But I think my pelvis is broken along with my legs and perhaps a couple of ribs."

"Mitch, if you think you're in bad shape, you should see your poor horses."

Mitch grabbed his arm and squeezed it hard. "Before anyone else comes," he rasped, "I want you to know that this was no accident."

"What do you mean?"

"I mean that someone shot an ear off one of the sorrels and that caused the team to bolt and go over the side."

"Mitch, are you sure that . . ."

"See for yourself!"

"To hell with it!" Strobridge cussed. "You're the one that needs looking after right now."

"No," Mitch insisted. "I need you to look at the horses and tell me if I'm imagined that one was shot from ambush."

"All right."

A moment later, Strobridge returned. "You weren't imagining anything," he grimly reported. "Someone did ambush you. But who would do such a thing?"

"I think it was someone hired by the Sierra Mining Company, but I've no proof."

"Mitch, let's talk about this later. Right now, we've got to get you back up on top. Okay?"

"Sure," Mitch said, "but if something else should happen to me . . . well, I just wanted you to know."

"Right," Strobridge said, looking very worried.

Before Mitch could say anything more, Strobridge stood up and shouted, "Send down a litter of some kind that we can strap this man onto and drag up!"

"A litter?" Ford asked from up above.

"Yes, of course!" Megan exclaimed. "He might have a back injury and you can't wrestle him up there!"

Some of the men kicked the sideboards out of the buckboard and found some wire to bind them together. They dragged the rope back up and then they tied it to the crude litter, and it was quickly hauled back down to where the three rescuers and Mitch now waited.

Megan fretted terribly as Mitch was lashed securely to the litter and then slowly dragged up the steep shale slide to the top. The moment he cleared the edge of the road, she was at Mitch's side, cradling him in her arms.

"I thought you were dead for sure," Megan whispered,

hugging his battered face to her own.

"Me too," he gasped. "Megan, someone shot my horse and I think it was—"

"Shhh!" she whispered. "Don't say anything now. Do you understand?"

Mitch looked bewildered but, to his credit, he closed his eyes before murmuring, "Just get me to a doctor, Megan."

"I will!" she vowed. "We're taking you down to Sacramento."

"Don't you worry about a thing, Mitch," Ford said, squatting on his heels beside them as he rolled a cigarette. "You've had a hell of an accident, but I'm going to take it upon myself to see that you're out of the woods just as soon as is humanly possible."

Megan looked into the man's eyes, and it struck her in that very instant that he knew that she knew, and that soon the whole world would know, his murderous little secret. Megan shivered and turned her face away from Ford, who struck a match with his thumbnail and filled his lungs with smoke.

It was only later, when Mitch was safe in a hospital, that Megan broached the subject of the wreck. She came right out and told Mitch that she was sure it was Ford, and not the Sierra Mining Company, who was behind the ambushing.

"But . . . but why!" he exclaimed weakly from his hospital bed.

"Because Ford desired me," she said, knowing her words sounded conceited and shallow. "I . . . don't know how else to explain it. I only remember his face when I told him that we were to be married as soon as we were together again."

"Christ," Mitch whispered. "The man is a lunatic. We

have to warn Mr. Crocker and get him—"

"No," she said. "You see, we don't have any proof and we probably never will."

Megan quickly told Mitch about Ford's slipup when he'd first told her that a pair of sorrel horses and a buggy had gone off the cliff.

"But there's no way that he could possibly have known that," Mitch agreed.

"I know that, but you're a lawyer. Couldn't Ford just claim that he'd seen you leave the evening before and made an assumption that you were the likely victim?"

"Yes," Mitch was forced to conceded, "and without some hard evidence to the contrary, a jury would acquit him of all charges. They'd have to because there is no real proof of guilt."

"But do we have to just let it go?"

"I don't know," Mitch said. "Sometimes, things have a way of working out in the end. Right now, what I really need is time to recover."

"Of course."

Mitch looked around his hospital room. "I haven't got time to stay here. I have too much work to do!"

"You *have* to stay here until the doctors say you can leave," Megan insisted.

"But Megan, you saw the Emery family. I told them that I'd be back the next morning to help them pack up and come to Sacramento. They must think I've abandoned them."

"No," Megan argued. "I'm sure that they'll have heard about the accident. I'll help them move. Mitch, I *want to help*!"

He stared at her and his eyes grew misty. "The doctors tell me that I may never regain the full use of my legs. That the very best I can hope for is to walk with a cane.

That I'll always kind of shuffle around like a doddering old man."

Megan placed her fingers over his lips to silence his words. "The doctors can often be wrong. And even if they aren't, it isn't going to change anything between us because we won't allow it. Isn't that true, Mitch?"

He dipped his head and cleared his throat. "It's true. But I think we're going to have to forget about a honeymoon in the Canary Islands. In fact, I'm going to teach you more about the law than you've ever dreamed of knowing or even cared to learn."

"I say hooray for that and hang the Canary Islands," Megan told him. "And I want to be married today."

He sat up straighter. "Megan, are you *sure*?"

She kissed his mouth. "More sure than I've been about anything in a long, long time."

"Then send for a preacher. Any preacher will do."

Megan laughed and hugged his neck. She knew now what her life's work would be. Together, they'd win big and vitally important cases for people like the Emery family.

"You're going to hike up that steep hill from your office to our home again," she promised him. "You just wait and see."

"I believe that because I believe in *you*, Megan," he told her with a catch in his throat.

A month later, they were both back in Auburn and Mitch was trying to practice law again, albeit with some very important help from Megan. They had brought the Emery family down from the mountains and Clinton had undergone surgery for the gangrene. Amazingly, the doctors had managed to save the remaining fingers on his only hand.

"I don't know how I'm going to pay the bills and support that family given the shape I'm in," Mitch fretted.

"We'll do fine."

And they did. An unexpected letter came from the Sierra Mining Company the very day before the Emery court hearing was to take place. For the first time since the accident, Mitch whooped with joy and beamed.

"Don't tell me," Megan said. "They've made an offer to settle it out of court."

"That's right! And a very *generous* offer, I might add."

Megan took a deep breath. "How much?"

"Eighteen thousand dollars . . . and I'll get them up to twenty!"

Megan threw her arms around Mitch's neck and hugged him with all her might. "We're all going to do just fine," she promised. "Just wait and see."

When they told the Emery family the amount of money they would soon be receiving, it was one of the most emotional moments of Megan's life. The entire family almost went crazy with joy, even the youngest children, who really didn't understand what an incredible difference that kind of money would make in their lives.

"We want you to manage most of that money for us," Mrs. Emery said before they left. "We ain't good with money and we want you to take care of us."

Mitch looked at Megan, then turned back to the couple and said, "My wife is an excellent businesswoman. I'm sure she'd be happy to help you."

"I would," Megan said, meaning it.

Mitch nodded in approval, and then he took the whole bunch of them out to the finest restaurant in Auburn, where they celebrated until the wee hours of the morning.

CHAPTER
20

In the loftiest reaches of the high Sierras, one sure indicator of a fierce and early winter is that aspen turn colors in September. This year, Glenn Gilchrist and the huge advance tunneling crews assigned to the 1,659-foot Summit Tunnel anxiously watched the aspen leaves change to red and gold in late August as they furiously tunneled under Donner Pass.

"Damn the luck!" Strobridge swore one cold afternoon as rain and sleet poured down from the dark sky above. "I'll bet you anything we're going to have snow in another couple of weeks."

"In September?" Glenn asked.

"That's right. We're just over seven thousand feet of elevation here, and the Donner Party recorded snows sixty and seventy feet deep."

Strobridge dismounted from his horse and walked over to stare into the Summit Tunnel, which had to be roughly twenty feet in diameter and was buried hundreds of feet below rugged Donner Pass.

"Glenn, I really hate to ask this, but how is the blasting going?"

"Slow," Glenn answered knowing that Strobridge was more than aware of their pitiful progress. "Not only are we trying to bore through solid granite, but the black-powder smoke remains our biggest problem. We can't clear it out of the tunnel in less than a couple of hours so that the drillers can go back to work inside. On some days, we're lucky to make a foot of headway. At that rate, I figure this bore will take us about four and a half years to complete."

"By then," Strobridge said, "Congress will have lost patience and have given all their money to the damned Union Pacific and we'll be bankrupt. We can't let that happen, Glenn."

Glenn was as exasperated by their lack of progress as anyone. "I am acutely aware of that, but what else can we do? You've got more than a thousand Chinese up here drilling, blasting, moving rock and working from sunup to sundown."

"As you know," Strobridge said, "we got another crew over on the east end of the tunnel coming in from the Nevada side to meet you. But even at that, we're still only working two faces of this tunnel. So Mr. Crocker and I have decided to put a crew right up on top of Donner Summit and drill another bore straight down. When we come even with the lateral bores, we'll start working both additional faces. That way we'll double our progress."

"Do you want me to do the survey work?"

"Of course," Strobridge said. "Obviously, if we don't sink the vertical shaft exactly where it needs to meet both lateral bores, we're in deep trouble."

"Obviously," Glenn said, knowing that his calculations were critical. Just a few degrees off and hundreds of thousands of dollars would be lost when the three bores did not join perfectly under this rugged and unyielding summit.

"There's something else I wanted to ask you, Glenn."

"Shoot."

"Well," Strobridge said, picking his words carefully, "we may have found another way to really speed up the work on this tunnel."

"Nothing would please me more."

Strobridge's brow furrowed. "Glenn, have you ever heard of an explosive called nitroglycerine?"

"Can't say as I have."

"Neither has anyone else," Strobridge replied. "But a few weeks ago there was a terrible explosion in San Francisco."

"Really?"

"Yep. The blast was so powerful that it leveled an entire city block. It killed twelve people and sent a bloody arm flying through a third-story window."

"I never heard of *anything* even approaching that kind of power. Was it caused by this nitroglycerine you mentioned?"

"Yep, a couple cases of the stuff had been accidentally dropped near a Wells Fargo office and that was finally determined to be the cause of the explosion. The whole city was rocked, and the people of San Francisco were so upset that the town council immediately put a ban on any more nitroglycerine entering their port."

"What *is* nitroglycerine?"

"Beats me," Strobridge said. "But the minute we heard about it, Mr. Crocker raced off for San Francisco to investigate. From what he read, it's liquid."

Glenn's jaw dropped with surprise. "Liquid?"

"That's right, and unfortunately, it's pretty damned unstable. I'm not sure that it's something we can use, but we're ready to try anything."

"I just hope that Mr. Crocker doesn't get himself blown to bits. Where did this stuff come from?"

"It's a European invention. What Mr. Crocker is

hoping to do is to find a chemist who can manufacture nitroglycerine right up here in the mountains since it's been banned for import into California."

"How much smoke does it leave?" Glenn asked.

"That's another critical question, of course. But I'm sure that it's less than black powder. And I've heard that nitroglycerine is estimated to be eight times more powerful than black powder and, therefore, requires far smaller drilling holes."

"That would really give us a boost!"

"To say the least," Strobridge agreed. "But something that powerful could bring the whole tunnel down on us if we weren't extremely careful. We'd have to experiment outside for a few days just to take the measure of such a tremendous explosive."

"I don't see a problem there," Glenn said. "We've got nothing but trees and rocks and a few more or less isn't going to make any difference."

"My sentiments exactly," the construction foreman said. "I'm pretty excited about this stuff. Mr. Crocker is so confident that it will help that he's asked me to construct a log cabin just off a ways."

"For what?"

"For someone to brew the damned stuff in, of course. Can't have him doing that in the middle of us if nitroglycerine is that unstable, can we?"

"I should say not," Glenn readily agreed. "And while we'd all like to speed things up, we'd also prefer to be around to see the completion of this tunnel. It'll go in the record books as the longest and the highest railroad tunnel ever constructed."

"I know," Strobridge said with a tight grin. "But we've got to move faster. The Union Pacific sure isn't wasting time. They're already in the coal fields of central

Wyoming and planning on driving down into the Great Salt Lake Basin next year."

"But first they'll be having their own troubles when they finally reach the Wasatch Mountains," Glenn said with no small amount of satisfaction. "Not that I'm suggesting those mountains pose anything even approaching the challenges we face up here at Donner Pass."

Strobridge glared out at the cold falling rain. "I have a bad feeling about this winter. I think it's going to be a real hard one but I hope I'm wrong."

"Me too," Glenn said, before leaving the man and heading back into the gaping western entrance of the Summit Tunnel.

Two weeks later, Crocker arrived with an energetic and self-confident Scottish chemist named James Bowden. After being introduced around, Bowden strode into Summit Tunnel, grunted a few times as he surveyed the pitiful progress being made with black powder and made his announcement.

"Gentleman, I can assure you that my nitroglycerine will reduce this mountain summit to a molehill."

One of the foremen scoffed. "Sir, no offense, but this is pure Sierra granite. Rock just doesn't come any harder."

Bowden bristled. "I'll blast it to smithereens! Next spring, we'll be drinking from the Truckee River and watching the spring flowers sprout on the eastern slope."

"Talk is cheap, Mr. Bowden," Crocker said with a twinkle of amusement in his eyes.

"I can back my talk with results," Bowden said without hesitation. "I'll give you a little demonstration right now, if you'd like."

Everyone exchanged nervous glances and then Crocker said, "Of course, but at a distance."

"Of course," Bowden agreed. "But nitroglycerine is not as dangerous as some might think."

"Glad to hear that," Strobridge quipped, "but I believe that the people of San Francisco might take issue with that statement."

"Ba!" the chemist scoffed as if the loss of twelve lives and an entire city block were nothing of consequence. "That explosion was simply the result of carelessness and stupidity. You see, nitroglycerine is made up of glycerine, nitric and sulfuric acid. If kept apart, they are inert, almost harmless."

Bowden winked. "However, after you mix them, well, that is when you have to be very, very careful. Some fool mixed them and put them in shipping cartons and that is why the outcome was so tragic."

"Then you'll not mix them until they are to be used right in the tunnels?" Glenn asked.

"That's right. Oh, I might mix two of the three ingredients for convenience, but I'll not add the third element until it is ready to be poured into the drilling hole."

"What will set it off?" Strobridge asked.

"Anything," Bowden replied with a disarming smile.

Glenn looked around at the faces of his co-workers and he could see that they were more than a little apprehensive.

"Mr. Bowden," Crocker said, breaking the silence, "why don't you go ahead and demonstrate the power of nitroglycerine just as you suggested."

"Gladly!"

It took the chemist a mere fifteen minutes to go off by himself, combine his chemicals and carefully pour them into a flask. Bowden's flask held about a pint of the explosive, and he placed it under a huge boulder that was surrounded by some big pine trees. Everyone stared at the beaker as if it were some evil witch's brew.

Hurrying back to join the others, Bowden said, "I think we should move back a little farther for safety's sake."

No one objected. In fact, they stumbled all over themselves in a full retreat.

"What now?" Strobridge asked when they were a good hundred yards uphill from the flask.

"Inside the tunnel, I suggest that we initiate the explosion with a tiny charge of black powder and a long fuse. Anything that will shatter the beaker or even give it a good jolt will do. For right now, however, I suggest a marksman."

"I'm a good shot," Ford Hayward said. "And I've a rifle in the boot of my saddle."

"Then get it and let's proceed," Bowden said.

No one said a word as Ford hurried over to his horse and drew a Winchester from his saddle boot. He came back, levered a shell into the chamber and then took a deep breath. Ford looked very nervous. "Is everyone ready?"

The chemist slapped his hands to his ears and nodded. Everyone followed his example and several of the men ducked behind cover. But Crocker and Strobridge stood in the open and so did Glenn.

When the Winchester roared the flask vanished in an explosion so cataclysmic that it shook the entire mountain. Glenn staggered backward scarcely believing his eyes as the immense boulder vaporized and two massive pines were ripped out of the ground and then hurled down the mountainside in a hail of splinters and bark. Chinese who had been working outside dove for cover. Others who had been working inside Summit Tunnel came running out, eyes wild with fear.

"Well?" Bowden said as thunder reverberated across

the highest peaks and alpine meadows. "Gentlemen, have I made you all believers?"

Glenn, like everyone else, was absolutely speechless. *Never* had he dreamed that anything could be so incredibly powerful.

"You have indeed," Crocker finally said as a slow grin split his wide, meaty face. "And I'd like to show you your own private cabin."

Everyone looked at the ground, and then Glenn couldn't help himself for he began to chuckle. Soon, they were all laughing uproariously, even James Bowden.

In the days that followed, Bowden settled right into his lonely cabin, and he truly seemed to enjoy his work as he brewed his nitroglycerine and only appeared with the temperamental explosive when he was signaled. The Chinese, Glenn noticed, treated the chemist almost like a deity. They showed Bowden even more deference than they did Mr. Crocker, which obviously irritated their proud superintendent. But Crocker forgave them because he was so delighted with the great progress that the Summit Tunnel was making thanks to nitroglycerine.

Their headway under the summit proceeded far more rapidly as winter approached. The vertical shaft, which Glenn had supposed would be aborted because of their new explosive, was instead blasted out in record time using nitroglycerine. And when the first blizzard struck in October, four crews of Chinese were already deep underground, blasting and hacking away at the Summit Tunnel.

"I'm sending more Chinese over the top so they can start work on the eastern slope tunnels following the Truckee River down onto Nevada's vast sagebrush plateau," Crocker announced one snowy morning. "When we finally blast through this big sonofabitch in the spring, I want the way already cleared for us to start laying track toward Reno."

"Maybe we could even drag a locomotive over Donner Pass," Strobridge said jokingly. "That way, we could just leapfrog this mountain and *really* work the eastern slope."

"Excellent idea!" Crocker shouted, clapping his hands together. "Why didn't I think of that!"

Privately, Strobridge later admitted that he wished that he had not thought of the idea because Crocker was all excited and soon had several hundred Chinese dismantling a locomotive and preparing monstrous sleds to be dragged over Donner Pass so that track, locomotives and even flatcars carrying construction supplies could be ready to go when the weather looked good.

But the weather did not look good. Glenn had experienced terrible winds and Northern Plains blizzards while working for the Union Pacific across Nebraska and Wyoming, but they were as nothing compared to these lethal high Sierra blizzards. As October ran into November and November into December, the blizzards kept coming with the speed of fast-moving freight trains. There were twenty-three of them, every one packing deadly force and all dumping more than six feet of snow on the already buried construction camps.

"I don't know how your people survive in those snow caves," Glenn said from the warmth of his own little cabin one evening after summoning Ah Toy with some trumped-up excuse about needing Chinese medicine for a chest cold.

Ah Toy now wore the heavy winter clothing of her countrymen. Her outfit was very thick, almost like a quilt, so that she appeared to be as shapeless as a water barrel.

"My people have bad winters in China," Ah Toy

explained. "And famine. At least here they are well fed."

"I'm sorry that an entire camp was lost last week when it was buried by an avalanche."

"There will be much white death here this winter," Ah Toy said. "Snow caves collapse and Chinese die. Explosions and avalanches very dangerous too. There is nothing that can be done."

"I know that Crocker is doing his best to keep the Chinese from building snow caves and their camps wherever it seems that they are in danger of being in the path of an avalanche, but it's nearly impossible."

Ah Toy nodded in agreement and when she said no more, Glenn changed the subject. "Ah Toy, I suspect that you must keep the teapots boiling twenty-four hours a day."

"Yes, hot tea very important. Chinese drink much tea now. Keep insides warm."

Glenn nodded, pouring Ah Toy a cup of Chinese tea. He had become very fond of drinking it and it had largely replaced the acid-belly coffee that was always available in the company dining hall, now also buried under snow.

"How is chest cold?" Ah Toy inquired.

"Better," he answered, gazing at her beauty in the candlelight. "How are you feeling?"

"Good," she told him. "But Mr. Loudermilk come back."

"What!" Glenn lowered his teacup from his mouth. "He's back now?"

"Tomorrow," Ah Toy said, eyes dropping to her hands. "He send word that I am to meet him . . . alone."

Glenn did not have ask the reason behind the request. Ah Toy, while she never asked for favors or complained, was not afraid to tell the truth, even when it was ugly.

"You're not going to go meet him," Glenn said sternly. "I can't allow that."

"Must."

Glenn opened his mouth to protest, then closed it. He realized that Ah Toy meant that she had to do business with Loudermilk in behalf of her people. What happened after the business would then be beyond her control.

"Where are you to meet him?"

Ah Toy placed her teacup down and said, "Must go now."

Glenn took her arm and drew her close. "I have my own reasons to meet this man, Ah Toy. This has nothing to do with you. This is business. Do you understand? Unfinished business."

She looked right into his eyes. "Glenn, I leave at daybreak and go down tracks." There was a long pause and then Ah Toy added, "Maybe you follow."

"I will," Glenn promised. "You can just bet that I will."

Ah Toy decided to finish her tea and they talked of other, happier things. They had both grown very comfortable together, and had recounted the smallest details of their childhoods, which were so very different.

Finally, Ah Toy reached into her pocket and found a packet of herbs. "This help you," she said, extending it to him.

Instead of taking the packet, Glenn took Ah Toy in his arms for the second time and kissed her long and passionately. Ah Toy melted against him and returned his kiss, her passion every bit as great as his own.

"What is going to happen to us when this is over?" he asked.

"Don't know," she replied. "Be careful tomorrow. Mr. Loudermilk very dangerous man when angry."

"I'll be careful," Glenn vowed. "And I don't want you to worry about anything tomorrow morning. Just do your business and leave. If he tries to stop you, I'll be there."

Ah Toy gave him a warm smile. "How Chinese medicine for Mr. Townsend work?"

Glenn picked up a letter that he had recently received from Auburn. "Megan's letter arrived only yesterday. She said that the Chinese doctor that you had sent up from Sacramento was using needles to help bring back feeling to Mitch's legs. Can you imagine! Needles!"

"Ancient Chinese medicine," Ah Toy said. "Strong when used properly and with Chinese herbs."

Glenn sighed. "After reading this letter, I can't argue that. Megan says that her husband, after months of no evident physical progress, has suddenly regained the full use of his legs. The Sacramento doctors are calling it a miracle."

"No miracle. Acupuncture and herbs," Ah Toy said as if she knew all along that Chinese medicine would work wonders for Mitch Townsend.

Glenn watched his lovely Chinese girl vanish into the snow and the night. He went over to his bunk and picked up a copy of an old engineering text, but it held no interest this night. His thoughts were all on Ah Toy and Harry Loudermilk and what would happen tomorrow morning when they finally met.

CHAPTER
21

The weather was very clear but cold when Ah Toy left early the next morning as Glenn saddled one of the company horses and prepared to follow her.

"Mr. Gilchrist?"

He finished tightening his cinch and then he turned to see Tommy Farin, one of the newer surveyors. "Yes?"

"Mr. Crocker wants to see you right now."

Glenn glanced back down the road. Ah Toy was already gone, vanished around a bend. Glenn silently railed against this untimely delay. "Any idea what this is about?"

"He probably just wants to get a report on the drilling," Farin said. "Who knows?"

Glenn was torn. "I really need to be somewhere else," he said.

Farin just shrugged to indicate that it meant no difference to him. "I guess you'll just have to jump like the rest of us when the big boss calls."

"I guess so," Glenn said, leaving his horse saddled and hurrying off toward Crocker's cabin.

Superintendent of Construction Charles Crocker was seated at a big desk, smoking a cigar and pouring over survey maps. When he realized Glenn was waiting, he turned and said gruffly, "Come on over here a minute and show me on these damned maps exactly where each of the walls is facing right now."

Glenn curbed his impatience. Every day he or another surveyor precisely measured the length of each tunnel. The figures were always presented to Strobridge, who would deliver them to Crocker. In fact, as Glenn approached the man's desk, he could see the very latest figures penciled out on a pad of paper.

"Here we go," Glenn said, taking the figures and a measure, then quickly placing dots on the map to show the progress of the four tunnels. "As you can see, we've already completed nine hundred seventy-three feet of the Summit Tunnel."

"That's pretty good, isn't it!" Crocker exclaimed, obviously delighted.

"You bet it is," Glenn said. "And the work is going faster every day. We'll be through by next spring with our eyes fixed on Nevada. The only problem is that we're running your Scottish chemist half ragged working all four tunnel facings."

"He's getting paid a fortune," Crocker said without sympathy, "so let's make sure he keeps earning it."

"Very well." Glenn was frantic to start after Ah Toy. "Anything else?"

"As a matter of fact, yes," Crocker said. "Sit down, Glenn, I have something else to discuss with you."

Desperation about Ah Toy's safety caused Glenn to blurt out, "I don't suppose it could wait?"

Crocker was not a man who waited for anyone and his voice took on a decided edge. "Mr. Gilchrist, have you something more important to do than to meet with me?"

"No, sir. What is it that you wanted to discuss?"

Crocker drummed his thick fingers on the maps and studied his expensive Cuban cigar with distaste for a moment before he replied, "It's your ex-fiancée, Megan O'Connell, now Mrs. Megan Townsend."

Glenn forgot all about Ah Toy for the moment. "What about her?"

Crocker blew smoke into the air and leaned back in his chair, then kicked his feet up on his desk. "Please don't feel insulted, but is Megan always truthful?"

"Why, of course! Why would you ask such a question?"

"I didn't want to ask it," Crocker admitted, "but I was in Auburn yesterday on business. You may not have been aware of it but Mitch Townsend is on retainer for our railroad. Mostly, he's done right-of-way things. He's sort of smoothed our path when we've had reluctant squatters and landowners unwilling to sell us our roadbed."

"I see."

"Anyway, I'm happy to tell you that Mitch's recovery is progressing very well. In fact, he's starting to walk without the use of a cane and trying to build up his strength. He's predicting a full recovery and, after seeing him, I believe that will be the case."

"I'm delighted to hear that," Glenn said, knowing better than to tell this man that acupuncture and Chinese medicine were due no small part of the credit for Mitch's remarkable recovery.

"But that's not why I asked about his wife."

"I didn't think so."

"Glenn, the Townsends confided in me that they believe that Ford Hayward ambushed Mitch, thus causing his buggy to go over the edge of that cliff where we found him."

"Ford ambushed Mitch?" Glenn asked with surprise.

"Yes," Crocker said, "a nasty bit of business, isn't it? Anyway, someone shot an ear off Mitch's horse, and it seems that Ford was the only one that knew the details of the accident before they became evident to Mr. Strobridge or anyone else who was with that rescue party."

"I see," Glenn said, shaking his head.

"But the troubling thing is that Mitch admits that the evidence isn't sufficient to stand up in a courtroom. And yet, they both feel absolutely sure that Ford is the guilty party."

"Motive?"

"Megan claims that Ford was attracted to her from the moment that you arrived at our construction site at Cape Horn."

"I think he was," Glenn said, remembering Ford Hayward's hot eyes that first time they had all met.

"But enough to ambush and *murder*?"

"I don't know," Glenn admitted. "I do recall Megan saying that your assistant was extremely upset when she told him that she'd decided to marry Mr. Townsend."

"If he really was the man with the rifle, I'm going to have to confront him," Crocker said heavily. "And while I don't mind doing that, it's such a serious charge that I'd feel like a damned fool if this is all just a bunch of poppycock."

"What did the Townsends suggest?"

"They suggested that I do nothing since they cannot prove their suspicion," Crocker said. "And when I asked them the purpose of their confession, they told me that they believed that I ought to be aware that I had a potential killer for an assistant and should be careful."

Glenn could see that the big, gruff Crocker was somewhat shaken by the idea that his assistant was capable of ambush and murder. Furthermore, the man was probably torn between outrage and some kind of loyalty to his assistant.

"I wanted to ask you about Megan," Crocker said, looking away and smoking thoughtfully, "so that I could try and determine what course of action I should pursue in this delicate matter. As you know, Glenn, it is a terrible thing to slander a man's character and reputation without a shred of evidence."

"Yes," Glenn said, thinking of the injustice he'd suffered from Durant when he'd been fired from the Union Pacific, "I know."

"So," Crocker said, "having been yourself slandered and unjustly accused, what do you think I ought to do about Mr. Hayward?"

Glenn considered his words very carefully. "I think Megan is correct. She's not a woman who would make such an accusation lightly. My advice would be to take no action but watch the man closely. Perhaps I could ask around to see if Ford was seen riding out of camp shortly after Mitch Townsend delivered Megan and then headed back toward Auburn."

"Yes," Crocker said, nodding his head. "You could do that, but I could not. If I began to ask such questions, it would immediately arouse suspicion."

"But even if someone did see and remember Ford following Mitch," Glenn said pointedly, "it wouldn't be proof positive that he was the ambusher."

"No," Crocker agreed, "but it would give me enough circumstantial evidence to fire the man. I'll not have someone capable of ambush working for me. Glenn, be discreet and see what you can find out."

"I'll do that." Glenn stepped back. "Since we're on the subject of right and wrong, I might as well tell you that I'm on my way to confront Harry Loudermilk."

Crocker's bushy black eyebrows shot up. "What's he doing in these mountains instead of in San Francisco?"

"I have no idea."

Crocker frowned. "He's not here to see me."

"I think he's here to see someone else."

"Oh, yeah, who?"

Glenn took a deep breath. "A young, half-Chinese girl that I've become very fond of and who . . ."

Crocker couldn't help but chuckle. "You're talking about Ah Toy, aren't you."

It wasn't a question and it caught Glenn by surprise. "You know about her?"

"Of course! Half my staff is secretly in love with Ah Toy, but the inside gossip I hear is that she's your new girl. Is that true?"

"I certainly hope so."

"Well," Crocker said, coming to his feet and clapping Glenn on the shoulder. "When you find Loudermilk, tell him that I want to see him at once. Tell him to get up here today."

"Yes, sir!"

Glenn started to leave, but Crocker's words stopped him at the doorway. "Glenn, be careful. Loudermilk is a very tough man. He can be pretty ruthless and is not someone to be taken lightly."

"Thanks for the warning."

"You're welcome," Crocker said, sitting back down in his chair and tracing the progress of the tunneling again. "I'm just dying to punch through this damned Summit Tunnel and get out of these mountains so we can really move next year."

"Me too." Glenn started to leave but, again, Crocker's words stopped him.

"Glenn?"

"Yes, sir?"

"Good luck." Crocker was smiling, eyes back on the

maps as he puffed rapidly on his cigar.

Glenn practically bolted out of the door and ran back across the packed-down snow to his horse. Untying the animal, he swung up and sent it galloping down the road, each stride cupping clods of snow and hurling them into their wake.

He only had to travel a mile down the snowy road to a tiny town where the Irish laborers spent their wages every Saturday night in the saloons or upstairs at the Ridgetop Hotel.

"You see a Chinese girl come walking into town a few minutes ago?" he shouted as he rode down the only street.

"You bet!" a man answered, looking excited. "Tall, pretty young thing. She gonna start working a mattress at the Ridgetop Hotel today?"

"Hell, no!" Glenn responded angrily. "Where is she?"

"Went into that hotel just like she'd been doin' it every day," the man said. "Maybe you're wrong about what she does, huh?"

Glenn didn't deign to answer the man, but booted his horse into a gallop through the mud, snow and slush. He reined it up so hard that the horse skidded into the hitching post, almost knocking it down. Glenn tied the animal and dashed inside the hotel. The only man he saw was wearing an apron and was sweeping the floor.

"Where did they go!" he yelled, craning his head upstairs.

"Who?"

Glenn rushed over to the man and grabbed his broom. "The tall Chinese girl and the man she was with!"

"Give me back that broom!"

Glenn cocked his fist. "Not until you tell me what room they went to."

"First door on the right, top of the stairs." When Glenn turned and darted toward the stairs, the man yelled, "I own this place, you crazy sonofabitch! If you bust things up, you're gonna pay!"

Glenn went up the stairs taking them two at a time. He was at the door in seconds and grabbing the handle. The door, not surprisingly, was locked.

"Ah Toy!" he yelled, banging on the door. "Ah Toy, open up!"

When there was no answer, Glenn reared back and kicked the door as hard as he could. It splintered at the hinges but did not come free, so he kicked it again and this time the top hinge was torn loose and the door twisted inward. Glenn started inside, but the cocking of a six-gun brought him up short.

Harry Loudermilk stepped out from behind the damaged door and growled, "The thing of it is, I want to know who the hell I'm about to kill."

Glenn's hands shot up over his head. Harry Loudermilk was a thick wedge of a man with a square, meaty face and deep-set eyes that held no kindness or mercy. He was short, maybe five-foot-eight, but stocky and in his forties. His nose had been busted and he had a wicked scar on his right cheek. The gun in his hand was as solid as the granite under Donner Summit.

"Who are you!" he shouted as Glenn turned his attention to Ah Toy, who was standing beside the bed with her lip bleeding and her pale face already beginning to swell.

"It's all right," he assured Ah Toy before he turned back and said to Loudermilk, "Does the name Peter Arlington arouse a few memories?"

Loudermilk blinked and tried to guess where the conversation was heading. "Yeah, sure. He was a young dandy who came to San Francisco looking for stories and adventures. A real fancy feller, that one. What about him?"

"He was spying on the Union Pacific and sending you his information."

Loudermilk laughed outright. "Even if that were true, who the hell cares, anyway!"

"I do," Glenn said, "because I was implicated as being part of your little spy ring and I was fired by none other than Thomas Durant, the Union Pacific's president. My name was slandered and my reputation sullied."

Loudermilk kept laughing until he could say, "So is that what this is all about? You bust in here to die over your gawddamn silly little reputation!"

"It's also about you taking money from the Chinese in order to line your own pockets."

"You can't prove anything," Loudermilk sneered. "Are you armed? Sure, you are. Keep your right hand up in the air and drag out your gun with your left. Easy now, or you're a dead man."

Glenn had no choice but to comply. He had been packing a six-gun in a shoulder holster.

Taking the gun and tossing it on his bed, Loudermilk said, "Now, get the hell out of here before I really do shoot you for breaking into my room!"

"I'm not going anywhere," Glenn said.

Loudermilk raised his pistol and took aim. "Mister, you are going to the cemetery in about three seconds if you don't get out of here."

Glenn looked at Ah Toy, who was silently pleading for him to leave.

"One," Loudermilk counted, his lips now stretched in a wicked smile. "Two."

"Glenn, please go!" Ah Toy cried.

"All right," he said, spinning on his heels and hurrying downstairs with Loudermilk's mocking laughter ringing in his ears. Then, he heard the sound of the door slam, and knew that Loudermilk had jammed it back into place and that he was going to abuse Ah Toy no matter how hard she fought him.

Glenn ran to the hotel owner. "I need a gun!"

"Go to hell!"

Glenn grabbed a fistful of the man's shirtfront and propelled him around and behind the registration desk. He began to yank open drawers until he saw a pistol.

"Don't touch that!"

Glenn grabbed the weapon and checked to make sure that the Colt revolver was fully loaded. It was. He pointed it at the owner and said, "That man up there is hurting the Chinese girl and I'm going to stop him. If you yell a warning or try, in any way, to stop me, I'll shoot you. Is that understood?"

The owner stopped struggling. "Mister, I don't want no trouble."

"Good," Glenn said. "Then don't make any."

He hurried back upstairs, and sure enough, the door was jammed back into place. But this time, when Glenn reared back and kicked it, the thing crashed in easily and Glenn caught Loudermilk in the act of beating Ah Toy, who was now sprawled across the bed crying.

"Get away from her!"

Loudermilk dove for his gun, which was resting on a bedside table. Glenn waited until the man had hold of his gun, then coolly took aim and fired. Loudermilk howled in pain as blood blossomed at his side. He staggered badly, but still managed to grab his gun and even fired an errant bullet. Glenn shot the man again, this time through the forehead, and Harry Loudermilk slammed up against the wall, eyes rolling, thick legs twitching as he began to slide down into a sitting position. The gun spilled from his hand.

Ah Toy cried out in fear, and then she was jumping out of the bed and racing into Glenn's arms. "It's all right," he soothed, clutching her tightly. "It's all right, my darling."

Ah Toy shuddered and then looked up at him. "But he's dead!"

"That's right," Glenn said, "and his gun is fired and that proves that I killed him in self-defense."

Out in the hallway, doors flew open and half-dressed women peered out and began to yell and curse.

"Ah Toy, let's get out of here," Glenn said gently. A few minutes later, he was leading Ah Toy down the stairs into the lobby, already filling with curiosity-seekers.

"You killed him, didn't you!" the hotel owner shouted. "You just went up and shot that man to death."

"Get a marshal over here," Glenn ordered. "I want to make a statement that I acted in self-defense."

"There ain't no marshal here! Nearest one is in Auburn, almost seventy miles away!"

"Auburn," Glenn said quietly, thinking that would be perfect because, if there were any problems, he'd have a first-rate attorney.

"All right, then," he announced to the swelling crowd, "we'll take the body down to Auburn and make a statement to their marshal."

The owner yanked off his apron. "Dammit, I don't care about none of that. I just want damages."

"One door broken," Glenn said, reaching into his pocket. "How much?"

"Oh, five dollars for that, and then there's probably bloodstains and—"

"Here," Glenn said, tossing the man ten dollars. "That ought to cover everything."

"Yeah," the hotel owner said, eyeing the bill warily before reaching to pick it up off the floor. "I guess it will. You're going to remove the body now, aren't you?"

"That's right. Find me a wagon to rent and we're on our way."

"I'll do it," the man said. "This ain't good for business and I just want you two out of here."

The hotel owner got his wish. But before leaving the town, Glenn sent a terse telegram to Charles Crocker which read:

KILLED HARRY LOUDERMILK IN SELF DEFENSE. TAKING AH TOY AND BODY DOWN TO SEE MARSHAL IN AUBURN. BE BACK IN A COUPLE DAYS TO START WORK.　　GLENN.

"You killed Harry Loudermilk?" the telegraph operator exclaimed with surprise.

"I did."

"Good riddance! He was one rough customer."

"I know," Glenn said as headed off to Auburn.

Their arrival caused no small amount of excitement. Megan and Mitch were shocked when Glenn asked them to accompany him and Ah Toy to the marshal's office.

"I hope," Glenn said, "that your services aren't going to be necessary."

"I doubt they will be," Mitch said, walking slowly but with very little of his initial paralysis. "Marshal Tate is one of my best friends and Harry Loudermilk had a bad reputation. In fact, he was jailed on more than one occasion by Marshal Tate."

Mitch's prediction proved accurate. Marshal Tate, a man in his forties whose hair was already silver, just said, "Good riddance to bad rubbish. We'll plant Loudermilk in our cemetery. Did he have any relatives?"

"I wouldn't know."

"Well," Tate said, "I do know that Harry damn sure didn't have any friends, so if you could chip in a little to help the city pay the costs burying him, it would be appreciated."

Glenn paid the marshal and Mitch added a ten-dollar bill for good measure.

And that was it. The next day as Glenn and Ah Toy were preparing to return to Donner Summit, Megan came out to join them and said, "After all this time, you just end up having to kill the man."

"He deserved killing," Glenn said, helping Ah Toy back into the wagon. "How are you two really getting along, Megan?"

"We're so happy together it's shameful."

Glenn smiled broadly. "I can't tell you how glad that I am to hear that."

"I wish you as much happiness," Megan said, eyes shifting to Ah Toy for a moment before returning to Glenn.

"We're going to be fine now," he said. "And about Ford Hayward?"

Megan's smile died. "Yes?"

"That'll be taken care of in due time."

"Like with Harry Loudermilk?"

"No," Glenn said. "But justice always seems to find a way to be served."

"And what about Donner Summit?" she asked.

Glenn had a ready answer. "My second promise is that we're all going to have a picnic in the spring and collect wildflowers blooming along the Truckee."

"Are you sure?"

Glenn squeezed Ah Toy's hand tightly. "Bet on it, Megan."

And then, Glenn waved good-bye as he and Ah Toy headed back up the mountain toward Donner Pass. Each in his or her own small way was determined to help finish the great and seemingly impossible transcontinental railroad that had began with the dreamer Theodore Judah, and would end when the rails joined somewhere in Nevada, or maybe even the Utah Territory.

If you enjoyed this book, subscribe now and get...

TWO FREE

A $7.00 VALUE—

If you would like to read more of the very best, most exciting, adventurous, action-packed Westerns being published today, you'll want to subscribe to True Value's Western Home Subscription Service.

Each month the editors of True Value will select the 6 very best Westerns from America's leading publishers for special readers like you. You'll be able to preview these new titles as soon as they are published, *FREE* for ten days with no obligation!

TWO FREE BOOKS

When you subscribe, we'll send you your first month's shipment of the newest and best 6 Westerns for you to preview. With your first shipment, two of these books will be yours as our introductory gift to you absolutely *FREE* (a $7.00 value), regardless of what you decide to do. If

you like them, as much as we think you will, keep all six books but pay for just 4 at the low subscriber rate of just $2.75 each. If you decide to return them, keep 2 of the titles as our gift. No obligation.

Special Subscriber Savings

When you become a True Value subscriber you'll save money several ways. First, all regular monthly selections will be billed at the low subscriber price of just $2.75 each. That's at least a savings of $4.50 each month below the publishers price. Second, there is never any shipping, handling or other hidden charges—*Free home delivery*. What's more there is no minimum number of books you must buy, you may return any selection for full credit and you can cancel your subscription at any time. A TRUE VALUE!